PALISADES OF THE HEART

Praise for Palisades of the Heart

"*Palisades of the Heart* **is a fantastic read** for historical fiction enthusiasts. This story of romance and the thrilling adventure that comes from living on the frontier is sure to capture the heart of readers. Whether you've read the previous books or not, the novel will keep you captivated from beginning to end."—Literary Titan

"*Palisades of the Heart,* **is an immersive,** thoroughly researched dive into the frontier of western Virginia in 1776. This YA historical romance is a window into the past. Chock-full of young love and adventure, you'll be rooting for Mary and her beloved the whole way."—Brooke French author of Inhuman Acts

"**I've enjoyed every book in the *Dangerous Loyalties* series,** but I love the way this one pulls so many things together, including the budding romance between the two main characters. Wonderfully researched with interesting details and characters based on real historical figures, *Palisades of the Heart* was a delightful read!"—Amazon Customer Amanda

Palisades of the Heart

Dangerous Loyalties Book Four

Phyllis A. Still

Climbing Tree Publications

Palisades of the Heart is a work of historical fiction. The author's fictitious use of historical people and events are used for entertainment and educational purposes.

Copyright©2023 by Phyllis A. Still
First Edition
Climbing Tree Publications
phyllisastill@gmail.com
Cover design by K.M. West Creative
ISBN: 978-1-958674-09-3
eBook ISBN: 987-1-958674-10-9
Library of Congress Control Number: 2022913379

PRINTED IN THE UNITED STATES OF AMERICA

All rights are reserved. No part of this book may be reproduced or transmitted in any form or by any electronic or mechanical means, including photocopying, recording or by any information storage and retrieval system, without the written permission of the author, except where permitted by law.

To McKaylee, Brandon, Midori, Elaina, Sawyer, Nikolai,
Zachary and all descendants of the brave men, women,
and children mentioned in this historical novel.

Be strong!

BOOKS by PHYLLIS A. STILL

Dangerous Loyalties Series

Defiance on Indian Creek, Book One

Fleeing the Shadows, Book Two

Warrior on the Western Waters, Book Three

Palisades of the Heart, Book Four

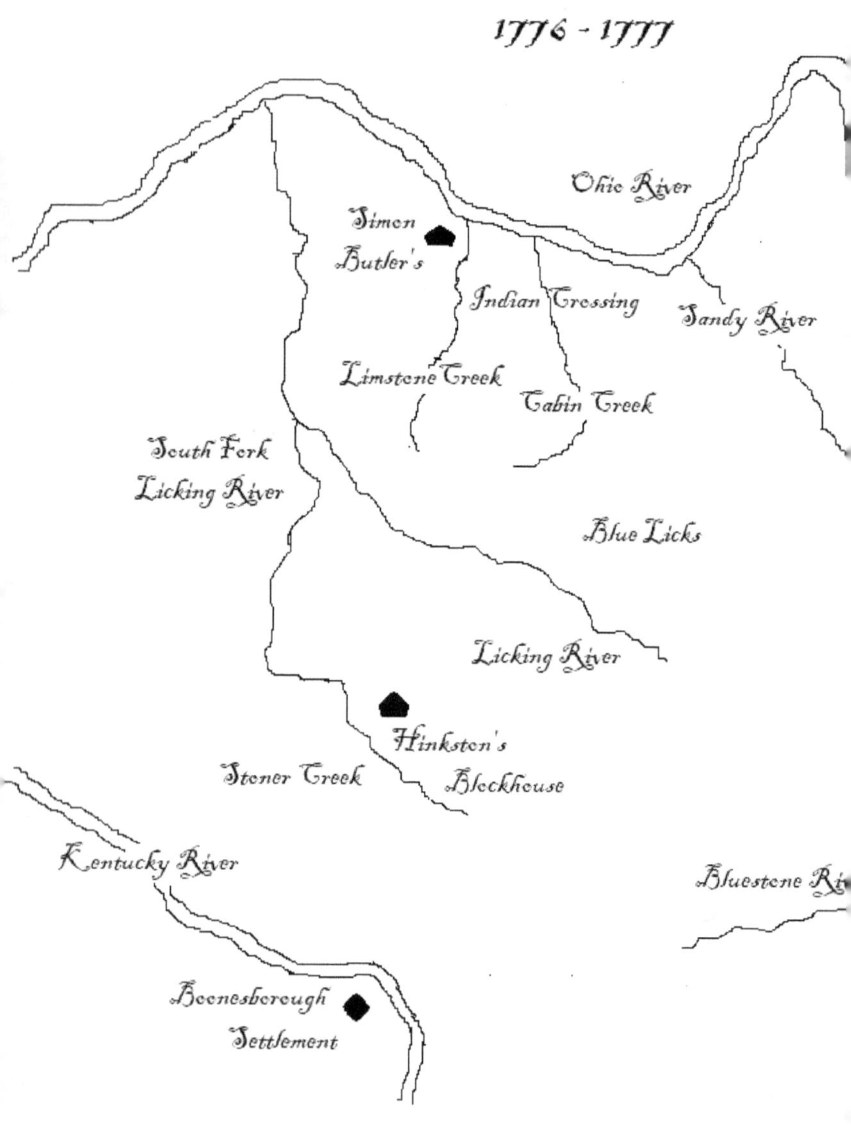

Western Waters
1776 - 1777
Ohio River
Simon Butler's
Indian Crossing
Sandy River
Limstone Creek
Cabin Creek
South Fork Licking River
Blue Licks
Licking River
Hinkston's Blockhouse
Stoner Creek
Kentucky River
Bluestone Ri
Boonesborough Settlement

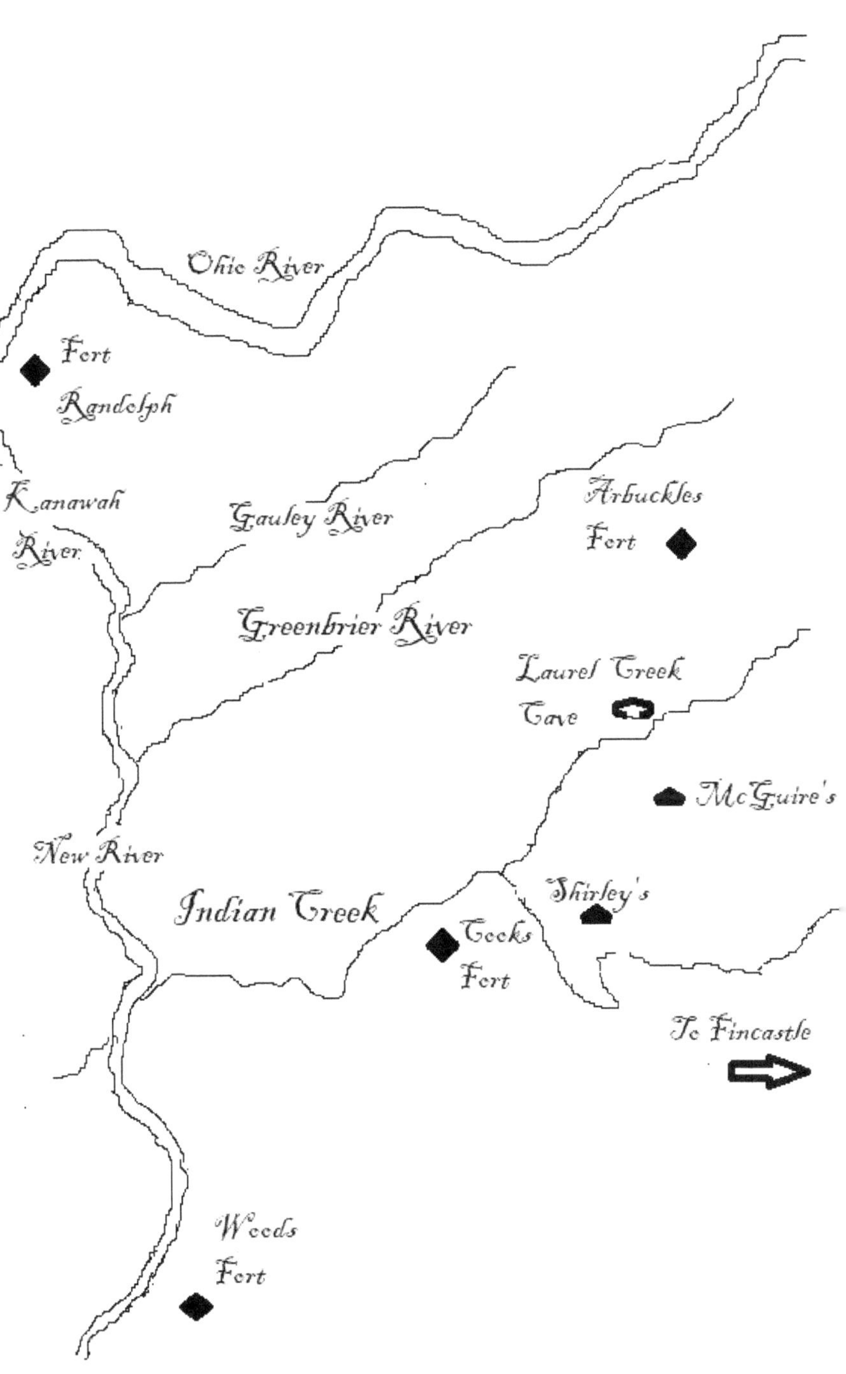

Ohio River
Fort Randolph
Kanawah River
Gauley River
Arbuckles Fort
Greenbrier River
Laurel Creek Cave
McGuire's
New River
Indian Creek
Shirley's
Cooks Fort
To Fincastle
Woods Fort

Chapter One

August 8, 1776: Cooks Fort

A humid breeze rippled my white mop cap and tattered brown petticoat as I stood atop a ridge and raised my face toward the shimmering yellow and gold sky. *Thank you, God, for bringing us out of Kentucky.*

When we crossed back over the stony gap in the Cumberland Mountains three weeks ago, I shook the territory's vile soil from the hem of my skirt and vowed I'd never return to the unprotected territory.

I couldn't return. The Shawnee warrior, Loud Hawk, spoke a stern warning: "A curse on your firstborn son if you ever return."

Huzzahs rang out from my parents, seven younger siblings, and the Gatliff family of four. My surge of joy sprang from reaching the safety of the Greenbrier Valley. My belly fluttered like hundreds of butterflies, anticipating the sight of William McGuire, the man I hoped to marry someday.

I gazed down the gentle ridge to the diamond-shaped palisades of Cooks Fort, remembering his playful manner, polished-oak eyes, well-groomed dark hair, and well-proportioned body. *Like a prized thoroughbred.* I chuckled and wondered if he'd still make me giddy.

My family moved forward, and I clucked my tongue at Jasper—an old bay gelding who survived the twenty-one-day trip from the Boonesborough settlement.

"Come on, boy. I promise it's an easy walk down. We're at our new home. You'll enjoy a thorough grooming, a full belly, and a long rest."

I held a corner of my petticoat and took small steps toward the stockade with my chest pounding like a Shawnee drum in a celebration dance.

To the southwest of the worn path, we passed a ripening field of gilded tobacco leaves, cornstalks, and wheat near a blockhouse-style home with a stockyard of cows, horses, and chickens. I daydreamed of a similar home with William, then shook my head.

Why do I want a husband who's always gone and in danger as a fort scout?

When I asked him to stay at Boonesborough until we could travel with him, his answer stung.

"I'm a scout, Mary. Leaving is what I do." Then he rushed into the dark forest to warn other settlements about the threat of Indian raids, come spring.

The hickory smoke aroma from the fort made my stomach growl, and my horse rubbed his face on my sore shoulder.

"Ouch!" I pushed him back. "What's perked you up?"

I rubbed the tender bullet wound, and willed the memory of the event not to surface by repeating, *I'm safe, and all is well.*

The north-facing gates of Cooks Fort stood open, and the sentries on the left corner platform welcomed us inside. We passed under a thick oak beam connecting the towering palisades and peace surrounded me as if I'd entered the gates of heaven. I stared into the sky, grateful and exhausted.

My thirteen-year-old sister, Katie, stopped and looked back at me with her sparkling green eyes as I neared. Her dark-brown hair shimmered in the sunlight as she used her bonnet as a fan.

"Are you excited? Do you think Papa will allow Mr. McGuire to court you before you're fifteen?"

Heat rushed across my face. I shrugged. "He prefers I wait until my birthday."

"Yes, but maybe he will." Katie laughed and walked beside me. "I'm looking forward to our new home. And I long for at least one handsome young man wishing Papa would allow me to dance."

I laughed, remembering my whims at her age. "I'm sure you will. You are pretty."

"Thank you." She twisted toward me. "If William doesn't work out, you'll have plenty of others to choose from, I'm sure."

I frowned and refused the thought of anyone else.

Papa directed the family to gather. He turned to Momma.

"What do you think, Katherine?"

She stepped into his arms. "I'm pleased to feel safe again."

My nine-year-old brother, George, shouted, "Yippee," and tossed his black felt hat into the air, then caught it. "I like this fort. It's smaller than Boonesborough, but enclosed."

Several giggling children played chase in one corner of the yard. Pleasant-faced residents scurried around tending to various chores. A few women stood talking and turning spits of sizzling beef and pork. The juices dripped into the fire, creating savory hickory smoke that brought back memories of the Shawnee village and the women I called friends before escaping a month ago.

I gulped, then drew a deep breath and their faces faded.

I'm no longer Shoots in Knee.

Ten lean-to-style log cabins, with covered porches and a shuttered window, nested between three picketed walls. Most appeared tidy, and a few posts displayed spiraling pea vines with dangling pods. One large blockhouse sat inside the southwest corner.

Katie tugged on my sleeve and pointed toward a barn with a small corral along the western wall—and William striding closer.

Giddiness washed over me like the day I accidentally breathed smoke from dried hemp leaves. Heat rushed up my neck and burned my ears. Suddenly, the memory of being shot and him lifting me into his arms returned. I closed my eyes, remembering his warm chest and the comforting scents of a rain-fresh forest, and I longed for his embrace.

"Aye, and I'm thanking God you're safe and well."

His deep musical brogue included the G unlike most Irish and still thrilled me.

He flashed a crooked smile and a wink my way, but greeted his sister, Letitia Gatliff, with a hug and kiss on the cheek, then shook his brother-in-law's hand. After he rubbed the copper heads of his two nephews, he turned to my papa.

"Glad for the sight of you all, but you're looking a mite dreary-eyed. I'll take you to a cabin."

I expected a personal greeting from him, not the slight smile and wink. Doubts of his affection for me made my eyes water with hurt. I hesitated to follow until my family moved ahead with the horses in tow.

William led us across the spacious fort yard, where at least a dozen smiling women shouted welcomes as we passed. My throat tightened from another bout of missing the Piqua women. I stood still, breathing deeply for a moment.

"You sick, lass?" A soothing voice from the nearest woman caught my attention.

"Nee-wee-see-lah-seh-mom-moh."

The woman frowned, and her mouth dropped open.

My face burned. "Oh, I'm ... sorry. I meant to say I'm feeling well."

I curtsied, then hurried to catch up with my family, allowing the woman to form her own conclusions.

On the way to a row of cabins built into the south wall we passed roughly twenty soldiers, who tipped their tricorn hats and gawked. I averted my eyes, but Katie and ten-year-old Lizzy grinned at them, then at each other.

I focused on William, desperate for a chance to tell him about my firm stance on settling in the Greenbrier Valley and my objection to living in Kentucky. Then he could verify his lack of interest in me in his future.

William stopped in front of two slanted-roof cabins and pointed. "Gatliffs on the right and the Shirleys here." He stepped onto the covered porch closest to my family and opened the door. "There's table and chairs enough, is all."

I took a step toward him, but Momma rushed past me, carrying an armload of quilts and calling out, "Don't dawdle. Let's get the horses unpacked so we can eat and make our pallets."

"Yes, ma'am." I pressed my lips together, stepped toward Jasper, and untied the bundle of blankets.

William came beside me and lifted them off. "Glad to see you, puny girl."

The first time he called me that I almost smacked him. This time, his greeting restored hope, and I stared at his mouth, dreaming of a first kiss.

He cleared his throat and stepped back. "How's your shoulder?"

I gazed into his eyes, remembering the fear in them when he first saw the wound after a camp guard mistook me for an Indian.

He tilted his head. "Mary?"

My face flushed. "Healing, but a little sore from the trip. It's ... wonderful to see you."

He leaned his head closer to my cheek.

My heart thumped, expecting a kiss.

He straightened, handed me the blankets, and hurried away. He helped Papa unload sacks of milled corn from the mule and stacked them on the end of the porch.

I lingered in the daydream of him kissing my lips, then, on a whim, I shifted the blankets to my left hip and picked up an acorn. *Might as well give him a reason to call me a puny girl.* I bounced it off his hat as a playful gesture.

He raised his eyes, nodding.

"Leave the man be." Papa laughed and lifted a sack of corn seed. "Get back to work."

Amused, I strolled to the porch. Papa's wise advice to leave William alone flew over my shoulder as I contemplated the conversation with him about Loud Hawk's threat to my life.

I peered back at the man I desired and stepped onto the porch.

William

Mary rushed into the cabin, leaving me lingering in the thrill and commotion of her rippling current.

When she entered the fort with her family, I blessed God for bringing her safely. I hated leaving her at Boonesborough—almost went back for her twice, but her gunshot wound needed tending to.

I wanted to whisk her into my arms when she fixed her bewitching brown eyes on me, but drew a breath and calmed.

"You all right, Will?"

Michael's question snatched me back to reason, but my face burned.

"Aye." I sucked in the humid breeze, lowered the heavy sack of seed corn in my arms onto the stack, and wiped sweat from my forehead.

"Dazed by the heat or my daughter?" He smirked and shook his head as he untied another bundle from his horse.

I squared my shoulders and waited for eye contact. "Well, sir. I'm interested in courting Mary when you allow."

He nodded. "I noted the bond forming at Boonesborough. You're welcome at our table for supper."

"Obliged, sir, but I best keep my distance for now. Seeing her often, and her wanting me to, makes not eloping more difficult. Aye, and I'm saying so now, so you won't shoot me later." My ears burned. "But you know me as an honorable man."

Michael moved closer to his horse. "I got me a new rifle too." He raised a sly smile and slid it from the sheath on his saddle. "Shoots sure."

I grinned in return. "I'll not be testing you."

"You've never given me cause to doubt your word. You are welcome to visit with the family around. I'm sure Katherine will agree." He rubbed his chin.

"Is there a problem?" I knew his *leaving something out* gesture. I met him four years back while on the same scouting crew ahead of the surveyors to this area.

"Mary won't like you staying away," he said. "I've seen the gleam in her eyes when you're nearby. Her headstrong manner grew more so living among the Shawnee women."

"Aye." *The reason I'm setting the boundaries.* "I noticed when she insisted on traveling back to Boonesborough with a day-old gunshot wound—whether I came along or not. Then, she faced off with the Shawnee warrior like a bobcat, and he allowed us to leave with one horse." The memory knotted my stomach. "I'll do my best to keep my distance."

He grinned. "I'll appreciate your attempt."

Michael pulled an ivory pipe from his shirt pocket, along with a long twig. "Follow me to the fire pit and tell me the news."

I fell in step behind him, then stood back from the fire's heat and waited while he lit the tobacco, sucked in draws, and released the sweet, beechnut-scented smoke. A slight smile accompanied his nod.

"The Cherokee alliance with the Shawnee fell apart and the Clinch Valley settlers speak of returning, but Dragging Canoe escaped farther south. I met with my Shawnee source, Hiding Turtle, a week ago, who insists Shawnee warriors will raid this spring."

Michael frowned. "Is he the man who took Mary to the village instead of the British outpost?"

"That he is. Please let Mary know he inquired after her and said Turkey Claw is being questioned for poisoning Chief Lone Duck."

He emptied the pipe into the fire. "Alright, but she'd want you to tell her."

"I best not. She'll want to hug me. Would you like to see the land we discussed in the morning? I've men willing to help in the cabin raising."

Michael nodded. "First thing after breakfast work for you? I'll draw out my plan on parchment tonight."

"Aye. I'll come by here in the morning."

He reached for my hand. "Thank you for the help. Have a pleasant evening, Will."

We shook hands, and I strolled toward the cabin I shared with my brother Thomas, who thinks me daft about the lass when there are others desiring me as a husband. I shook my head at the thought of finding a docile woman to marry instead of the strong-minded Mary who had held my heart since I met her a year ago. Strong, brave, and beautiful—even after the long trek, with dirt smudges on her tired but sweet face. Wisps of her loose dark hair had shimmered like crow feathers in the last glint of sunlight. I yearned to smooth them. Her shiny brown eyes widened as I leaned toward her, then resisted kissing her cheek. But I longed to kiss her lips, and wanted her by my side, cultivating Kentucky land, raising horses and a passel of children. *I'll wait for her, but I best stay busy cabin building.*

I arrived at the cabin and forced a frown so Thomas wouldn't tease me for grinning.

Mary

Unable to breathe in the cramped, hot cabin, I remade my bed on the porch. I preferred my own space under the starry sky and the croaks of frogs to the snores of my family. In the Shawnee village, I shared a wigwam with Whispering Leaf until she left with the war party. *I hope she is well. I owe her my life.* My throat tightened, remembering her stepping up to adopt me.

Exhausted, confused, and at the end of endurance, I closed my eyes and inhaled the fort's smoky scent, allowing the familiar smell to calm my frazzled nerves from all the life-altering changes in a year. I rolled to my side, peering over the northern palisades at the flickering stars against a moonless sky. Crickets played their sweet love songs, and the deep-throated tree frogs announced their intentions to court. As I wondered if William would wait for me, I waved off the fretting along with a buzzing mosquito and pulled my blanket over my head.

Chapter Two

August 9

Papa and my brothers came from the woodpile, dusting shavings from their clothes as I placed the platter of bacon on the outside table for breakfast. When I looked up, the sight of William strolling toward us made a wonderful way to start the day. When he glanced my way, I widened my grin.

He carried a pail in one hand and his large sleek bay, Babcock's Boy, followed behind him without a lead rope.

Momma stepped toward him first, blocking my view.

"Good morning, Will."

"Morning, Mrs. Shirley. Thought you might enjoy a bit of fresh milk."

"Indeed. Thank you." Papa took the pail, then handed it off to me.

Charlie cheered, "Yippie," before plopping onto the bench beside two-year-old Sally.

I carried the heavy pail to the table and turned back. "Please, join us for breakfast."

His eyes sparkled at me as he smiled. "Thank you, but I've already eaten. I'm getting on to the land." He clucked his tongue and strolled away with his horse.

My heart pattered, watching him, wishing I could spend the day handing him cups of water and wiping sweat from his brow.

"Are you coming, Mary? Milk is strained—come to the table," Momma said.

I heard but didn't look away.

Papa placed his hand on my back and leaned toward my ear. "He intends to wait until your birthday for courting. He will keep his distance until then, but he relayed a message from Hiding Turtle that Blue Jacket is investigating the chief's death. Easier on him if you stay back a bit. Come, eat." He stepped around the table to his chair.

I sucked in a deep breath as frustration festered. "Well, he hasn't asked me about courting, and I'm not a little girl. Maybe I don't want him courting."

I slid beside Katie on the bench.

My family stared at me as if I had two heads.

"I'm sorry for my outburst." I clasped my hands together and bowed my head, still smoldering.

Papa prayed, "Thank you for our blessings. Give us wisdom for the day's decisions and keep all safe. Amen."

As we echoed the amen, he reached for two slices of thick bacon and wrapped them in his napkin.

"George and I will view the land before hunting game for supper." He swigged down a cup of milk.

George rushed his last bite and shouldered his rifle.

Charlie stood. "Me too?"

Papa kissed Momma's upturned cheek, then addressed Charlie. "You're responsible for filling the kindling box and helping your momma."

"Yes, sir," he said through a mouthful of honey-saturated hoecake.

They left down the same trail as William.

I stood from the table, seconds away from following and seeking William's mind on Kentucky, before desiring him any longer. But Letitia Gatliff's cheery voice called out, "A fine mornin' 'tis."

I scooted from the bench, excited by her visit and ready to hug her, but Letitia approached with an older woman who favored her.

The woman wore a soft blue cap over silvery hair and a pleasant smile. A bushel basket full of pea pods swung from the handle in her hand.

Momma dusted off a chair with her apron and offered it. "Welcome."

Letitia stood still. "And I'm pleased to be introducin' my ma, Tessie. They live north of your new place."

Mrs. McGuire placed the basket on the table and took Momma's hand. "I've been hearing of the Shirleys for a month and a day." Her Irish brogue matched Letitia's. "And now I'm pleased to meet ya."

"Happy to meet you too." She chuckled. "Please sit. Would you like coffee?" She looked at eight-year-old Susie. "Bring two clean cups for our guests."

"Yes, ma'am." She darted toward the cabin.

"And a container for these peas, lass," Mrs. McGuire said and beamed at Momma. "If ya' don't mind me sharin'."

Momma smiled. "Thank you. These will make a fine addition to our supper."

Mrs. McGuire remained standing as she scanned over us all and returned to me, grinning.

"And you'd be William's Mary."

My mouth dropped open. *William's Mary?* Heat radiated to my cheeks. Katie and Lizzy giggled behind my back.

Mrs. McGuire chortled as she took my hands in her warm ones. Her brown eyes sparkled with the same playful glint as her son's. "He boasts of your bravery and strong-mindedness. And you're a pretty lass as well." Her smile rose.

My lips numbed. I looked at my feet, unable to bear her scrutiny. *He's spoken to his ma too?*

Mrs. McGuire gave my hands a gentle squeeze, released them, then held the edge of the table before lowering into the chair. I drew a deep breath and joined Letitia on the bench.

Susie handed the cups to Momma and placed two large bowls on the table.

As green pods tumbled into the bowls, Mrs. McGuire's words spilled into the air. "He'd be shy sayin' so, but it's plain as plain my Will's fancyin' your daughter a might. A mother knows these things."

I glanced up as Momma gave me a wry smile and poured coffee into the clean cups. "We think Will is a fine man. We're grateful for his help. Would you like milk and sugar?"

I squirmed and wiped my palms on my apron, thankful Momma changed the subject.

Letitia leaned toward my ear. "Sorry Ma embarrassed you." She straightened, then sipped her coffee. "Thankful for a break from my sons. Charles took them fishing."

I folded my hands, pressing my lips, annoyed at being the last to know his mind.

"How far is your land from us?" Momma asked.

I didn't listen to the answer but turned to Letitia.

"Why did your ma call me William's Mary? I don't belong to him."

Her eyebrows raised. "She meant no slight. Aye, my brother is smitten with ya and always mentionin' your name." She grinned.

The happy news also set my mind on speaking to him about ignoring me.

Letitia patted my hand. "Have I said too much, lass?"

"No." I smiled. "Sorry for judging your ma too quickly. Now, I'd like to know why your ma calls you Christina."

She sat back. "'Tis my name. But Charles said he wouldn't call me by it because another lass named Christina spurned him a year before." She finished her coffee and gave me a firm stare. "I allowed it for the sake of keepin' peace. But I've a mind to put my foot down. I've already informed my brothers."

"I'll make the change too." I clasped her hand. "You've every right to insist on your name."

She beamed. "Aye, and so I will."

Mrs. McGuire eased from the chair and stretched her arms over her head. "Time I head home. There'll be game of some sort waitin' to be cooked by now—and your da frettin'. Would you like to stroll along, Katherine? Your place is on my way."

"Yes, thank you." Momma stood, brushing off her lap.

Christina rose from the bench. "And I'll enjoy an hour alone before the lads return."

I slid out after her. "Be strong."

"Thank you." She chuckled and squeezed my hand. "Don't ya rush into courtin'. You've plenty of time to consider my brother and others castin' their eyes on ya."

Others? My face burned as she waved then scurried toward her cabin.

Mrs. McGuire placed her hands on my shoulders and kissed my cheeks. "Pleasure meetin' you, lass. Look forward to more visits."

Her smile and acceptance warmed my heart. "Thank you ... Mrs. McGuire."

Momma turned toward us with a childlike joy. "Please finish the chores while I'm gone. Shouldn't be more than an hour."

My eyes misted for her happiness. *She deserves a break and some fun.*

She and Mrs. McGuire chatted like long-lost friends along the same path the men had traveled.

I helped gather dishes and pondered the certainty of William's interest in courting and my need to speak with him before day's end. I didn't want his ma thinking so highly of me if I'm not the one to marry her son. My chest ached with the possibility of life without William, while I washed dishes and handed them to Lizzy.

"We should shell the peas," Katie said as she scraped off the last plate and added it to the wash pile.

She cleaned her hands, handed Sally a bowl of peas, and pointed to a shady place under an oak tree.

"Sit under that tree and let the peas out of the pods. We'll come help in a minute."

Once finished with our chores, we carried containers of peas to the shade and sat.

"No moo." Sally showed me her empty pods while chewing a mouthful of peas.

I laughed and stood her up, brushing off her dress. "No more for you."

Lizzy stepped forward and took Sally's hand. "I'll take the children blackberry hunting. I saw some not far outside the fort. We should find enough for a pie."

Katie frowned. "Would Momma approve?"

"A blackberry pie sounds wonderful. I don't think she'd mind, and Lizzy is capable." I peered at Lizzy. "Stay south of Indian Creek."

"Watch for snakes," Katie said. "And don't let Sally wander off."

Sally nodded. "I be good."

They ran to the other three and announced the task. Charlie shouted, "Huzzah." Susie and Nancy rushed to retrieve baskets.

Katie gazed at me, smiling.

"Mrs. McGuire seems to approve of you for her son."

I sighed. "I think so too. Made me nervous." I raised a handful of peas to my mouth and chewed.

She laughed. "Why?"

I ate more peas while considering my answer. "I don't know if I'll marry him."

Katie stared as if waiting for more information.

I shrugged. "Life is uncertain and can change in seconds."

Katie peered behind me. "Momma's back." She pushed to her feet and helped me up.

Momma's smile stretched wider as she neared.

"Our new home is a five-minute walk." She beamed. "Flat and already cleared. The McGuires grew plenty of corn to share seeds, and your papa will survey for Mr. McGuire as payment. The men are hauling logs to the cabin's location now."

Katie grinned at me, then Momma. "Wish we could watch."

I chuckled at the thought, but watching William work would make what I had to say harder.

Momma noticed our bowls. "Best for us to stay out of the way so they can work faster. Thank you for the peas." She reached for a handful, popped one in her mouth, and scanned the yard. "Where are the other children?"

Katie answered. "Lizzy took them berry picking close to the fort."

She nodded, and Katie and I grinned.

"The McGuires' place is two miles north of us," Momma said. "Once we move in, Tessie will gift us with her extra flax wheel for thread making. We'll make new outfits for the harvest dance on October fourth."

"Why so early?" I calculated the moon days in my head. "The moon won't be full yet."

She tossed in another pea. "They want to celebrate early and not delay harvesting."

What does a full moon matter with no one to dance with?

"How long will our cabin take to build?" Katie asked.

"Shawnee women build their wigwams in a day or two," I blurted. "They're made with sturdy green saplings, weaved tightly, and covered with layers of bark and bison hides. Easy, practical, as well as dry, warm, and cozy." I smiled and imagined building one for me and William. Then the turmoil returned.

"A stick hut?" Katie tilted her head and frowned. "Logs make more sense."

Silent stares from Momma pricked my heart.

I forgot how my spoken memories seemed to cause her pain. "Sorry for interrupting. It would be wonderful if cabins took only two days."

She nodded and turned to Katie. "It could be as soon as a month because everything is ready. We'll settle on our own land, in a spacious new cabin." She smiled at me. "And focus on the future."

"Yes, ma'am," we said together.

She stood. "And we'll be close to this well-stocked fort with plenty of soldiers in case of trouble. Thank you for taking care of things here. I enjoyed my visit with Mrs. McGuire."

Plenty of soldiers? I remembered Christina's mention of others casting their eyes on me. The thought of unknown men asking me to dance twisted a knot in my stomach, but I supposed I'd accept—even though I'd wish each one were William.

Katie pointed toward the gate. "Here comes the children."

Susie and Nancy rushed into the yard with full baskets. Lizzy scowled and pulled Sally by the hand.

Charlie stepped around her and huffed. "She didn't obey. She ran into the woods searching for fairies. We found her at another creek, talking to a frog."

A surge of panic rose. "Do you remember falling into the creek at our old place? You almost drowned."

"I remember." Charlie knelt on one knee and peered at Sally. "The slave man, Adam, told me a serpent snatches children in when they get too close to the bank."

Her eyes widened. She grabbed Momma's skirt. "No serpent. I sorry. I stay 'way from keek."

"Land sakes." Momma shook her head. "The only thing that's going to get you is me. Go to your pallet." She pointed to the cabin and turned to the rest of us. "You may all go do something fun. I'm going to nap with Sally."

Something fun? All that came to mind was walking with Katie to meet other's our age, but she'd want to pass by the soldiers.

Chapter Three

As Momma went inside, Charlie plopped on the ground beside me, wiping sweat from his brow.

"Wish I could go fishing. But I can't make a fishing pole by myself."

Katie moved beside him. "You can barter one. Would you like me to go with you?"

Charlie climbed to his feet. "Yes, and help dig worms."

"We have time to make a four-pronged spear. Then we don't need bait." I pushed to my feet.

Curious stares prompted an explanation.

"The Shawnee chief's daughter, Corn Flower, taught me how to use one. It kept me from starving when I escaped."

The memory of her betrayal when I needed her most stirred crushing sadness.

Katie giggled. "I want to learn. Fish sound good for supper." She glanced back at our younger sisters. "Want to go?"

They shook their heads, but Lizzy spoke. "We're going inside to gather our sewing baskets, then sit in the shade and practice our embroidery. We wish to make pretty things for our new cabin. Then we'll help Momma make the pie."

"I want to make yellow flowers on my sampler." Nancy smiled and held Lizzy's hand as they stepped inside the cabin.

After retrieving a hunting knife, a hatchet, a tall basket, and two lengths of rope from the porch, we strolled out of the fort and crossed a footbridge over the creek into the woods. Charlie and Katie watched for snakes while I examined the young pine, oak, and elm trees.

"The sapling has to be straight and strong, and fit your grasp. Like this one." I pointed and handed the hatchet to Charlie.

Katie gasped.

"He's older than most Shawnee boys who chop saplings for huts and practice throwing them at trees, some as young as two. He'll do fine. Won't you?"

He nodded. "I won't tell Momma."

I sliced a mark on the bark. "Try to chop here each time and don't place your hand on the trunk."

With a few wild strikes, Charlie whacked the stick down and proceeded to hack on another.

I stopped his arm and took the hatchet back. "That's enough. Let's make the spear."

He pooched out his lips, but I led him to a large flat-topped rock used as a sharpening stone and laid the stick down.

I split one end of the spear into fourths with the knife and whittled sharp points on the end. Next, I wrapped thin vines around the cut end to prevent it from splitting.

"What is the rope for?" Charlie held up the cords.

I gave one to Katie. "Tie this around your waist, then tuck the hem of your petticoat and chemise through."

Katie's mouth dropped. "You mean show our bare knees?"

"Better than removing our garments." I laughed and Charlie giggled. "Once we are in the water, no one will think we're immodest. And I don't care if they do."

"Well, all right." Katie secured the rope and raised her skirts while scanning for onlookers.

I did the same.

"Let's go to the creek." I offered Charlie the spear. "Want to carry it?"

He beamed and held out his hand.

"Keep the point up and away from you. At the creek, I'll show you how it works."

We crossed back over the bridge, left our moccasins on the bank, and waded into the cold, slow current. I walked along the bank, pointing the spear at the water. As Charlie and Katie watched, I explained the procedure, and Katie followed me with the basket.

I stood still and waited for the silt to clear. "See that trout hiding in the snag?"

"Get him," Charlie whispered.

I plunged the spear into the fish. "Bring the basket—I'm pulling it up." The rainbow-striped trout flapped from two sharpened points.

"It's beautiful," Katie said.

I shook the fish into the basket.

"Lower it in the water a little, but don't let it jump out."

I gave the spear to Charlie. "Your turn. Use a light thrust. Don't break the points."

His first two tries failed, but he squinted hard at the next fish and aimed.

"I got one. I got one. Hurry with the basket. Huzzah." Charlie's excitement drew the attention of five soldiers wearing tan trousers and bleached linen shirts. They were William's age or younger.

Katie bumped my arm and giggled. "We have admirers."

My face flushed as I scanned them, but none sparked my interest away from William.

The men cheered each time one of us speared a fish.

Don't they have work to do? I shook my head after my turn and gave the spear to Katie, who relished the men's attention. Within the hour we had eight large trout, and I had an aching back and sore arms.

"Let's clean these back at the cabin." I splashed to the bank and lowered my skirts. "I don't want the soldiers lingering to speak with us."

Katie sighed, fluffed her petticoat, and stood with folded arms. "You're afraid Mr. McGuire will see and think you're not sweet on him. It won't hurt to be friendly. What if one of these men is his equal?"

I faced her. "You can't stay here without me. Let's go."

Before she could protest, I ran. I didn't want to consider replacing William in my heart.

After Katie, Charlie, and I finished cleaning, salting, and wrapping the trout, Papa and George stepped into the yard with William, who made his way toward the barn.

I rushed to dry my hands.

"I'll be back." I dashed away, giving Papa a quick glance.

As I neared the barn, I slowed, breathed deep, and eased inside.

William hummed a peppy tune as he brushed Babcock. The horse raised his head, and William turned with a bright-red face.

I caught my breath and tucked a stray hair behind my ears. I lost the nerve to bring up Kentucky outright. "Would you like to come for supper?"

He straightened with tight lips and raised eyebrows, then scanned behind my head as if expecting someone else to come inside.

I glanced back, but no one came. "Are you expecting someone?"

He shifted his feet like a nervous horse. "No. I'm surprised you've come alone."

"Why?" I glared, and he took a step back. "I've been alone with you many times. And why does my papa and your ma know you're interested in courting me, but you've not mentioned it?"

He stared a moment. "I'm ... sorry. I'm staying away and busy until your birthday. Respecting your da's rules. After finishing the cabin, I'll leave on a long scouting trip and come visiting when I return."

I gulped. "How long?"

"Hope to be back by Christmas." He stepped around the horse, brush in hand, and faced me. "Thank you for the supper invitation, but Christina is expecting me." He sniffed the air toward me, then waved his hand before his nose. "What have you been doing? Why do you smell like fish?"

Horrified by this, I stepped back. "I taught Charlie how to spear fish. I'd hoped you could share supper with us."

His smile widened as he returned to brushing. "We can visit while I finish grooming Babcock's Boy."

I eased closer and rubbed the horse's neck, still too nervous to speak the words I came to say. "Will we move into the cabin by the end of the month?"

"I hope so." He brushed the horse's hind leg and moved to the other side. "We have a good plan, and the logs are ready." He stopped moving and peeked at me over the horse's withers. "Headed for Kentucky the first week of September."

I held my souring stomach and frowned.

"Must you keep going back?"

He rubbed the horse's head and faced me. "Now that most of the Cherokee have agreed to peace, the Virginia Counsel wants Kentucky protected from British control. They need surveyors to go back and sort out the claims so settlers can return with militiamen."

I moved back and filled my lungs with dusty air, staring into his deep-brown eyes. My chest squeezed.

"Do you intend to be one of those militiamen?" My heart pounded. "Are you planning to settle in Kentucky?"

Please say no.

He stepped back, frowning. "Well ... I ..." He studied my eyes. "Not immediately. But I'll help keep the western territory out of British hands. And ... I thought I'd ask Daniel Boone for that piece of land you liked the day I escorted you back to your family." He smiled.

I shook my head and spewed, "No. I'll never return to Kentucky. I can't."

His head jerked back as if I'd slapped him, then his face and shoulders sagged.

I regretted my harsh tone, but the explanation he needed stuck in my throat as I fought the need to bawl.

"I ... I'm sorry." Embarrassed, I raced from the barn—hating myself for being so childish.

I ducked inside a privy and latched the door, crying and muttering to the flies, "He'll not want me now. Why do I build dreams from sticks only to have them blown away by devastating whirlwinds?" I covered my nose with my apron to block the stench.

The memory of his stricken face and joyless eyes strangled my throat. "I still need to explain."

I dried my face and stepped into the fresh air. My legs wobbled back to the stable, but Babcock's Boy was already nibbling grass in the corral with no sight of William.

Crushed in spirit, I strolled back across the yard toward my family's cabin.

"There you are." Papa grinned. "Did you ask him to come for supper?"

I stared at the ground, hiding my swollen eyes. "He has plans with his family."

I rolled a sharp pebble back and forth under my bare foot. But the pain didn't dull the agony in my chest.

William

Mary's fiery eyes and harsh tone wrenched my gut like a punch I didn't see coming. I waited five minutes, hoping she'd return and explain why she got so riled. Thought she'd be excited about the land. Didn't know she'd oppose settling in Kentucky. I know it's not safe yet, and she's still troubled by her experiences. Maybe she'll calm down.

I led Babcock out of the barn and into the stockyard, but the lass didn't appear.

My mind reeled as I sauntered toward Christina's, but I watched the Shirleys' cabin, willing myself not to seek her out, deciding she'd find me when ready.

I dusted off and entered my sister's place. She stopped slicing squash and gazed up. Then, after wiping her hands on her apron, she rushed toward me, placing her cold palm on my forehead. "You're pale. What's ailin' ya?" She felt my cheeks.

"Mary."

I hung my hat on a wall peg, thankful my nephews were with Charles somewhere. "She found me in the barn, and we chatted a bit. Friendly, until I mentioned buying a piece of land she liked in Kentucky. Suddenly enraged, she yelled she'd never return, then stormed out."

I shook my head and sat on a log bench at the table. "I'm a mite scuffed and bruised on the inside. What if she doesn't change her mind?" My gut knotted.

"Well, then." She stood at the head of the table. "Let her finish recoverin' her wits, and don't ya be holdin' on to hurt because of her wailin'. The lass battled at the gates of Hades itself, and she's young and tender." Christina's face softened. "She'll calm down."

Her sharp tone stung my pride. I expected sympathy, not a scolding, but my heart broke.

"It's true. Mary's not a seasoned soldier and scout, calloused from the fears of the fight. I'll focus on my duties and allow her peace."

The door opened with five-year-old Reese holding a string of fish over his head, followed by my brother, Thomas. Charles entered carrying the yearling James.

Before the door closed, I glimpsed Mary outside with her family. The desire to join them for supper caused an ache in my belly and a longing for her in my arms.

Mary

Inside the cabin, Papa touched my arm. "Has something happened? Your eyes are puffy."

"William wants to settle in Kentucky someday." My chest hurt. "I can't go back." Tears formed. "I ... I can't bear the dangers. I told him, but ... it hurts."

"I'm sorry, *liebchen*." He drew me into his arms and stroked my hair while I snuggled against his chest. "William desires the land for breeding fast horses."

More than me? The crushed sensation deepened.

Papa sighed and eased me back, his face solemn. "Plenty of time for sorting things out. Enjoy a time of peace and grow strong again. You are too young for such a troubled heart."

My head pounded and tears threatened to fall, but I nodded and stepped back. "Thank you, Papa."

I turned from him and retrieved the platter of fluffy hoecakes.

As I stepped outside, Christina's family passed and entered her cabin. I focused on my siblings gathering around our table and chattering about new friends, but my insides felt squashed like a June bug.

"Did you hear me?" Momma patted my hand.

I smiled at her tilted head. "I'm sorry, no."

"For the rest of the month, we'll help work the community garden for a share of the harvest and preserve as much as we can." She waited for my nod before lifting her fork and saying, "Eat, Daughter."

"Yes, ma'am."

I set my mind on staying busy, but a tear slid down my cheek just the same, and I quickly wiped it away.

I'll tell him of Loud Hawk's warning at the next opportunity. Maybe he'll understand and forgive me.

Chapter Four

September 5

After a long month, we rose early and packed our belongings for the move. The happy day also sparked sorrow over the inability to speak with William before he left.

He'd stayed at the building site instead of returning to the fort each night. I imagined him still hurt and avoiding the sight of me, though I understood.

While the rest of the family carried loads of household items to our new wagon, Katie and I rushed to the community garden with a tow sack.

Christina Gatliff stood up from the steamy fog hovering above the ground and waved. "Good mornin' to ya."

"And to you." I scanned the area, expecting to see and hear her sons. "Where are your boys?"

She carried her full basket closer. "Fishing with their da before he's away scoutin' here, there, and yon."

"Is William still here?" My stomach fluttered. "I'd like to speak with him."

She smiled. "He's waitin' at your new place to unload. Come back and see me when you can. I'm off to enjoy a moment of peace before my rowdy critters return."

"I will." I kissed her cheek, then hunched along the dew-soaked row, snipping squash from prickly vines in a rush.

After dropping the last one into my sack, I stretched a kink from my back and rubbed my itchy hands.

I wiped sweat from my brow and spied my sister giggling at a large elm tree in the back corner of the garden.

What is she doing?

I slogged closer and heard her whisper, "Stay safe."

I cleared my throat, then shouted, "Who's there? Show yourself."

Katie startled, shouldered her bag, and darted in front of me, wide-eyed. "He's just saying good-bye."

A soldier stepped out and tipped his hat. "Private John Baughman, miss. Heading out on patrol but saw her here. Meant no harm." A coy grin rose as he gave her a nod. "Good day, miss."

"I'll pray for you." Katie waved as he marched away.

I waited for him to move from earshot and turned. "Katherine Shirley. How long have you been speaking to the man in secret? You're only thirteen. Has he asked Papa?"

"No." She peered into my eyes. "John saw us spearfishing, and I met him the next day. Isn't he handsome?"

All I could do was glare. Not angry but ... jealous.

"Please ... don't tell Papa." Her voice trembled. "John's been busy but will talk to him when he comes back from patrolling."

I shook my head and calmed. "Papa won't approve if you sneak around."

"I know." She shifted the bag to her other shoulder and trudged forward.

I hung back, gulping down the grief of losing William's attention all because of Kentucky and Loud Hawk's very real threat of death if I return.

As I hurried toward the wagon, I glimpsed Thomas McGuire enter the barn, and panic gripped my stomach.

Not much time left.

I peered beyond the canopy of fire-colored leaves and prayed. "Grant me time to explain everything in my heart. I'm hoping he'll consider remaining in the Greenbrier."

"There you are." Papa took my sack and lifted it up to George, who arranged our wares in the narrow wagon.

Not only had George grown a foot taller during my absence, his manner matured into one of strength, wisdom, and bravery. Pride swelled in my chest, but I missed his fun-loving nature.

Momma handed me a stack of blankets, and I transferred them to my brother.

Papa climbed onto the seat and motioned for George. "Come drive the wagon, Son."

"Me?" His smile beamed as he scooted into place and took the reins. After a few instructions, he said, "Giddyup," and the creaky wagon lurched forward.

I gave Jasper a light tug and followed the rest of the family and horses east across the meadow, then north toward Indian Creek. The wagon crossed a newly built bridge over the slow-moving stream as it sparkled in the sunlight and trickled over scattered rocks.

After Momma and my sisters scurried across, Charlie stopped and backed. Before I could grab his arm, he jogged down to the water's edge in front of the bridge, hurled himself into the waist-deep water, and floated under the bridge.

I held my breath until he climbed the bank and planted his feet.

"Momma won't let you drip on the new cabin's floor."

He giggled and squeezed water from his clothes, then darted along the trail through a maple grove.

I strolled across the bridge with my horse and grinned, tempted to try it but shook my head.

No one would believe I fell in. And then there's William.

I quickened the pace past blackberry thickets, wild plum groves, and other foraging places and reached the wonderful sight of our two-level home in the middle of a meadow and my family speaking with William.

Nerves twisted my stomach as I trampled through the grass, growing more breathless as I neared the majestic home with a wide covered porch.

My family removed items from the wagon and horses, and I crept closer, admiring our new home. All my life we'd lived in small, cramped cabins.

William gazed at me without smiling, then turned away and helped Papa unload the salt barrel.

His reaction stung but didn't detour my quest.

"Mary, are you alright?" Momma carried a bag of milled corn as she passed.

"Yes, ma'am. I'm coming." I dropped Jasper's lead rope and grabbed an armload of blankets from the wagon.

I veered toward William and brushed his back with my bundle, then turned and smiled, hoping my flirtation would hold him until I returned for another armload.

"Good morning, Mr. McGuire. Thank you for the beautiful cabin and for helping us move in."

His deep brown eyes widened, and a slight grin raised. "Morning."

Delighted by his reaction, I sashayed toward the covered porch where the others waited in front of George, who blocked our entrance.

"You're going to be so happy." He beamed and whisked the oak plank door open. "Follow me."

George led us inside the spacious dwelling with a hardwood floor. A spruce-scented breeze swirled through the door and the two front windows.

A unanimous gasp filled the air. Then Momma ended our silence with, "Oh, how wonderful."

A polished cedar mantle adorned our fireplace in the western wall, and the knee-high hearth stones from Indian Creek were a lovely smoky gray.

"I want to see." Charlie wedged through, and Momma moved aside.

My eyes squinted at the bright whitewashed log walls that ended at the ceiling. My mind flashed back a year.

"Like the Mueller's house on the Bluestone River, only ours is better." I straightened with pride.

"It's butiful." Sally pointed and grinned.

Nancy clapped. "I love it."

To my left, a steep stairway with a banister led to the loft with guardrails. A large rectangular table made from planed pine boards sat in the space before the stairs. I placed the blankets there.

My excited brother rushed across the wood floor and opened a door on our right. "This is Momma and Papa's room." Scooting to our left. "And this room is for Susie, Nancy, and Sally." His smile widened. "Now come see a surprise."

He stopped in front of a three-shelved cupboard to the left of the fireplace, reached for one of its two drawers, and looked at Momma. "Watch this." He yanked one forward.

I clasped my mouth, expecting the drawer to land on his foot.

His chest puffed out. "There's a ledge at the back. I figured it out, and Papa helped me make it."

"Clever boy." Momma hugged him.

Clomping boots on the porch preceded the door opening. "How do you like the place?" Papa grinned and hung his hat on a peg.

"Everything is wonderful." Momma rushed into his arms. "I hate to make it dirty and smoky."

"But I'm hungry." Charlie moaned.

I glanced out the window as William headed toward his grazing horse.

No! I turned to my family. "I need to speak to William before he leaves."

I rushed outside, down the same path, then ambled toward him. Desperation drove away fear. *Be strong.*

He stood beside Babcock, tugging on the saddle. As my foot snapped a twig in half, he flinched and turned stern-faced, but his horse nickered a greeting.

"Please wait." I caught my breath. "I need to tell you something."

He removed his hat and pressed his lips.

My throat tightened, and my eyes blurred. "The day Loud Hawk allowed us to live"—I clutched my chest—"he threatened me, saying, 'A curse on your firstborn son if you ever return to Kentucky.'" Suddenly, the warrior's icy glare appeared in front of me, and a swirling sensation made me dizzy.

As I wobbled, William clasped my forearms.

"Take a breath, lass. Do you need to sit?"

His soothing tone calmed me. I shook my head and sucked in the steamy air.

He released my arms but stood near and shook his head. "I'm not believing in curses."

I stepped back and dried my cheeks with my apron. "Me either, but if Loud Hawk encounters me again, his retaliation will be swift. I can't bear the consequences of losing my future children to Indian raids." My soul screamed, *No*, as the words I had to say squeezed out, "I care for you. But I can't be your wife in Kentucky."

He stepped back, frowning.

Heat shot across my face. "Not that you were going to ask." I stared at the ground like a silly fool.

He shifted closer and held my hand. "I didn't understand the words Loud Hawk said that day. Aye, and I'm sorry you're afraid."

I stood still, relishing his warm touch and tantalizing brogue as he continued.

"Appreciate the explanation. It helps me understand."

I flipped my hands over in frustration. "I've been wanting to talk to you all this time, but it seemed you were avoiding me."

A wry grin raised on his face. "Thought it best to stay away and give you time to settle in." He studied me, and the corners of his mouth straightened. "I'm off to Kentucky now. I'll be wishing to speak again when

I return." A slight grin rose. "Be expecting me before Christmas."

His softening gaze deepened the slicing pain in my gut. He clasped my hands and lifted them to his lips. A mischievous glint shone in his eyes. He kissed the top of my fingers, and prickles ran up my spine.

I watched his lips and wanted them on mine. A first kiss I could treasure forever.

He stared at my mouth, released my hands, and cupped my face. I studied the shades of rawhide in his brown eyes. When his thumbs caressed my lips, I gasped as if he'd tossed me into the sky while my stomach stayed on the ground. *Do it again.*

One hand slipped behind my head while his other rested on my back. His cheek brushed past my lips and rested against mine. Warm breaths whispered low and raspy, "I want to kiss you."

My stomach fluttered. *What do I say? What do I do? Did I just nod?*

With a slight move back, he gazed into my eyes and smiled. Then eased me toward his lips. I closed my eyes and slipped my hands around his back.

His lips pressed warm and soft against mine, while I delighted in the sensation of floating. He pulled me closer.

The kiss deepened, and everything around me silenced until I moaned.

The kiss ended, but he hugged me before pushing away with a raspy voice, saying, "I shouldn't have done that."

I staggered back, confused and panting.

He steadied me and glanced around. "I promised your pa I'd keep my distance."

"I'm glad you kissed me." My smile widened, and I stepped into his arms and lay my head against his pounding chest, relishing the scents of leather, witch hazel, and pine resin. My heart thumped a quick steady rhythm, and I imagined swaying around him in a Shawnee courtship dance.

He kissed my cheek and stepped back. "Well, I'm not sorry, but I can't be doing that again. I'd want to marry you now ... and, well ... I'm needed to keep the British out of Kentucky. I'd like to buy that land we saw and raise horses."

My breath caught. "What?"

His eyes widened, then he shifted his weight. "I'm sorry to mention it again, but I hope you change your mind about going back." He kissed my hand, then picked up his hat, brushed off the dirt, and frowned. "I better go. Thomas and Charles are waiting for me."

With chest-crushing panic, I lunged back into his arms, breathing him in again, and wishing I could take back my vow, but didn't. "Maybe there will be peace in Kentucky someday, and I won't be afraid."

His face brightened. "I'll pray peace comes before your birthday, puny little girl." He eased me back and winked.

I peered through watering eyes. *I want to be with you—forever.*

He donned his hat, swiped a tear from my cheek, and kissed it off his finger as his polished-oak eyes glistened. "Wish I could take away your pain." He rested his hand on my forearm and caressed it with his thumb and stated the Shawnee farewell. "Somewhere I'll see you again."

"Until ... we meet again." I sniffled and clutched my chest, keeping my pounding heart from spilling to the ground. "Stay safe" floated out in a whisper.

As he clucked his tongue, Babcock followed him away and down the trail.

Tears fell as the man I desired strode out of my life.

Songbirds flitted overhead, chirping their love songs, and the hole in my heart deepened. I wandered toward a clump of hedges that resembled a short wigwam and crawled inside. I cried until the pungent blends of earth and nearby wild sage calmed my sorrow. Memories of my time in the Piqua Shawnee Village, of Whisper and Moon

Flower's kindness, and of God's protection, reminded me to be strong and keep going, even when afraid. But the voice of wisdom still warned against settling Kentucky.

I emerged from the hedge and strolled back to my family, picturing William. The sensation of his kiss still made my lips tingle.

I've given him my first kiss and can't take it back.

I don't want to, God.

He's the man I want.

Chapter Five

I couldn't stop grinning, even though my cheeks ached. Several quick steps later, my breaths calmed. Kissing Mary was a foolish thing to do, but what a kiss—more potent than moonshine.

When Babcock snorted behind me, reason returned.

I slowed and turned. "Sorry, boy, didn't mean to ignore you. I'm a mite distracted."

I shook my head and led him on toward the creek, sharing the muddle in my mind. "I only meant to soothe her sadness by holding her hand. She trembled at my touch. But when she fixed a longing stare on my lips while I kissed her fingers—I lost my mind."

My bay whinnied, and I imagined him chiding, "Sober up, lad. She'll still be pining when you return." I laughed.

Babcock waded into the creek and drank. I stood on the bridge and stared at the sky—somber for the mission ahead. "God, help us foil the British plans to subdue liberty. We desire peace, but we'll secure freedom or lose our lives."

I watched a bright-yellow hickory leaf tumble through the cool breeze and land in the water, where it caught a ride in the trickling current toward New River with no idea what's waiting downstream. *Like me and my mates. Come what may.*

I entered the fort and maneuvered around a group of new people with horses and mules but didn't recognize anyone.

By habit, I glanced at the now empty Shirley cabin, missing the sight of them and aching from the dagger-deep pain of holding Mary in my arms and her fearing the words Loud Hawk seeded. *If I encounter the fiend, I'll take him out myself.*

Thomas and Charles stood with their horses and a pack mule in front of the Gatliffs' porch.

My brother grinned and raised his chin. I expected a jeer.

"Thought you moved in with the Shirley clan, so we did."

I nodded with my jab back. "Aye, and miss scouting Indian country with you ruffians?"

Charles chortled as he ruffled his son Reese's bushy red hair and shook the lad's hand. "Take care of your ma and mind."

The toddler, James, leaped into his da's arms and squealed when tossed heavenward, nearly hitting a tree branch. I gasped with a sensation of flight and concern.

Charles stood the child on the ground again, slipped an arm around Christina's waist, and kissed her firm and purposeful. *The way I kissed Mary and plan to again.*

I turned away to curtail the desire to stay.

Sis stepped back, rubbing her belly. A sure sign of another young'un on the way.

Her eyebrows raised as she sassed, "I'm wantin' you back with your scalp, if you please."

"Aye, lass." Charles turned to his bay.

I eased to Sis's ear. "Mary explained her fear, and we've mended the fence." My heart thumped, remembering the feel of her in my arms and the sweetness of her kiss.

Sis smiled. "And I'm glad to hear it. She'll be longin' for you, for sure and certain. I'll see after her. Now, git." She grinned and raised her chin. "They're leavin' ya."

When I turned, my brother had Babcock in tow, halfway through the gate. I ran to catch them.

Thomas dropped the lead rope as I neared. "Crazy eejit. Can ya forget that Shirley lass long enough to make it to Woods Fort?"

My brother-in-law stopped outside the gate and turned to us.

"When we arrive at Woods, we'll be needin' updates from Williamsburg about settlers' petitions. There should be news from Maj. Clark concernin' troops and gunpowder."

Thomas nodded. "Aye, they'll be givin' him flack for not sendin' more volunteers for Virginia regiments."

I moved ahead, enraged by the need for another war because His Majesty refused to lift his boot from the necks of his subjects. And his officials keep us from the lands acquired by Lord Dunmore's treaty by paying the Shawnee and other tribes to raid.

I want the land and Mary.

I reached into my haversack for a slice of venison jerky for distraction more than hunger.

When an acorn hit the back of my head, I scowled at Thomas.

His eyes narrowed. "You didn't see that?" He pointed back a few paces to an elm tree. "How you goin' to find Indian signs?" He scoffed, "and you in the lead."

Along the drooping branch I'd passed under lay a large copperhead, inching toward a silent cicada laying eggs. I gulped, ashamed and shocked.

"Maybe you should go a courtin' instead of scoutin'. You're gonna get us all killed, and we've a long journey."

I shook my head. "Won't happen again."

Charles stepped up with his horse and the mule in tow and handed me its rope. "Be in charge of Ol' Bess awhile, and you'll understand marrin' a woman." He chuckled. "I'll lead now."

I'd observed him and Sis enough to know which stubborn mate caused the most resistance in their home, and it wasn't Sis.

"Come on, Ol' Bess. Make friends with Babcock." I tethered her to my horse, put him on a lead rope, and fell in step behind Charles.

After a calm hour with nothing amiss, we left the main trail and headed up a ridge. If Shawnee scouts were prowling, they'd be watching from the crags and shrubs. I scanned for anything out of place—overturned rocks, broken twigs, scuffed ground, or a careless human footprint.

I'd dislodged a stone or two in my early days. Four years ago, Captain Henderson assigned me as a scout with Mr. Shirley, tasked with securing the Greenbrier Valley ahead of the surveyors. Michael taught me the patience needed for spending hours blending into the foliage, sitting still, and listening.

When the steep rocky incline changed, my foot slipped on loose rocks. I landed hard on my knee and dropped the rope. I dusted my pants and shook off the pain. I righted overturned rocks and tugged on the mule's rope, but she balked. I stroked her neck and whispered softly. "Come on, Ol' Bess."

She wouldn't budge. "If you stay here, the wildcats, coyotes, and wolves will eat you. Best to trust me and follow."

I draped the lead rope over her back and clucked my tongue. My horse moved forward with me, then the mule followed and I mused, *maybe Mary will too.*

Within the hour, we arrived at the Hans Creek crossing. Thomas stood guard while I inspected trees for Indian carvings used as signals or warnings.

Charles examined the ground near the bank, then returned. "Small game tracks. Good place to graze the horses and mule. Any markin's?"

"Only scratches from a mid-sized bear." I propped my rifle against a tree.

He nodded and pulled the jerky from his coat pocket. "How you gettin' along with the mule?"

"One disagreement. But she yielded."

"Humph. Just gettin' familiar with ya. Could balk anytime without warnin'. Like your sister the other day. Up and changed her name. Said I can't call her Letitia no more." He shook his head and plucked large hickory leaves off a tree on his way to the bushes. "I'll be back."

You deserve Christina's balk—you ol' mule. Many a time I'd raised fists to punch him in the jaw. But Sis managed him her own way and I leave them be.

The sudden thought of Mary ending up with someone like Charles instead of me twisted my gut. A grin rose as I sat on a stump, confident the man would meet his maker sooner than expected.

Thomas plopped on the ground beside me and stretched out his legs. "I'm hankering' to go on a bear hunt before we return. Take my mind off joinin' a regiment."

"Bear hunt's a fine idea." Charles returned and sat on a log across from us. "We can hire on as guards with a huntin' party for a share of the meat. Keep the Shawnee from takin' it and the men's scalps."

My empty belly rumbled for hickory-smoked bear bacon. I gulped from the canteen and handed it to Thomas. "I'm itching to sneak into a British fort for information. Or we can waylay their couriers taking supplies to Blue Jacket." I stood and dusted off. "I'll take the lead again awhile."

Thomas and Charles eyed each other without comment.

"I've come to my senses. See if you lads can keep up. I want to make Woods Fort in two hours. We've a war to help win." I proceeded to my horse and retrieved a hoecake from my saddlebag before leading Babcock away from the creek. I ate while my kin readied their horses and Charles took charge of Ol' Bess.

Wreaking havoc on the British outposts would relieve my pent-up frustration about everything complicating a future with Mary.

Chapter Six

As we approached the closed gates of Woods Fort, Charles shouted at an armed guard on the bastion, "Scouts comin' in. McGuires and Gatliff."

The message echoed inside until the doors creaked open.

Thomas entered first and yelled back, "Crowded with families and horses."

Not good. Hairs on my neck prickled.

I glimpsed Capt. Archibald Wood weaving through the maze of people and coming our way.

He spat out his plug of tobacco and halted in front of us. "Glad to see you men. Where ya comin' in from?"

"Cooks." Charles dismounted and shook his hand. "What's happened?"

"We received news of scattered raids south of the Holstein River by Dragging Canoe's rogue Cherokee."

I gripped the reins, prepared to gallop back and protect Mary despite my orders. My horse shifted his feet, as if expecting my intention.

The captain eyed Babcock, then me, as he concluded, "But they're on the run now, and our local settlements are safe."

My battle stance required several deep breaths to calm.

Capt. Wood tilted his head toward a row of canvas tents. "You men settle in and come to my quarters. I'll explain more."

Thomas and I climbed from our horses and trudged along until we arrived at a urine-soaked corral.

I turned to my mates. "I'm not leaving my horse here breathing the foul air. I say we leave after we hear the news."

Thomas stood beside me. "Aye. This crowded place is more dangerous than facing a raiding party."

"Come, lads." Charles held his nose.

We led our horses to the blockhouse, where Capt. Wood finished addressing five men, then turned to Charles. "Not staying?"

"No, sir. Heading west. What's the situation?"

The captain raised his chin. "Shawnee are retaliatin' for the Cherokee defeat in the Clinch Valley. They killed families and livestock along the Bluestone River a week ago. Men found a survivor—a Dutchman named Hans Mueller."

He pointed to a young man hunched over a wooden plank. "I put the lad to work makin' a cupboard for my wife. He's still squeamish, but at least he speaks English. I think Blue Jacket's involved."

"I hope not." I handed my horse off to Thomas. "I'll speak with the lad."

The young man stood hunched over a board propped on sawhorses. He focused on carving until my approach alerted him. He straightened and stared from stark blue eyes. His blond hair and chalky skin matched his bleached linen shirt. But muscular arms contradicted my impression of weakness.

He'd be a ghost if not for his eyes. No more than twenty.

"Name's William McGuire." I held out my hand.

He dusted his palms down the front of his shirt and exchanged handshakes.

"Hans Mueller ... Junior."

"Capt. Wood conveyed your loss. I'm sorry. I'm a scout from Cooks Fort, heading to the western settlements with my mates. Mind telling me about the raid?"

He staggered to a ladder-back chair and sucked in a deep breath. "Last Wednesday afternoon, *Jah*, and no warning."

His accent was more German than the Shirleys.

"I worked with my papa inside the barn. Brother Fredrick entered, shouting, 'Indians,' then fell forward. Five arrows in his back."

Hans's breaths heaved as he peered at the ground.

I touched his arm to calm him. "Take your time."

"Papa rushed outside pointing his rifle. He fired but collapsed, holding his chest of arrows. I dove through loose boards in the wall and rolled into the bushes, hiding like a child."

He covered his face and wept.

"No shame in surviving." I sat on a nearby stump. "Shooting a man's not like hunting. Take your time."

As I waited for him to recover, the unwelcome face of the first man I'd killed showed itself. Thomas and me, ten and eight, defended Ma and Christina from French soldiers with muskets, while Da fought off Indians. The soldier's scowl became an empty stare as he fell backward.

'Twas months before I fired the musket again without trembling.

I took deep breaths to slow my pulse.

Hans cleared his throat and sighed. "When quiet came, I raised up enough to see our cows dead in the field. A dozen Indians led our horses away, and a few more lit fires. I thought it all a dream." He rolled up his shirtsleeve, showing a scab-covered gash on his left arm. "Then an arrow grazed my arm, and I knew."

"I'm amazed they let you live. Do you recall their garments or markings?"

He closed his eyes. "*Jah.* Some wore fringed buckskin shirts and pants. Most wore black breechcloths with silver medallions, including the one who shot me."

Hans's face paled again. "Him, I remember in nightmares. White-painted face with a black line from his right eye down across his nose to his left cheek. A red line from each eye down to his chin. Long black hair with a large black-tipped eagle feather dangling on the right." Hans pushed to his feet and shuffled toward a water bucket. He drank from the dipper, then said, "Called himself Loud Hawk."

The name raised goose bumps.

I leaned backward. "Did you say Loud Hawk?"

He nodded. "Told me to flee like a frightened child. Said, 'Tell the white forts Blue Jacket is coming back soon … will take away women and children.' Then he mounted with a blue-coated man and rode off."

The lad offered me the dipper.

"Thank you." I drank, then stood. "I'll leave you be now, but how did you make it here?"

He swallowed hard. "When they left me, I sat in a heap on the ground, shaking and crying. I don't remember how long before uncovering a shovel blade from the smoldering ashes of the barn." He shook his head. "Images of my family are horrible. The worst ..." Hans lowered to the ground and held his trembling hands over his eyes. "My sweet momma. They ..." He wept a moment. "I can't say it."

I swallowed to keep my emotions in check. "You don't have to."

Hans grasped a sawhorse and stopped wobbling. "I dug by moonlight. Then ... had to roll their bodies into the grave. But too exhausted to cover them, I sat, weeping and fighting off coyotes. In the morning, I finished and placed charred stones from the hearth on top."

As he sniffled and wiped his face, I watched a beetle crawl on the ground. My stomach soured with memories of the occasional ravaged bodies encountered on the trails.

He cleared his throat. "Then I picked up my rifle and headed east. I don't remember collapsing near the river, but a Mr. Jones and a black man named Zeke revived me and brought me here."

I leaned forward. "Did these men have a coyote-looking dog with them?"

His head tilted. "Yes. Mean, lame dog. Growled every time I came near. They're leaving for Cooks Fort in a few days to find its owner."

The Shirleys.

He studied me. "Please. If you arrive at the Boonesborough settlement, tell the Shirley family what happened and where I am. Do you know them?"

I gulped and shrugged. *Isn't staying silent better than a straight-up lie?*

Hans straightened. "Big family with a pretty daughter named Mary. They stayed with us one night on their way to Kentucky territory. A year ago."

My gut knotted. "I know them."

I turned, but the nudge to tell him the truth stuck my boots to the ground. I released a loud sigh. "The Shirleys didn't stay in Kentucky. They're at Cooks Fort now, and the dog is Mary's. She'll be happy to have him back."

The lad's face went from drooping to beaming. His grin annoyed me.

"I will go there." He jumped to his feet. "Thank you for telling me this." His eyes watered. "I need their comfort at this time, and I'm excited to see Mary again. Please, Mr. McGuire. How do we find them?"

His enthusiasm raised panic. "Sorry, I need to report to my mates."

I moved forward, but guilt stabbed my gut, then my skin crawled as I answered. "From Cooks Fort, head northeast across the bridge and follow the trail."

He grabbed my hand. "Thank you, sir."

I glanced down at the intricate carvings of flowers and swirls on his work. I ran my hand over the smooth finish of the cabinet door.

"This is impressive work, Hans." I meant the praise. "You should go on to Williamsburg and open a shop." *And leave Mary alone.* "People will pay top prices for such beautiful furniture."

"Thank you, Mr. McGuire. Others have suggested this." He grinned and nodded. "I'll visit the Shirleys for a while, then consider the move."

Tarnation. My stomach churned imagining him winning Mary because he's not going to Kentucky. *He could become wealthy and lavish her with gifts I could never afford.*

I turned away. "I must leave you now. Safe travels."

Panic gnawed at me all the way back to where Charles and Thomas stood waiting. I wanted to ignore my orders and escort the men to Cooks and make sure Hans didn't pursue Mary.

"What did he say to make you so pale?" My brother frowned.

I relayed the details of the raid, but not the agony of his quest for Mary.

"Let's get away from here." I marched off, whistling for Babcock.

When the horse shouldered up to me, I confided, "If Mary's meant to be mine, he won't turn her heart. He only has until I return in December, anyhow. I hope my kiss keeps her longing for me." I shook my head. "I sound like a fool. I need to keep my wits about me and stay alive."

I pushed away the worry and focused on the trail.

In an hour, the sky swirled with sunset shades above the ridgeline west of the New River.

"Hold up," Charles shouted. "Let's make camp here. No need to cross until we make a plan."

Thankful for his command, I dismounted.

Charles handed me his horse. "Tether our horses and the mule. I'll take Thomas to check the area."

I led the horses to a place between two thin trees near enough to water and grass. After securing them to a tether line, I found an oak tree and sat, stretching out my legs. Within seconds, something needled my mind. I chewed on a slice of jerky. *Am I jealous?* I stroked the stubble on my chin. *Maybe I am a bit, but that's not it.*

"All clear of Indian signs," my brother said as they returned. He carried a writhing, bleeding rabbit by the feet. "But came across a lone hunter's snare. If they're around and come 'fore we eat it, we'll share." He grinned. "And I say we're not on official scout duty tonight, and we might as well enjoy our last hot meal from a fire."

I raised my chin. "Aye, tomorrow is soon enough for obeying our Oaths of Fidelity, and the Duties of a Spy."

Charles laughed as he dropped an armload of sticks and raised his right hand. "I swear never to directly or indirectly divulge information or give away our location by building a fire—startin' tomorrow when there's need."

He knelt and arranged the kindling for a small fire. "I've a mind to make our way north. Learn the news from the new fort on the point."

"I'm agreed." Thomas laid the cleaned rabbit on the hot coals.

Sparks blew toward my face.

"Sorry, Brother." He laughed.

I stood and dusted off. "Glad men finally agreed to rebuild the defenses there. I'll look for Hiding Turtle on the way."

"A hard week ahead, for sure," Charles said. "Proud we helped cut the trails in '74. Well-traveled by now."

I stepped toward the river. "Let's double-check the area, then turn in. I'm weary, and that roasting rabbit smells ready for eating."

When Charles and I returned, Thomas lifted meat from the fire with a stick, placed it on a tin plate, and cut the meat into three portions.

The rabbit made a tasty morsel but didn't satisfy my belly. I gnawed on a slice of venison jerky from my saddlebag while I retrieved my bedroll. I found a semi-flat spot and unrolled. After my last swallow, I lay on my back and watched the sky fill with stars. Night hawks, owls, and distant coyotes lulled my mind, until I remembered Hans saying he had a rifle when he left.

Did he have it when he hid? Too scared to shoot?

I rolled to my side and stuffed my extra blanket under my head, sure that my Mary wouldn't fall for a man too scared to fight. I snorted. *She'd end up saving him.*

We journeyed northward along the New River for a day and a half, riding and trekking up and down steep ridges and crossing creeks.

Upon reaching the confluence of the Gauley and Kanawha Rivers, we dismounted and crept along the trail, staying quiet and alert for Indians. Thomas stopped ahead of me and pointed to a birch tree bearing fresh hatchet scars. Long strands of a silver-haired scalp-lock dangled from a forked twig. My skin prickled at the display left as a trophy.

There's been a raid.

About ten yards ahead, the cries of a child and a gruff man's voice speaking Shawnee words sent us into thick shrubs with our horses. We hunkered down in damp, moldy leaves, barely breathing for five minutes while twenty warriors from different clans passed within five yards—mostly Shawnee, but I recognized the symbols of Delaware and Seneca among them. All carried fresh scalps, but one carried a sobbing child—a boy, no more than five or six years old.

I'd seen captives among raiders before, but this boy tugged at my heart. I saw his terrified face and a resemblance to Mary, like seeing her future child.

My gut knotted as I fought the desire to rescue the lad. A rushed attempt would result in the child's immediate death and the warriors delighting in our screams while they skinned us like fish.

I cringed but sat still, fighting nausea, anger, and uselessness.

Charles whispered, "Let's go, lads. Two days to Fort Randolph, and we'll report this."

I stood, but wobbled.

Thomas grabbed my arm. "Breathe. You know someone in their tribe will adopt the lad."

I nodded, but each footfall in the opposite direction twisted the dagger deeper in my gut.

Chapter Seven

September 14

Our new rooster announced his dominance to the flock at dawn. My sisters rose and dressed, but I turned onto my back and stared at the log beam above my bed. *Is William alive or dead?*

I waited for inner peace or dread.

Peace came. I waited a few seconds more before concluding he was safe.

I rolled off my platform bed and onto my knees, then slid a small rectangular box out from under the bed frame. Without tilting it, I placed it on my straw-stuffed mattress. Inside lay a rolled swatch of linen cloth, a small ink bottle, and a goose-feather pen. I unfurled and smoothed the cloth on the bed, then uncapped the black ink and dipped the sharpened tip of the feather inside. After tapping a drip back into the bottle, I marked the ninth line since he left. I blew on the mark until it dried, laid the cloth flat on the bed, and turned to my sisters.

"*Ho-wee-see-wah-pah-nee,*" I said in Shawnee. "That means, good morning." Lizzy's eyes widened as I continued. "*Hah-koh-wee-see-lah-sah-mom-moh?* Do you feel good?"

"Why are you speaking in Shawnee?" Katie frowned and tied the end of her braid.

I grinned. "I hear the words in my head sometimes. Learning Shawnee saved my life, and I know I'm not supposed to forget." I put my tally cloth away. "Would you like to learn morning greetings?"

"I want to learn too." Lizzy smoothed the front of her bodice.

Katie shrugged. "Alright."

I taught them both the first part while I dressed and braided my hair.

"How do we answer?" Katie asked.

"Say, *Nee-wee-see-lah-seh-mom-moh.* I'm feeling well."

"*Nee-wee—*" She held her belly, laughing. "Now, my tongue is twisted. Time to go downstairs. I hope my life never depends on asking a Shawnee attacker, 'How are you feeling?'"

I chuckled. "They'd adopt you as Makes Us Laugh."

"Why are you girls giggling?" Our momma smiled and watched us descend the stairs while she mixed the batter.

"Mary is trying to teach us Shawnee." Lizzy attempted the Shawnee morning greeting as she took a stack of plates to the table.

Momma turned from us to the hot griddle. "I'd rather not remember your captivity, if you please. No need to teach us the language."

Her curt tone unsettled me while my sisters glanced between us.

I eased toward her side. "I'm sorry ... I didn't think."

She swiped her cheek with a finger and dried it on her apron. "I'm sorry too. Still a raw memory." Despite wet eyes, her lips raised in a small smile. "Please cook the bacon."

"Yes, ma'am."

I didn't mean to stir her sad memories. But an unknown need to retain what I'd learned from the Shawnee remained.

After breakfast, I stepped outside into the biting breeze with a bowl of coarse ground corn for the chickens. The squabbling brown hens scurried around my feet. A gust of wind whipped my mop cap off and down the trail onto a tree branch. Movement caught my eye. A man with unbound shoulder-length blond hair approached on a gray mule. I dislodged my wayward cap from a twig as he continued approaching. Two more men—one white and the other black, followed him on horses.

I yelled, "Company's coming."

Papa stepped from the barn, dusting hay from his hat. My sisters and brothers rushed up from the garden and woodpile while Momma stepped onto the porch, holding Sally's hand.

The mule plodded forward, and the young-faced man smiled and tipped his wide-brimmed black hat. He wore a bleached linen shirt and dark-blue trousers. His tidy appearance intrigued me, but I couldn't figure out why he looked familiar.

The excited chatter from my family greeting the man confirmed a recognition. But before turning to learn his identity, I spotted the slave I knew as Uncle Zeke. My coyote-mixed dog lay across his saddle but lifted his head when the man stopped.

"No Name!" I rushed to greet them. "You've come with my dog. Thank you."

The slave's owner, Mr. Jones, dismounted. "We had some trouble getting here, but Uncle Zeke took fine care of your dog. He's the only one can touch him." He glanced at the man. "Hand him down and dismount. I'll go say hello to Mr. Shirley."

Zeke lowered the growling dog toward my raised arms, but hesitated.

I spoke to the coyote in Shawnee. "I'm so happy to see you. Don't you remember me?"

The dog whimpered and wagged his tail.

When Zeke released him into my arms, I placed the dog on the ground, scratched behind his ears, and examined the healed wound on his hind leg.

When the man dismounted, I stood and stretched my hand toward him. "Thank you for bringing him."

He jumped backward, twisting his head toward Mr. Jones, then back. "No, miss. I mustn't touch you."

"Oh, sorry." I withdrew my arm. "I forgot about the slave rules. I don't want you in trouble. Thank you for caring for No Name."

The dog hobbled to a tree and hiked his weak leg. "He's moving well."

"Yes'm. Still an able watchdog and hunter." He lowered his head. "I be sorry to leave him, but he b'longs to you." He sighed. "Good dog too. I asked masta' Jones 'bout buyin' him, but he say, 'Don't want no lame dog a'slowin' us down.'"

Sorrow for his situation crushed my chest. I remembered the good men Big Jim and Adam, who Papa borrowed from a neighbor for a season. After being returned, they fled to join the British Army, who promised them freedom. But it was a lie.

I pressed my lips tightly as my eyes watered. Big Jim drowned crossing the river, and when Adam found the loyalists, they sold him to a trading company sending slaves to the West Indies.

Mr. Jones returned. "Well, miss. We're headed to the fort. Mr. Shirley compensated me for makin' the trip, and the lad's stayin'. Seems he's acquainted with your family."

I turned toward my family and studied the blond man speaking to them.

Hans Mueller?

The joy of seeing him again flipped upside down like a pancake when I remembered the hurt from him and his twin, Fredrick, not saying good-bye.

What's he doing here, anyway?

Mr. Jones held his horse steady. "Found the lad near dead on the bank of the river. Toted him across and to Woods Fort. He said his family died in a raid."

I clasped my chest. Shock turned to sorrow.

Dead? His family is dead? Why? How?

I saw their faces and remembered the sweet visit the day they welcomed us into their beautiful home for a night. I pictured his loving, boisterous momma smiling at Katie and me when Momma told her we were giddy over her sons.

It's not fair, God! Why was this sweet family butchered? Will there ever be peace?

I dried my cheeks with a clean corner of my apron.

"'Twas Will McGuire told him your family came here," Mr. Jones said.

William? My mind whirled.

"Good day, miss." He mounted his horse and moved forward.

"You too." I smiled. "Thank you again for bringing my dog."

I knelt and stroked No Name's neck. His tail brushed the ground as I soothed him in Shawnee, then switched to English. "So happy to have you back. I hope you like my family. Promise not to growl or bite anyone. I must introduce you to Papa first. Come." I patted my thigh, and he followed.

Momma and my sisters entered the cabin while my brothers returned to the woodpile.

As I neared, Papa stared at the dog a moment, then back to me. "You remember Hans Mueller?"

I nodded as the man grinned and focused his shimmering blue eyes on me. His face was gaunt and ashy. His clothes hung loose from his too-thin frame.

No Name grumbled when Hans stretched his arm toward me and returned my mop cap.

"Shh, it's all right, boy. Thank you, Mr. Mueller."

I swallowed hard and held back my secondhand knowledge of his lost family—not wanting to hug him and cry because I wasn't supposed to know.

His cheeks flushed. "Please call me Hans. I am happy to greet you again." He turned to Papa. "I'll go to the barn and groom the mule."

His deep, sad tone stabbed my heart. His slow stride and drooping shoulders stirred a deeper understanding of his grief and the need to seek friends.

Papa stared at the dog.

I gathered courage. "This is No Name, the Shawnee dog that helped me escape." I bent down and rubbed his fur. "I'd like to keep him in a stall until he settles in."

He pressed his lips, stepped to my side, and placed his hand on my shoulder.

No Name watched but remained quiet.

"Good boy." He knelt in front of the dog and removed a piece of bacon from his coat pocket, then offered it from his hand.

The dog sniffed and eased closer.

I held my breath and prayed.

No Name's teeth locked on the meat. Papa stood and bobbed his head.

"Keep him in the barn until he accepts the family. Must have reacted to Hans's fear but seems trusting."

"Thank you." I looked at my papa. "Has Hans said why he's come?"

"No. Momma greeted him before he could say. Then you came traipsing up with that coyote. Plenty of time, though. Momma insisted he stay with us instead of the fort."

I nodded and released my misgivings. *For now, he needs my family.*

We entered the barn, but I avoided looking at Hans by grabbing an armload of hay. Sympathy for him watered my eyes.

No Name followed me into an empty stall, where I dropped the bundle in a corner, then closed the door. "I'll bring you food and water soon. In the meantime, rest." I patted the hay, and he plopped down. When he rolled onto his back, I rubbed his tummy. "I missed you."

As I walked to the door, he whimpered. I turned. "It's all right. Stay. I'll be back."

I rushed out, shut the door, and then slid the latch in place. All was quiet. I expected to hear the men speaking, but they had gone.

Relieved, I stepped back into the yard.

Katie met me with a basket of yellow squash in one hand. "Why are you frowning?" She bumped my arm, beaming. "Aren't you excited to see him again?" She placed her free hand on her hip. "Or are you afraid he'll take your mind off pining for William?"

I shook my head as her eyes grew wide. She pointed behind my head. "A ... wounded coyote is coming." She gulped.

I spun on my heels. "That's No Name. Be still. He won't hurt you. He's the dog that saved me. Looks like he's not staying in the stall. Go inside. I'll come in a moment."

"Al-alright." She rushed into the cabin.

I pulled my knitted shawl tighter around my shoulders. "No Name, come." I led him down the path to my wigwam place in the hedges and crawled inside. I sat, and he lay down. "Please stay here. My family will fear you. After supper, I'll bring you food and water."

I scurried out, but he followed. "Papa might make me leash you."

We shuffled back through the autumn leaves. No Name hobbled onto the porch ahead of me and lay to the left of our entrance. I shrugged my shoulders. "We'll see."

I neared the door, hearing sobs inside.

When I opened the door, Katie fell into my arms, weeping. "Fredrick is dead. His whole family is dead. Killed by Indians."

My gut wrenched as I stroked my sister's hair while my own tears dripped onto her shoulder. "I know. I'm sorry."

She and Fredrick had shared a forbidden kiss. Her first kiss. We had daydreamed of marrying the twins someday and being sisters-in-laws. The memory made everything worse. Then I remembered Hans almost giving me my first kiss, but didn't. It upset me then, but he told me my first kiss should be from the man I love. That I'd be glad he didn't steal one. William's came to mind. *I am glad.*

When Katie moved back inside, I closed the door, then glimpsed Hans sitting in a chair at the table with Momma hunched over him in a hug as she cried. Papa stood before the hearth, staring at the fire. My sisters held each other, sniffling, while Charlie stared at everyone. George stood alone, peering out the window. He had enjoyed the twin brothers' company.

He stared at the steaming mug Momma gave him. "*Danke schon,* Mrs. Shirley."

When I approached, he set the cup on the table and stood. I took his hand in mine. It was warm from the mug. "I'm ... sorry about your family. Mr. Jones told me. What will you do now?"

His eyes glistened, then brightened with his face. He cleared his throat. "I made furniture at Woods Fort."

The hopeful tone in his deep voice made the skin on my forearms prickle. It was the one from our first meeting. Deep, smooth, and steady.

"Mr. McGuire said it is fine work and suggested I open a shop in Williamsburg. But I would be alone there. He told me your family was here now, so I came. Yours is the only German family I know."

The lonely quaver returned. His eyes watered as he placed his hand on top of mine. "Thank you. It's comforting to be with you and your family."

My chest ached remembering how devastated I was as a captive, hoping I'd return to my family. *Here he is, knowing he'll never see his again. We are all he has.*

I released his hand as my eyes burned with tears. "I'm glad you found us. Please excuse me. I need to talk to Papa."

He nodded and sat back down, taking a few sips from his cup. Momma sniffled nearby. "You'll share the room upstairs with the boys. Stay as long as you like."

When I turned, my eyes caught sight of the front door ajar. I gasped as Charlie squat-walked toward No Name with an outstretched hand.

"No. Wait." I lunged out onto the porch.

No Name lay still as my brother buried his face in his fur.

Momma gasped behind me. "A coyote."

"I'm sorry. He keeps following me to the porch." I sat beside Charlie.

Katie peeked over Momma's shoulder. "Is he dangerous?"

Papa stood behind Momma. "He's a coyote mix, so maybe he's more domesticated. Looks like he's accepting Charlie."

"Cody mix? I love Cody." Charlie rubbed the dog's belly.

I stroked No Name's head and laughed. "Sounds like you have a real name now."

"What if he tries to eat the chickens?" Lizzy asked.

George knelt beside me and scratched behind the dog's ears. "Fine-looking dog." He looked up at Papa. "Can we take him hunting?"

I nodded and stroked the dog's back. "But he'll limp. Shot by the black man by mistake. But he healed him for me."

"Why did he shoot him?" Susie squatted beside me and ruffled his fur.

My eyes watered as I recalled the incident. "He didn't know the coyote was tame."

"Oh. I'm glad we have a new dog. I think he's pretty." Susie patted him a few more times, then moved away.

George stood and folded his arms. "I'll take him with me to check the traps in the morning."

"That will be fine. But it's time to start on chores now." Papa headed to the barn with the boys.

When I rose, my youngest sisters, Nancy and Sally, stayed back, holding each other's arms.

"Do you want to pet him and make friends?"

They shook their heads and followed Momma back inside, where Hans had remained in the chair.

Why is he afraid of the dog? I glanced at Cody, who had laid his head on his paw. "We'll have to work that out, won't we?"

Cody raised his head and gazed at me, wagging his tail. I sat on the porch beside him and scratched his neck. "A lot of changes today."

I hugged my knees and remembered Hans as muscular, square-jawed, with a bright smile and intense blue eyes. He wore his hair long and braided down his back at that time, but now it's short. I imagined his handsome features would return once he regained weight and color returned to his face.

A smile raised with the memory of his plea to find me at Boonesborough when of marrying age. I stood, peering into the sky and shaking out my skirt.

Why is life so complicated and fragile?

Chapter Eight

September 28

A gusty northern breeze carried a smoky scent of roasting beef through the woods ahead, and the blaze-painted sky shimmered off the Kanawha River. I glanced back at Thomas and Charles.

"Don't dawdle, mates. I'm tired, hungry, and ready to make our report."

I quickened my steps despite sore feet and weariness from the day's hard travel.

As Fort Randolph came into view on the south bank of the Ohio River, my stomach growled louder and my mouth watered. I pictured a glazed hunk of beef rotating over a campfire and didn't blink until my eyes dried out.

When the guards heard our names, they opened the gates enough for us to pass. The scent of fresh-cut oak followed us into a yard teaming with uniformed soldiers.

Some wore the red shoulder ribbons of sergeants, in accordance with the new militia laws.

One approached, squinting his eyes under his hat. "Check in with Capt. Arbuckle at that blockhouse yonder." He pointed and continued toward a cabin in the middle of the western wall guarded by six soldiers.

"They're 'bout to hang someone." Thomas pointed at a tree where a man tugged on the noose end of a rope.

Poor wretch. Traitor, murderer, or horse thief?

We reached the blockhouse as a young private stood in front of the door and held up his palm.

"Hold, sirs. State your business."

Charles stepped up to his face. "Stand down. We'll tell the captain our business."

I slid beside my gruff brother-in-law. "We're scouts from Cooks Fort."

The private turned to the door and knocked before opening it a crack. "Capt. Arbuckle, sir. Three men reporting from Cooks."

The man scowled at Charles, and we shuffled inside the dimly lit blockhouse.

Two sergeants and a private scanned us as the captain extended his hand toward Charles.

"Pleasure to see you again, Mr. Gatliff. Who are these?"

"Thomas and William McGuire, sir. We've news concerning the Bluestone raids at the end of August."

I tipped my head in respect as the captain gave a nod and then turned back to Charles and frowned.

"August, you say?"

"Yes, sir," Charles said. "A witness confirmed Blue Jacket and his men." Charles motioned me forward.

I moved up and briefed him on Hans's account, then added, "We saw a raiding party leaving the Gauley River, heading north with a young captive boy, two days ago—mostly Shawnee, but also a few Seneca and Delaware."

Capt. Arbuckle studied me a moment before turning to the young private. "Hand me the map, Boggs. How old of a child?"

"I'd guess five or six."

The man unrolled the parchment on the table and weighted the corners with river stones. I leaned over the map with the captain, retraced our route to the location, and stepped back.

He lingered, shaking his head. "Could be John Nichol's boy, Benjamin. I warned that dang fool not to settle on the Gauley. I'll send word to his relatives at Arbuckles Fort." He glanced up. "Think you can lead a rescue party?"

Before I could affirm, Charles came beside me.

"Depends on what's happenin' from Detroit and what's stirrin' up Blue Jacket's raids."

Capt. Arbuckle straightened. "Not sure yet. Scouts captured a Shawnee spy yesterday afternoon. They saw him meeting with those renegade Girty brothers on the Scioto River." He frowned. "He put up a fight, but the men roped him and brought him in. Calls himself Hiding Turtle."

My heart sped. *He's the one they're about to hang?*

"Says he's a friendly—working for the Patriots. But won't give names or why he's with those loyalists. Even with the threat of hanging, he won't talk."

"He is a friendly, sir." I calmed my harsh tone. "One of my contacts. Please, let me see him. He'll tell me."

The captain's eyes narrowed. "If he doesn't, I'll expect you to stand down." He brushed past us and out the door.

My gut knotted. Charles stood in front of me. "Hope he ain't been workin' both sides. How will you know?"

"Never given me reason to doubt his loyalty. But if he's lying, I'll slit his throat." I hurried to catch up with the captain.

Two men stepped inside before we entered but left the door ajar.

I gagged at the stench and seethed at the sight of my long-trusted informant. He sat in the dark corner of the cabin with knees to his chest and chains on his ankles and wrists.

The captain crossed his arms and glared at the man. "Stand up. You've five minutes to prove you're not working for the Girty brothers. Why were you meeting with them?"

Hiding Turtle clenched his jaw. The chains rattled as he pushed to his feet, naked and shaking. He shuffled toward us and stopped.

I marched past the captain, looking for a blanket. Rage brewed at not finding one. I removed my wool coat and draped it over Hiding Turtle's shoulders.

I stepped back, shocked and disgusted by his swollen, blood-caked lips and right eye. I observed multiple cuts and bruises and doubted the soldiers wasted water on the man they expected to hang.

When he focused on me, his eyes watered. He straightened and cleared his throat.

"I am friend of ..." His hoarse voice gave way. He pointed at me, swallowed, and spoke again. "*Match-squa-thee Wee-pek-wha,* One Not Seen. I will tell him my words."

All eyes turned to me. I'd never heard him call me a Shawnee name, but *One Not Seen* made my pride swell. "I'm honored to be your friend." I moved closer. "Tell me about the Girtys."

He stared at the floor a moment before answering. "Swift Foot ... you call Simon Girty—he found me at river." His voice grew stronger but remained calm. "He told of Blue Jacket meeting with Hair Buyer Hamilton."

He held his gurgling stomach and continued. "Hamilton informed chiefs of gunpowder low at white forts. Encourages raids and wants Flaming Hair captured with new supply."

I rubbed the prickles from my neck and turned to the men behind me. "He's speaking of the redheaded major, George Rogers Clark. His capture would embolden every tribe between Fort Detroit and the Greenbrier to wipe us from the land."

When my gaze returned, he spoke.

"I camped with men. Next day, Swift Foot went to Fort Pitt. He will give Hamilton's words to Great White Elk." He stared at the floor and sighed. "I would go to wife, but men bring me here." He raised his head and scanned our faces. "That is all."

"Who is this Great White Elk?" Capt. Arbuckle asked.

Before I could reply, Charles blurted, "That devilish Alexander McKee. So much for his pledge of parole. He's not supposed to communicate with the Indians. He's a traitor, for sure."

Hiding Turtle nodded, lowered his eyes as he wobbled, then straightened. "McKee gives Hamilton news through your Simon Girty."

I grabbed a nearby stool and placed it behind him. "Sit before you fall." I looked at the captain. "Sir, please allow him food and water. We need this trustworthy man to continue working on our side. I'll swear he's not a traitor."

Charles stepped before the captain. "Release him to go with us to Limestone. Instead of rescuing the child, we need to find an old friend of Girty's named Simon Butler. If he's not in with them, he'll send a warning to Maj. Clark."

"I'll vouch for our Indian scout as well." Thomas pulled a long slice of beef jerky from his pouch and handed it to Hiding Turtle.

The captain's lips pressed as he stared at the Indian, then he turned to the man on his right.

"Remove the chains and fetch fresh water in the bucket."

He focused on Charles. "I'll send out scouts to relay the warnings to Fort Pitt and Williamsburg. Since you're headed west, you can warn your contacts that way. Hopefully, this Butler can warn Clark to watch his back."

"Yes, sir. We'll be needin' a place to stay the night." Charles studied the cabin. "Any reason we can't stay in here? Just need to burn some pine needles and air it out. Bring us firewood and a share of that roasted beef we smelled comin' in."

Capt. Arbuckle pointed to Hiding Turtle. "What about him?"

"He'll stay with us." I rushed toward the man carrying the water and filled the dipper.

Hiding Turtle drank and pushed to his feet, shaking. I steadied him and addressed the captain. "He needs looking after and his clothes. Bring medical supplies and extra bedding."

The captain nodded on his way out with his men.

"Stay with him," Charles said. "Thomas and I will bring in the packs 'fore we take care of the horses and mule." He moved outside.

Thomas looked at our friend. "Sorry 'bout this trouble." He tipped his hat and went with Charles.

I strode to the fireplace, lifted the poker, and uncovered the few remaining coals. "Dad-blame idiots. Can't wait for them to bring in kindling." I stomped toward the door. "I'll grab some and be back." I stared at him and grinned. "Don't run off naked with my coat. I mean it."

He attempted a smile. "I stay."

The latch lifted, and Boggs arrived with an armload of sticks, chopped wood, and a branch of pine needles.

"Captain is gathering garments." He unloaded. "We burned the Indian's clothes in case of lice. Be back with pans and more water."

"Bring lye soap and bandages too." I hurried to build a fire before the coals died.

He sauntered out, leaving the door open.

"Thank you, One Not Seen." Hiding Turtle sat on the floor. "Today and forever, you are my friend."

I smiled and blew on the coals until the kindling lit. "And you, mine. You've always called me Will Man. Why the change?" I added sticks and sat beside him.

He removed the coat from his shoulders and sat covering his mid-parts. "Others call you One Not Seen. Today I agree. Suddenly, you are here. Suddenly, I will live."

I laughed and added larger logs on the fire. "Guess I'm good at my job."

"What of Shoots in Knee? Is she well?"

Mary's name. "She was when I left Cooks Fort. Left Boonesborough. Two moons ago."

He nodded and studied my face. "You will wed?"

I adjusted the fire with the poker and spoke to the sparks. "She's afraid to return to Kentucky. Loud Hawk spoke a curse over her firstborn child if she ever returns. So ..." I stabbed a log before looking at him. "Not sure on marriage."

He chuckled. "Tell her she is Piqua warrior, Shoots in Knee. Her God is greater than Loud Hawk's evil."

A surge of hope rushed through me. "Powerful words, my friend. Thank you, I'll tell her. Maybe she'll change her mind."

Boggs stepped inside with a kettle of hot water and a bar of soap. Another man entered with cloth strips and a small clay jar of salve. A few minutes later, two more men came with plates, forks, a pot of stew, and a heaping platter of carved beef.

Thomas and Charles entered with our supplies, and Thomas tossed garments to Hiding Turtle.

"There's a flatboat taking supplies downriver early in the morning," Charles said. "They'll make room for us."

Hiding Turtle handed me the coat. "Boat is good—until Cabin Creek. Must stay on buffalo trail after." He plunged his chestnut legs into the britches and stood. "White man clothes smell. Will get me killed."

"Too cold for loincloth." I snickered and helped him clean up, then dabbed his cuts with the turpentine salve until my eyes burned and teared. It made a good ruse for my thankful emotions to God. He directed us here in time to save our friend from that noose.

My mates dipped stew into bowls and placed them on the table. I wet a clean strip of cloth and soothed my eyes before joining everyone.

Later, with my bed made on the smooth warm floor, I stretched out full-bellied and expected to fall into a sound sleep, but questions came. *Will Hiding Turtle's words make a difference? What if Mary's sweet on Hans?*

I rolled to my side. *Fool, go to sleep. Traveling through Indian territory tomorrow.*

Chapter Nine

September 28

My brother George shuffled through the leaves midmorning with his head down as he came into the side yard and leaned against a tree.

"Just a minute," I said and lifted my linen cloth from a dye-bath, draped it over the clothesline, then poured the last of a beautiful shade of cornflower-blue dye onto yellow hickory leaves. After righting the copper kettle, I dried my hands and acknowledged him. "What's wrong?"

He shifted closer. "Poor Hans will never be a good provider."

"What a mean thing to say." I stepped back, frowning. "Why judge him so?"

He shrugged. "He's been here two weeks. Every morning he goes out with us, but when there's game to shoot, he stays back staring at the ground."

His harshness raised my sympathy for Hans.

"Then this morning, he flinched when Papa took down a buck." He crossed his arms, frowning.

Poor Hans. "It's only been a month since the attack on his family. Remember when I froze in fear before the cougar lunged at us? Even Papa returned from the Indian campaign at Point Pleasant still dealing with memories of the battle."

"Yes." He flailed. "You were afraid of the gun blast because you almost shot Papa."

Not what I meant.

He continued. "But you shot that big cat when it mattered, and Papa still hunts."

"And that's my point." I grinned. "Hans will recover in time, so you be nice."

"I'm not so sure he will, but I won't tell him so." He peered at my face for a moment. "I've seen you and Hans eyeballing each other during breakfast and at other times. And—"

He paused when I glared. "And what? My glances are because I'm curious. Not from interest."

"Is that supposed to make sense?" He shook his head. "Anyway, he's fine as a friend, but I've seen you watching Mr. McGuire like he's the one you want to run off with. He suits you better and isn't afraid to fire a rifle."

I gasped. "George Shirley, mind your manners and your own business. Mr. McGuire's not going to ... well ... Hans might go to Williamsburg and open a furniture shop. He's not meant for frontier life. Maybe I'm not either."

What am I saying? I'm not interested in Hans.

He gaped, closed his mouth, then turned back toward the barn. "You're not thinking straight."

Maybe I'm not. I plopped down on a stump. *But why not consider Hans?*

His appearance was pleasing. Average height, well-proportioned since eating again, muscular arms, a square face, shy sweet smile, alluring blue eyes, and thick blond hair I wanted to touch.

I shrugged and confessed into the breeze, "Oh, alright, so I'm attracted to Hans."

A twig snapped behind me. I leaped to my feet and gasped at Hans.

Did he hear?

He edged closer, wearing a shy grin. "Sorry to startle you."

Heat swept up my face. I gulped at his low, controlled voice, but it didn't quell my irritation.

"Good thing I didn't grab my rifle."

His eyes widened as he nodded. "I should have called out."

"Yes." I squinted, annoyed. "How long have you been there? What did you hear?"

He bit his lip, took one more step, and stopped. "Everything with George." He wiped his hands on his thighs. "Are you angry?"

"Yes." I glared. "You heard private things I wouldn't have shared with you, and now I'm too upset to talk." I backed to the log and sat.

"I'm sorry. I shouldn't have listened, but I couldn't move. I'm interested in you as well."

His shining blue eyes and grin lured as he reached for my hand, but I resisted. *Not ready for trusting or touching.*

He backed a step, no longer smiling. "I've thought of you often since meeting you a year ago."

"I remember you not saying good-bye when we left the next day."

His face turned to stone. "Too hard to face you, and Fredrick was ashamed for stealing a kiss from Katie. Please forgive me." He took a deep breath and gazed into my eyes. "I wish to spend more time with you, but what are your feelings for Mr. McGuire? Should I step aside?"

Stunned by the question, I pressed my lips hard.

His face and voice softened again. "I'm sorry. Please forgive my intrusion. I'll pack my things and move on to

the fort. I don't want to cause trouble. I ... I care for you."
His sorrowful expression returned, and, once again, my
heart pricked.

"You don't have to leave. I forgive you. But don't rush
me." I brushed a fallen acorn from my lap. "We can
become better acquainted. As for Mr. McGuire ... well
... he's planning to live in Kentucky, and I'm not." The
words crushed my soul.

He beamed. "Good. Then, you don't mind if I come
visit?" His upbeat tone returned as he continued talking,
while I considered his question and wished he'd be silent
so I could answer.

"I enjoy making furniture. If I start a shop at this fort, I
can make money enough to move to Williamsburg. What
do you think of my plan?" Hans stood and offered me a
hand up.

"You'll do well there." I stood on my own, ready to be
free of him. "I'll see you at supper. I have things to do."

He grabbed and kissed the top of my hand. "I'll speak
to your papa."

I nodded and sped to the clothesline.

*He's like a blustery whirlwind. Makes it hard to think
straight.*

When I arrived at the clothesline, the beautiful blue-gray material rippled in the breeze. Perfect for the new bodice I'd wear with my pecan shell petticoat for the social. I checked the cloth for dryness, then swooped the linen from the clothesline, sending a nearby squirrel fleeing up a hickory tree. The creature rested on a branch, chattering as I rushed toward the yard.

Cody raised his head but remained near the chopping block with Charlie. A pang of guilt surfaced for being too busy for him.

I caught sight of Hans and Papa speaking in front of the barn on my way inside the cabin.

Momma and my sisters looked up from their sewing projects. I closed the door out of breath, then turned, holding up the material. "What do you think?"

Katie took one corner and held it up to my neck. "It's perfect for you." She leaned closer. "Too bad William won't be here, but you can dance with Hans."

She nudged my arm and giggled, but my heart ached.

"I suppose." I turned my watering eyes away from my joyous sister and reasoned dancing with Hans would be better than with soldiers I didn't know.

After spreading the cloth on the table, I took a sharpened edge of chalk from my sewing basket and the notched strip of cloth with my measurements, ready to mark a pattern.

Boots stomped on the porch and the men and boys entered, hanging their hats on the rack. Papa placed his rifle in the corner.

Hans smiled at me, clutched the brim of his hat, and blurted, "I have permission to court Mary."

What?

Heat rushed to my face as all eyes stared. I scanned their various wide-eyed, gaping-mouth reactions.

When did he ask me?

"Mr. Shirley asked me to move to the fort now. I'll begin making furniture as a business. If all goes well for a year, I'd like to move to Williamsburg and open a shop."

He gazed at me as if wanting my approval for something.

I turned away, rolled up my cloth, and placed it on my sewing basket out of the way.

Surely he doesn't think I'd marry him and live so far from my family.

Papa moved toward Momma. "Hans wants to secure lodging today. I've loaned him a few shillings."

"I will start making chairs in the morning," Hans said. "I can pay you back in a few weeks. I'll gather my things now." He approached me and bowed. "I look forward to seeing you at the dance next Friday." He sprinted up the stairs.

I stared at my feet and pinched my arm.

Not a dream. He thinks I agreed to court him.

My family remained silent while I stared out the window. *Do I give him a chance or break his heart now?*

Hans rushed back down with his belongings and plodded to the door before facing us. "Thank you for allowing me to be part of your family and comforting me these two weeks over my loss. Good day." He flashed another beaming smile my way and left.

I stayed still, but the room threatened to spin. *What am I going to do?*

Silence lingered a moment more, then whispers and giggles came from Susie and Nancy as they returned to embroidering.

My head felt detached, as if watching my family from afar.

Sally wrapped scraps of cloth around wooden clothespins beside the rocking chair.

"May I take Charlie fishing?" George waited for a nod, then the brothers plodded outside.

I wanted to go with them and ignore Papa coming toward me with a slight grin.

"Five months before you're fifteen. You'll see what he makes of himself by then. Plenty of time to decide if he's the man you want."

I gulped. "But I ..."

What's wrong with being courted by someone who cares for me? It won't take five months. William will return in three.

Papa kissed Momma's cheek. "I'm loaning him a few tools and helping him to the fort. I'll check on news and tobacco prices before I return." He grabbed his gun from the corner, placed his hat on his head, and stepped into the yard.

"Let's go wish him well." Momma laid Charlie's mended shirt on the sewing basket and stood from her chair. She glanced at me and went outside, holding Sally's hand.

I followed her before my sisters could pepper me with questions.

The men emerged from the barn with the mule and Papa's chestnut gelding.

I stepped closer. "Have a pleasant week, Hans. See you Friday."

His smile widened. "I'll be watching for you. *Guten tag.*" He tipped his hat and gazed at Momma. "Thank you for everything, Mrs. Shirley."

"Stay safe and well," she said.

My sisters echoed each other's good-byes, and I waved.

Momma hurried to the porch and retrieved a half-bushel basket from a peg on the outer wall and turned to me. "Grab a shovel and come help me dig ginseng roots."

Her tone hinted at a serious discussion. *Most likely about Hans.*

I hurried to the barn, brought back the spade, and followed her along a wooded trail to a shady hollow with an abundant patch of red-berried plants.

"I've never seen so many in one place," I said.

She brought the shovel. "It takes years of careful tending and guarding. Mrs. McGuire started this one. We'll give her a share. Store owners in the east pay nine shillings a pound for the invigorating roots." She turned her face toward me. "Greedy people don't leave the tender ones." Momma stood in front of a cluster. "Did you accept the request for courting?" She wiggled the shovel into the ground and loosened a large clump.

I sighed. "I didn't mean to. I don't remember him asking."

She knelt and dug her fingers into the soil, then lifted the hay-colored root with her fingers.

I sat beside her, crossing my legs. "I don't mind getting acquainted—not sure about courting." I studied her face for a response.

She pulled a paring knife from the basket and sat with her legs to the side.

"I thought as much." Her pleasant smile calmed my speeding heart. "Papa wisely asked him to move to the fort and begin his business. We believe he'll become successful because of his quality work and powers of persuasion."

She worked her fingers through the plants and pointed to the shovel as she stood, brushing off her skirt. "I need a full basket of mature roots only. They give the best benefits."

"Yes, ma'am." I grinned. "It's been a while, but I remember."

She placed her hand on my forearm. "Greed leads to choosing the immature with later regret. But the wise choose maturity and enjoy goodness for many years."

I frowned and studied her. "Yes, ma'am. You've always taught us to leave the smaller plants."

She handed me the knife. "I'll leave you with the task while you ponder the deeper meaning of my lesson. Take your time. This is a lovely place to seek the wisdom of God."

Momma stepped back toward the cabin.

What am I missing?

I focused on digging up plants with three five-pronged leaves but couldn't figure out what ginseng had in common with Hans wishing to court.

I huffed and spoke to a wiggly slug. "Is she suggesting Hans is immature?"

I continued filling the basket and decided I'd have fun visiting and dancing with Hans as a friend but say no to courting.

When the basket heaped with earth-scented 'seng, I headed home.

But what if it becomes courting? He is sweet, kind, gifted for business, and won't traipse off into the wilds like William—leaving me to worry.

I reached the porch, determined to have fun at the social and enjoy Hans's company. Momma's ginseng lesson may have hinted at William being more mature than Hans, but he may not be in my future.

I carried the basket to the barn and dumped out the roots on the drying table.

Hans will become a shop owner in Williamsburg. What would it be like to marry him and socialize with the wealthy gentry?

I entertained the idea of us being well-off and dancing among the rich. Me, in a fancy rose-colored silk and lace dress with matching slippers. Hans, in a white shirt, navy-blue jacket with tan trim, white stockings, and shiny black shoes with silver buckles.

Am I greedy for desiring a safe home and provision?

The image of William in the same clothes sparked laughter. *I like him best in linen shirts and buckskin pants—rugged, muscular, and—Why am I thinking about him?*

Chapter Ten

September 29

Under the flickering light of a lantern, I finished packing my horse for the day's travel to Limestone Creek and turned to Hiding Turtle.

"Will the Shawnee trade the captive lad to the British post on the Great Miami?"

He smirked. "No. Outpost much raided by Mohawk people and Patriots like you. Redcoats flee to Fort Detroit. Shawnee carry child to Blue Jacket town."

I schemed a rescue plan but couldn't get past the certainty of failure.

Only a daft fool would sneak into the largest Shawnee village north of the Ohio River to snatch a captive child.

Hiding Turtle grabbed the sleeve of my wool coat and peered at me with searing dark eyes. "Friend. You are One

Not Seen, but you cannot save child. Promise you will not try."

His stern tone and stare made my blood run cold.

"I promise."

But I wanted to. The boy's fate stung in my chest like a bull nettle.

Take care of him, God.

I led Babcock to the gate, appreciating Hiding Turtle's wisdom in making me promise.

We walked the horses out of the fort and down to the riverbank, where at least a dozen men held lanterns on poles beside the swaying flatboat, taking supplies to the forts downriver. Crewmen rolled barrels into the craft's center cabin, along with a few small kegs and other supplies. Several soldiers took up positions around the boat with rifles ready.

Anxiety grew, not from the danger of entering hostile territory but from the misery of being unsteady on my feet.

After boarding, we kept our horses calm at the stern, and the boatmen shoved off the bank. My gut sloshed up, down, and sideways with the boat, threatening to unsettle my meager breakfast of thick, greasy salt pork.

The swift current of the Ohio River carried us westward, away from Fort Randolph and closer to

Shawnee strongholds. I turned my face into the crisp breeze and watched the first beams of a rusty-gold dawn shimmer on the river's gray ripples until queasiness passed. I found a pile of grain bags and stretched out for a nap.

For six hours Hiding Turtle watched the southern bank for the best place to disembark, then shouted, "This place," and pointed at a clearing a few yards past the Sandy River.

Three helmsmen standing atop the boat's cabin steered toward the bank and six crewmen leaped out, pulling and holding the wobbly craft in place with long ropes.

I mounted with my mates, jumped ashore, then dismounted again so we could walk through the middle of Indian territory.

Charles waved to the crewmen. "Thank ye for the ride."

I stood still for a moment, allowing my head and belly to settle.

"This way. No talk. We cross warriors' trail." Hiding Turtle motioned us forward.

The tension in his voice knotted my stomach.

Sunlight glared above the forest as we moved through the wooded area across a well-tramped buffalo path running north and south.

If I didn't already trust him, I'd question my sanity.

We matched his quick pace to a marshy area around a spring. I slogged behind him as he checked trees for fresh markings of stick-people or messages from nearby warriors. His occasional checks for moccasin prints prickled the back of my neck. He never indicated trouble. Once back on hard ground, the forest thickened, and Hiding Turtle slowed and watched the ground.

Before I could ask what he suspected, a faint whimper alerted us to stand still.

Hiding Turtle motioned for us to secure the horses and stay down before he stalked through shrubs like a wolf.

I tied my horse to a branch, then lowered to my knee, preparing for a skirmish.

In a moment, he crouched back and whispered, "Five men ... and small white boy ... cold camp. Not far. They leave soon."

Nervous energy surged with a readiness for action. "Could be the boy from yesterday."

He placed a hand on my shoulder. "Give me long knife. I will make talk—tell story. When my arm lifts—come quick. I kill two men and grab boy—meet back here."

"Risking your life for a white child?" I slid my butcher knife from the sheath.

He raised his chin and took the knife from my hand. "I must, or you will try."

"'Tis a dang-fool idea all around." Charles glared at me. "We've important information to learn from Simon Butler. Can't, if we're all scalped."

Thomas examined his blade. "But the lad needs rescuing. Not the first time we've dispatched a party of Indians."

"Never this far into their territory." I stood and retrieved a spare knife from the saddlebag.

Charles straightened. "Godspeed to us, lads."

"Slow and quiet to bushes." Hiding Turtle led the way.

We crept along the ground and stayed hidden as our brave friend stood at the edge of a clearing until we got in place. I focused on breathing shallow, but my heart beat hard.

Hiding Turtle approached them, speaking in Shawnee.

The braves bolted to their feet, yelling with guns in hand.

He spoke more words, pulled at his garments, and held his nose.

They laughed and gestured for him to sit. One offered him a chunk of their brown meat cake. He declined the food and pointed to the young boy who might be the captive we saw, but either way, we were rescuing him.

While the warriors took turns telling Hiding Turtle their stories and reenacting their brave actions, the rest of us waited for the signal to attack. Charles pointed to his chest, then at the Indian on the far end. I chose the one in the middle. My brother would assist our friend with the last three.

I sucked in air and re-gripped my knife as Hiding Turtle spoke with exaggerated movements.

God, help us save this child, and have mercy on these men when they see you today. Or on us if we fail.

When Hiding Turtle waved his knife and moved closer to the warriors guarding the sniffling lad, we sprang from cover.

I grabbed the crow-feathered scalp lock of my target and jerked him backward off the log. One half-moon slice to the neck, and he fell to the ground in a heap. Hiding Turtle dashed past me, carrying the boy.

I wiped my blade on the dead man's shirt and observed the crumpled bodies of the other four stilled by my mates, then snatched a wool blanket on my way back to the hollow.

No one spoke while our breaths labored, but I gagged from the horrible stench reeking from the boy.

Hiding Turtle sat him on the ground and moved away. The lad held his knees, shivering and rocking while staring at nothing.

I wrapped the blanket around him and turned my head. "We need to hurry to Simon's blockhouse. The lad's cold and in shock."

Charles rose first. "He's not strong enough to walk, and that's for sure. We'll ride the horses, and you can hold him. He'll warm up between you and Babcock."

"I go back." Hiding Turtle headed toward the dead men.

"Why?" I asked.

He gestured at his garments. "Need Indian clothes. Also rifles and food for trip home. You go. I will come, fast."

I adjusted the load on my horse to accommodate riding with the boy, then knelt before him and clasped his trembling hands. "Can you tell me your name and how old you are?"

Wide green eyes studied my face and pierced my heart. His head bobbed and his lips parted. "B-b-benny ... N-nichols. Six."

"You're safe now, lad. Be brave a bit longer. I'm putting you on my horse, and we'll ride fast." I eased him to his feet.

He nodded and wrapped his arms around my neck, weeping.

I lost the ability to breathe for a second, then adjusted his blanket and lifted him into the saddle. "Hold tight while I climb on the horse behind you."

He sniffled. "Are you taking me home to Ma? I want my ma."

"We're going to a safe place." I moved my horse forward. "You're going to be alright."

He's not strong enough to hear his parents are dead, and I can't say it.

In a few minutes, his body went limp against my arm. "Are you sleeping, lad?"

I clasped his wrist and released a sigh of relief at the faint pulse then urged Babcock into a canter.

Hiding Turtle caught up to us within an hour as we drew closer to a blockhouse on Limestone Creek. A chilly breeze carried the sweet aroma of fried bear bacon, and Benny stirred from sleeping in the crook of my arm, rubbing his eyes.

Woodland sounds gave way to a sorrowful fiddle playing a familiar Irish tune, but I couldn't remember its tragic tale.

When dogs barked, we halted.

"Hello in the yard," Thomas shouted.

A shrill whistle hushed the yapping, and a scruffy man stepped closer, squinting. "Who you be?"

"Scouts from Fort Randolph," Charles yelled.

The man backed as his voice crackled, "Come on in."

Charles led the way but paused again at the edge of the woods. "We're comin' in with a friendly, so don't shoot him."

He and Thomas rode in first, giving their names and asking to dismount.

I waved Hiding Turtle beside me to make sure he'd be safe and entered the area. The elderly man, clad in tan buckskin clothes, hat, and leggings, eyed the Indian but lowered his rifle.

Thomas and Charles filled the man in on our rescuing the boy, but not on our mission.

"Mornin'. Name's Dewy Little. Sorry, can't offer vittles or shelter. Mite short on provisions and space. The others are checkin' traps."

"Can you spare a bite for the lad?" Charles tilted his head at the child.

The man peered at him. "Sure 'nough. Looks sickly. Sit 'im by the fire to warm."

I handed him down to my brother and slid off Babcock. Thomas stood him on the ground and backed away.

"Lookin' for Simon Butler," Charles said. "He around the place?"

Mr. Little spat a wad of tobacco downwind. "Nope. Gone on ta Hinkstons Fort on the south fork of the Lickin' River. He don't let the dust settle long 'fore he's off. Left a week ago."

He stepped toward the campfire, then squinted at Benny as he handed me a warm, thick, crispy strip of bacon. I stared at it a moment, tempted to taste, but released it to the starving child and smiled at the man. "Thank you. We'll push on before dark. The lad needs tending to and out of this weather. It seems colder than usual."

"Y'all be welcome." Mr. Little chuckled. "Poor critter."

Charles offered his hand. "Good day."

The man eased forward and gave it a shake. "Any news of Maj. Clark comin' with gunpowder?"

Charles shook his head. "Couldn't say if we did."

"Shoulda know'd. Well, watch ye scalps ahead. I heard there's trouble." The man headed to the blockhouse.

Hiding Turtle grasped my arm. "I go home now. Somewhere, I will see you again."

I laid my hand on his shoulder. "Safe journey."

"I will speak for peace." He nodded. "But Blue Jacket accepted a peace wampum from Hamilton to make war on rebels. Stay low."

He waved at the others, then slinked through the brown and gray forest. Pride in our association raised a wide smile as I watched his back until gone.

I plucked a handful of pine needles from a sapling, crushed them in my palm, and rubbed the pungent oil under my nose before mounting. Thomas lifted the lad into my saddle.

"Good boy. We'll be at a safe fort by supper. Then you'll bathe while I find clean clothes for you."

"Will ... Ma ... be there?"

The quaver in his voice wrenched my gut. "Someone will care for you until your uncle comes. Stay brave." As soon as the words left my mouth, my skin crawled.

His head bobbed. "Aye, and he'll take me home."

"Yes, lad, he will. Hold tight, we're riding fast now." I looped my arm around his small body and urged the horse forward.

He grabbed a handful of mane as we galloped behind the others. I welcomed thoughts of a family at the fort caring for him so I could shake off a growing attachment to the lad.

Billowy clouds grayed throughout the afternoon and hung low and dark. We stopped at a large spring so the horses could graze and drink.

I lifted Benny from the horse, but he teetered when I stood him on the ground. His eyes drooped, and his face paled. I walked with him into the bushes to relieve himself and carried him to a dry spot near the trickling stream. He sat while I filled the wooden canteens.

"We've a couple more hours, lad. Then we'll be warm, rested, and fed. Can you be strong a bit longer?"

He raised a weak smile as his body wobbled.

Tough for such a small mite. I shouldered the heavy canteens, offered the lad my hand, and lifted him to his feet.

"Can you hold yourself on the horse while I let him walk?"

Benny stumbled over a root but said, "Yes, sir."

His parents would be proud.

I loaded him into the saddle and lifted Babcock's lead rope while saying no to the desire to keep him.

The horse dipped his nose for one more drink and followed me back along the trail.

My brother stepped in front of me, pointing above the trees. "We won't make Hinkstons Fort before those clouds burst."

Charles mounted. "The horses must endure a hard, fast ride. We ford the Lickin' River before the storm, or we're stranded for days and the lad sickens and dies from being wet, cold and starvin'."

I climbed behind Benny and rubbed Babcock's neck. "Aye, let's git to Hinkstons Fort."

A few blustery hours later we forded the wide river, but Benny didn't wake.

"Benny?" I shook his shoulders as my teeth chattered from a sudden chill.

He raised his head and mumbled, "Da?"

"Hang on, we're close to the fort." I shivered and tightened my grip.

As my wet pants made my legs numb, I clicked my cheek, and urged my exhausted horse past Thomas and Charles in a gallop, shouting, "Lad's weaker. I'm riding ahead."

I didn't wait for them.

Gusty winds blew black rumbling clouds over the ridge, and a burst of lightning released a crack of thunder and a cold storm. Panic took control as a new danger surfaced. I couldn't feel my hands, and my body no longer shivered.

Must stay awake.

"I see the gates, Benny." I shouted, "Do you hear me?"

A guard lifted his long rifle. "Hold there."

I slowed. "Will... McGuire ... Sick boy. Mates coming."

My horse stopped, but I weaved.

The man signaled the men at the gate and allowed me through. I trotted to the main blockhouse as people gathered.

I locked eyes on a stout fellow rushing to my side. "Take the child ... rescued."

The man cradled the boy and whisked him toward a middle cabin on the eastern wall. When I slid from the horse, my legs folded. Two men lifted and held me up. Babcock lowered his head, trembling from the sweat and cold. He sounded wheezy.

"My horse." I pointed and reached for his reins.

"I'll take care of him, mister." A young man took my horse's rope.

"Th-thanks."

"You need tendin'," a man said. "What's your name, lad?"

I shivered, and my throat itched like I'd swallowed hay. "Will ... McGuire."

"Name's Edward Tully." He stared over my shoulder. "Help me get him inside, Joe."

I stepped, but my feet were numb. I landed on a straw-stuffed mattress. Someone pulled off my boots and wet wool socks. My teeth chattered. "W-why am I s-so cold?

My hat floated before my eyes, then something heavy covered my shivering body.

A small hand lifted my head, and a warm salty broth found its way through my lips and down my raw throat. A light flickered from a lantern. I squinted, then focused on a woman's face, but my eyes kept drooping.

"I'm Mrs. Tully. You're goin' to mend, Mr. McGuire. And so shall the lad. Poor mite is hungry and exhausted, like the lot of ya. Though your mates fared better. Sleep now."

Benny's going to make it. My eyelids closed. An old Irish prayer came to mind.

May it be three days 'fore the devil knows I'm here.

Chapter Eleven

October 4

Many horses, wagons, and carts surrounded the meadow outside the fort where people gathered for the harvest celebration. Lanterns hung from tall posts within the wide dance circle. Women and children carried food inside the gates to tables, and others came out empty-handed and beaming.

I spotted Hans exuding a delightful smile as he approached. His determined cadence matched the peppy fiddle tune. His cheeks flushed when I grinned.

He scanned my outfit and spoke German. *"Du bist schon."*

I chuckled, then returned his "you are beautiful" with the English, "Many thanks. I prefer English."

He reached for the bowl of beans in my hands. "May I carry your dish?"

When I released it to him, he kissed my cheek. He lingered near my ear and whispered in a deep, soothing tone, "I've missed seeing you every day."

His breath on my neck sent heat across my face. I took his arm and strolled beside him, feeling pampered and proud. "I've been looking forward to dancing with you all week."

"*Jah*, we will dance, but please come see my shop and meet my customers." His words sped. "People are complimentary of my work, and orders are coming in each day."

I pulled him to a full stop and searched his face for signs of teasing, but he remained serious.

"I'm here to dance and enjoy your company first. Show me your shop later."

He studied my eyes. "Alright. One dance, then I'll introduce you and show you my work. Shall we take the food now?" He moved toward the tables located inside the fort.

I stepped beside him but felt less important.

We entered the bustling fort, where more lanterns hung above the tables. The aromas were tantalizing. Momma arrived ahead of us and pointed Hans to an empty spot.

Momma scurried toward a group of women, which included Christina. I waved, and she smiled and nodded as if in approval.

Hans placed the bowl of beans on the table with all the other vegetables and turned his sparkling blue eyes on me, offering his elbow. "Please let me introduce you to one of my customers."

Shyness flustered my nerves as we approached a gray-haired gentleman I didn't know. They shook hands.

"Hullo, Mr. Smyte. This is Mary Shirley, my intended. Well, in a year, I hope." Hans winked at me.

I curtsied and smiled, but anger simmered.

Intended? Now I'm his intended?

"Miss." The man flashed a pleasant smile. "You are Michael Shirley's daughter?"

My heart sped with a danger warning.

Why is he asking? Is he a loyalist spy after Papa?

I noted his German accent and gazed into his steady eyes.

He's not acting shifty. I calmed. *It's an innocent question. Why did I panic?*

I took a deep breath and forced a smile. "Yes, sir."

"Honored to meet you. I've heard of your contribution to the Patriot cause. Well done."

I curtsied again. "Thank you." My stomach remained knotted by his knowledge of Papa and me connected to secret matters he and Hans shouldn't know.

I'll tell Papa about this later. I'm here to have fun.

Mr. Smyte tipped his hat to me and turned to Hans. "You've a good eye for strength and beauty, Mr. Mueller."

I clenched my jaw and stared at Hans, wishing he'd read my mind. *Stop showing me off.*

Hans beamed a smile at his customer. "Thank you, sir."

The man engaged him again. "My Helen loves the cedar chest you made. Fine carving skills. I know you will have a successful business in Williamsburg someday." He gazed beyond us and grinned. "Now, I must dance with my beauty before she accepts dances from others. Blessings to you both."

He chuckled and stepped toward a woman nearby who chatted with a soldier.

"You were just about to lose me, Johann." She winked as he approached.

I couldn't help grinning. *I'm not alone in feeling annoyed.*

Hans took my hand. "Shall we join the dance? That private thinks you smiled at him. Now he's gawking at you as if I'm not standing here."

"Well, we can't have that." I turned my back on the young man.

Hans held out one hand and bowed. *"Mien liebchen."*

I stepped back. "It's too soon to call me sweetheart."

He straightened. "I'm sorry, but it's how I feel. You are special to me."

"Well, it's not acceptable yet." I laid my palm lightly on his and pushed away the gloom.

He led me to the designated dance area as if I were a princess.

I didn't know the name of the reel, but we stumbled and laughed as we twirled and skipped along with the other dancers. Soon no one noticed our mistakes. I loved this relaxed and fully abandoned side of Hans.

We were out of breath when the song changed to a waltz. Rather than end, he led me into slow gliding steps. An easy flowing rhythm beat in my heart. *Is this growing desire real?*

Hans stared over my shoulder with furrowed brows.

"You've grown quiet. What's wrong?" I asked.

"I'm sorry." He glanced down and walked me out of the crowd. "I'm troubled by what Mr. Smyte said—concerning your contribution to the Patriot cause. Please tell me what happened while you were in Kentucky."

The abrupt request and turbulent voice ruined the sweet mood. I stepped back. "It's a story for another time. May we continue dancing?"

"But if I'm to continue courting you, I must know what happened. I've heard others refer to you as the Indian Captive. Did a warrior violate you?"

His accusing tone sent heat raging up my neck. I fixed a glare on his blinking eyes. "How dare you assume. Would it matter?"

Hans stepped backward, squaring his shoulders. "No. But hearing half-stories troubles me." His face softened as he dared a step closer. "Please, understand my need to know more about you."

His calm tone didn't lower my defenses.

In the faint light of the half-moon, I narrowed my eyes. "I'll tell you everything while we eat. Then you owe me an uninterrupted waltz."

"*Jah.*" He swallowed hard, sighed, and offered his elbow.

I took it, still seething.

After filling our plates, we found Momma speaking to a few ladies near the tables.

"Hans wishes to show me his workshop, and we have a few things to discuss. Do you object?"

She shook her head, but added, "Leave the door open and be wise."

"I will stay honorable, Mrs. Shirley." Hans bowed.

When we reached his cabin, he entered and propped the door open with a sawhorse.

"Wait here."

He carried our plates inside, and within a minute a golden light shimmered from a lantern. He offered his arm. "Come in."

Our meal sat on a small table, and new ladder-backed chairs awaited us. Along three log walls were various saws, axes, chisels, hammers, and planers. Two sawhorses hung from the ceiling beam. His bed set centered on the back wall beside a chest with drawers.

He dipped water into two wooden cups and placed them next to our food, then scooted a chair back. I sat, and he lowered into the other.

I took a few bites and mulled over which details of my troubled past he needed.

Hans listened wide-eyed as I started with discovering Papa's coded surveys and our trip to Boonesborough. I explained my capture and how No Name saved me from being violated. Then I ended my tale with how William helped me return. Reliving the emotions of those times depleted my enthusiasm for dancing.

Hans stood and offered his hand. "I owe you a waltz."

I eased to my feet with his help while he placed his free hand on the small of my back. As we waltzed around the tiny space of the shop to the faint tune of distant fiddles, I felt safe and accepted.

Then he stopped dancing, wrapped his arms around me, and whispered, "I'm in love with you, Mary Shirley."

In one quick motion, he tilted his head and pressed his lips on mine, uninvited and too hard.

I groaned and pushed against his chest, but couldn't free my neck from the crook of his arm. I couldn't breathe. Rage freed my fist. I punched his ribs and shoved away.

He moaned and stumbled backward, holding his side and scowling. "That hurt."

"Yes, it did." I glared. "My mouth is throbbing. You didn't ask to kiss me, and that's not how it works."

I retrieved my plate and moved toward the doorway, needing fresh air and space from Hans.

He stepped in front of me, wide-eyed and out of breath. "Forgive me. I've never kissed anyone before. But how do you know how kissing should feel?"

I stood still and watched the softness return to his face. He appeared contrite.

I can't mention William.

"I know it's supposed to be gentle and sweet. You held me too tight and pressed your lips too firm."

His gentle touch on my arm released the knots in my stomach.

"Please. May I try again the way you said? I wish to learn."

I raised the back of my hand to him. "You may kiss the back of my hand for now. I don't wish to kiss you so soon. Let's return to the dance and have fun."

His light peck on my hand didn't send tingles anywhere.

We stepped outside into the crisp air and lively music. My smile rose as the memory of William kissing my hand and fingers ignited a longing for his return.

What am I doing with Hans?

After leaving our plates with the young girls at the washtubs, we weaved through the crowd. As we entered the dance area, cheers rang out between sets of lively fiddle music and rhythmic heel-to-toe shoe stomping on a board.

I glimpsed Christina step on the wooden square. I pulled Hans with me to watch her, adding my roar of approval to the others.

"I didn't know she could do those back-steps."

Hans nodded. "I saw people practicing all week. They call it buck dancing." He slid his feet backward.

I attempted the moves but couldn't stop laughing.

"Mary, there you are." Christina rushed toward us, still out of breath.

I hugged her. "Did you win?"

"No, but I enjoyed tryin'. Last time to dance for a while." She caressed her belly, gazed at me, and winked.

"Oh, congratulations. Maybe a daughter this time."

"And I'm praying it is so." She looked at Hans.

"This is Hans Mueller. Our families met two years ago."

He clutched my hand. "She's accepted my courtship."

I cringed, too dumbfounded to refute him in public, but heat crawled up my neck.

Christina's mouth opened, and her eyes widened. She curtsied. "Pleasure to meet you."

"And you, Mrs. Gatliff." He bowed.

She turned to me. "Have a good night." After kissing my cheek, Christina whispered. "He's a fine-lookin' man."

I smiled but needed to explain the friendship away from Hans's hearing.

"Have you heard anything from ... Charles?"

"Aye. Scouts report Charles and my brothers left Fort Randolph headin' west."

Relief lifted my spirit but not my worry. *How does she live, never knowing if her men are alive or dead?*

"Glad they're safe. Good night." I slid my hand over Hans's arm, hoping he wouldn't discern my personal interest.

I spotted Papa loading my younger siblings into our small cart while speaking to a man who looked like an older version of William.

I gazed back at Hans. "My family is preparing to leave. Thank you for the dances. *Guten tag.*"

"May I come see you soon?" The sad, deep tone returned. "I bought a horse yesterday. We can take rides together."

I smiled. "Of course you may. Riding will be fun." I stretched my face to his cheek.

His lips landed soft and sweet on mine. "Was that better?"

When the shock wore off, I nodded. "But I aimed for your cheek."

He chuckled. "Is it wrong of me to say I'm glad I misunderstood?"

"It's still too soon. Good night." I hurried toward my family.

William's kisses are better.

I enjoyed dancing with Hans but did not enjoy his dominating and anxious manner. He mellowed when confronted, but I couldn't allow him to rush things.

Papa turned from a gray-haired man and waved me closer.

"There you are, Daughter. This is William's father, Cornelius McGuire."

I curtsied. "Pleased to meet you, sir."

He bore the same playful twinkle in his eye as William.

"Aye, and I you, lass. I've heard your name oft, and it's a pleasure to meet ya. Hope to again soon."

Same smile as William's too.

He twisted toward Papa. "I'll see ya in the morn, Michael."

After shaking hands, Mr. McGuire sauntered away. I stepped in front of Papa.

"Something wrong, little polliwog?"

I snuggled against him and sighed. "Do I have to marry? Can I be an old maid?"

Momma chuckled from the cart where my younger siblings were covering up with the blankets. "I'd like to hold grandchildren in my lap someday. But I'm not in a hurry. You didn't enjoy Hans's company?"

"I enjoyed dancing but not—Well, his customers interrupted."

And he's rushing things.

Chapter Twelve

December 4

We recovered our health in a few days but remained at Hinkstons Fort through October and November, allowing our horses to regain sufficient strength. A week ago, I accepted a quarter-mile race to gauge Babcock's readiness for the long trip ahead. We needed to resume our search for Simon Butler.

My bay soundly beat the chestnut and maintained his reputation as one of the best racers around. I gained five shillings, a pocket watch, and a mild-mannered gelding for Benny. When I introduced the horse to the lad as his, he rushed me with a hug.

"I'll call him Johnny, for my da."

My heart ripped down the middle.

I spent six days teaching the lad the basics, and he and the horse bonded.

Last night, we agreed to move on to Boonesborough and then toward home before the weather worsened.

After checking Babcock's legs and hooves in the gray foggy morning, I strolled toward the fire pit for a cup of coffee.

I glimpsed six-year-old Benny, beaming as he toted kindling for Mrs. Kruger. She and her husband agreed to care for him until someone in his family could come in the spring. His smile pleased me, but the thought of leaving him behind didn't sit well in my gut because of the coming raids.

My mind insisted he wasn't my responsibility anymore. My heart disagreed.

Thomas poured a steamy brew into a mug and held it out. "Mornin'."

"Thank you." I grasped the cup and sat next to Charles, respecting his quiet mood. I sipped and closed my eyes, savoring the stout coffee before swallowing. It soothed my throat and erased a dull headache.

A twig snap alerted us to a man strolling our way. I recognized the tall and brawny Simon Butler by his bushy brown ponytail flicking like a squirrel's tail under his fur cap. I had become acquainted with him shortly after the skirmish at Point Pleasant two years back but didn't care for the cocky scrapper much.

"Mornin'. I heard you blokes were soon off for Boonesborough seekin' me."

His enthusiastic greeting matched the sky-blue sparkle in his eyes but clashed with my preference for a gentle morning. He didn't sit or speak any softer.

Charles greeted him. "That we are, lad. Want coffee?"

"No, sir. Come ta see what you're needin' from me, then headin' southwest on to Boonesborough."

"What do you know of Simon Girty's association with Alex McKee?" Charles asked.

He frowned and shook his head. "I've only heard rumors. No firsthand knowledge." He took a knee and warmed his hands. "I've not seen nor spoken to that wild man since serving with him at Fort Pitt in '74. What's he done now?"

Perhaps it was his mellowed tone and his more mature manner, but I believed him.

Charles continued. "Tell Maj. Clark that Blue Jacket's men plan to ambush him for the gunpowder he's bringin'. Alex McKee is passin' information through the Girtys to Hamilton at Fort Detroit."

Simon straightened. "I'm off now to seek him with this report. I'll inform the men at Boonesborough of the trouble comin' and about Clark bein' seen. Stay safe, friends." He held out his bear-paw-sized hand. "Where you off to now?"

We stood, but I answered. "Back to Cooks Fort in the Greenbrier Valley."

Charles and Thomas exchanged vigorous handshakes with Simon. I controlled the speed of mine and didn't spill a drop of coffee.

"Safe travels, Simon," I said as he turned. *Still a brassy fellow, but I'd fight beside him.*

I downed my last warm swallow. "Since we're headed home, I'll tell Benny good-bye."

"I'm ready." Thomas stood and shouldered his rifle.

I checked my saddle and rubbed the horse's neck.

"Don't leave me." Benny's shout crushed all reason. He sat tall on his horse with a firm stare and a clinched jaw as he rode toward us, then dismounted.

My grin rose despite an attempt at firmness. "It will be a hard, long trip."

"Yes, sir. Me and Johnny are ready." His beaming smile nailed my commitment to see him rejoin his family at Arbuckles Fort before heading south to home.

I faced Charles's glare.

Thomas shuffled up beside me. "I agree with bringin' the lad. Full-on raids are coming by spring, and these Kentucky forts don't have men enough for defense." He squared his shoulders and continued. "The lad proved his toughness on the way here. I say he comes along and learns trackin' skills. I'm ready to go." He spun on a heel and strode to his horse.

Charles growled, but I ignored it.

"It's final. We're taking Benny to family. You wouldn't leave one of your sons here." I strolled toward the Krugers to explain the situation as Benny followed.

Might be a bad idea, but it's done.

Mrs. Kruger cried but said she understood, and Benny thanked her with a hug.

He held my hand back to the horses and reality hit.

"We'll cross many rivers and creeks on the way to your family at a fort called Arbuckles. You ready to be brave and strong again?"

His eyes widened. "How long?"

"At least three cold weeks without a fire and staying quiet to avoid Indian scouts and hunters as we pass through their territory. Understand?"

He nodded, but Charles huffed behind me and stepped around.

"Give the lad a few swigs of coffee with his jerky. Warm him up good 'fore we near freeze him to death again." He scowled. "Still say we should leave him here. Let his family come for him." He stormed toward his horse.

I squinted and pressed my lips together. Benny peered at my fists. I uncurled them and exhaled. *Can't teach the boy to be a good man if I rush into a brawl.*

Thomas stepped to the fire and rubbed his hands in the heat. "Charles is ready to move on."

I nodded and passed him the bag of jerky. "Benny and I will keep our distance from him."

"He's mean." The lad's eyes narrowed. "Mr. McGuire wanted to hit him."

My mouth dropped.

Thomas frowned. "You told the lad that?"

"Of course not, but he saw my *want to*. Can't help it if the boy's observant." A grin rose.

Benny beamed. "Ob ... sir ...ob ... sirbent." His head bobbed.

I fought a smile and forced my face to squinch. "Sometimes men settle things with their fists or guns. A good man tries to keep peace." I took a deep breath. "Mr. Gatliff says mean words, but he tries to be good too."

Thomas knelt in front of him with a relaxed expression but firm eyes. "If you're a wise lad, you'll not speak of this to Mr. Gatliff."

"Yes, sir. I don't want a whoopin'." He gazed up at me. "I promise not to tell."

He held out his hand.

I shook it. "Good boy. Time to head home."

Hard being a parent. I thought about Mary and what a wonderful mother she'd be. *Already protective of the babes she hasn't birthed.*

I bit off a hunk of jerky and longed to see her at Christmas. *Hope that Hans hasn't won her heart.*

Chapter Thirteen

December 8

Momma wrapped a towel around the warm maple syrup pie on the table then placed it in my hands. I stepped outside and off the porch, making sure the towel remained taut as I joined the others holding food contributions.

"Ready?" Papa gazed behind me, grinning at her.

She passed me carrying a loaf of honey walnut bread.

We strolled through the silvery fog toward the fort for a special divine service.

A traveling Baptist minister had arrived from the Shenandoah Valley yesterday to hold a prayer meeting at the fort. Papa said the man deserved a hearing for braving the trip and for preaching without an approved license from the king's church.

As the cool breeze ruffled my pale-yellow skirt, I longed for a horseback ride with Hans after the service if he wasn't too tired.

At our last visit, two weeks ago, he lacked the energy for a stroll or a ride to the top of the ridge for a sunset view. But he shared details of his abundant orders coming in for Christmas. When I walked him to his horse, out of the view of my family, he deepened his kiss good-bye, but it still lacked the passion of William's.

William. I'd pushed him from my mind for a month, but he's due back. *How will he react to Hans courting me? Will he care?*

I hurried through the fort gates, then remembered the pie in my hands and slowed.

George reached the bridge first and shouted, "There are people and wagons everywhere."

Papa chuckled. "Thought there would be. A visiting minister is always a big draw."

We maneuvered through the crowds in the meadow and carried our food contributions inside the fort to the tables before gathering with the masses near the fort's eastern wall. Congregants sat on logs and quilts spread along the ground.

Hans waved at us from two long benches and greeted, *"Guten Morgen,"* before shaking Papa's hand.

He smirked at a group of soldiers as he approached me, then kissed my cheek.

I gasped and backed away restraining the urge to shove him down in front of everyone.

My family left as I glared at Hans, seconds from chiding him. But he clasped my hand and twirled me around, stating, "You're the prettiest girl here."

I jerked my arm free. "I'm not a prized horse to be shown off, Mr. Mueller."

Anger propelled me from him to the bench, where I plopped down beside Momma.

She stared forward but held my hand and gave a nod with a slight smile.

Hans eased in front of me, twirling his hat in his hands. "I'm sorry. May I still sit with you?"

I took a deep breath before answering, "Only because it's Sunday, and I'm expected to forgive."

Momma covered her mouth and turned her head with her shoulders shaking as she scooted over.

Hans sat and leaned toward my ear. "You're angry by my bragging. But you are the prettiest."

I turned to his solemn face and wide blue eyes. "You embarrassed me. Like you were staking a claim."

"I've heard those soldiers discussing the marriageable women in the area. Your name comes up often."

I gulped and stared at the ground. *Men are talking about me?*

Hans cleared his throat. "They need to know I am claiming. Why is this wrong?"

I didn't have an answer, but I bit my lip and concentrated on why I couldn't shove him off the bench. I couldn't explain why his showing me off embarrassed me so. *Would I be mad if William did the same?*

I sighed, slid closer to him, and slipped my arm through his. He leaned close to my ear. "I'm sorry I embarrassed you."

"Don't do it again."

Momma turned to us. "Shh, the service is starting."

Someone stood and led everyone in singing a lively version of "Come Ye Sinners." Those who knew the song joined in, along with a fiddle. My feet tapped on the ground, and I clapped with them. Then a few erupted in Scot Irish buck dancing, making it the best prayer meeting I'd ever seen, not counting Shawnee worship.

A gray-haired man stepped up on a wagon bed, making frantic downward motions with his hands. "No, please. Sit down. Stay reverent." He had to shout over everyone.

Silence fell, and people not used to stationary worship shrugged at one another.

He sang the same song, but in a subdued way that trickled over me like a peaceful stream. Then he suddenly stopped singing and shouted a prayer.

I flinched against Hans and thought of the Shawnee war yelps.

"Welcome, neighbors," he said, still loud but no longer frightening.

"I'm John Alderson Jr. from Linville Creek in the Shenandoah Valley. I'm here to share good news." He held up a large Bible. "Please let me share from this book."

He recited passages from Paul's letters, then spoke his mind about the words. I'd read the letters and heard Papa's explanations all my life and pondered them for myself. Mr. Alderson made some interesting points, but by now I had my own opinions—most from firsthand experience. I knew the one who saved me from death more than once, provided food, medicinal plants, comfort, and even correction.

When he finished speaking, many in the crowd surged toward the wagon and proclaimed their belief in the Savior. While some lingered and visited, Papa, Hans, and my brothers carried two benches inside the gate, and we joined others for lunch.

Hans and I filled our plates and strolled through a throng of people who praised him for his quality work.

Some engaged him in conversations, and those who didn't know me asked, "And who is this beautiful girl?" The sweet attention became overwhelming and a bit irritating.

When a man stopped him and chatted about trees, I lost patience. I curtsied and kept my tone polite. "Please excuse us, sir. We haven't eaten yet."

"Aye, sorry, lass. We'll talk later, Mr. Mueller." The men shook hands.

Hans grinned. "Thank you. I find pardoning myself from talkative people difficult. See, you're my perfect helpmate."

I took his elbow, appreciating his influence with people, but not my governess role. "I'm proud of your fine work and reputation, but someday your family must come first. Especially when someone wants to talk about trees."

He chuckled. "Indeed."

We sat near my siblings, eating and visiting. When I finished my last carrot and saw Hans's empty plate, I tugged on his shirtsleeve. "Shall we go horseback riding?"

"I'd rather enjoy a long, uninterrupted conversation with you."

Disappointed but curious, I nodded and finished eating.

In a few moments, he helped me stand and offered his arm. "Let's go this way."

We stopped outside the fort, and he turned, holding my hands.

"I'm moving to Williamsburg in April."

I gasped from the shock. "So … soon?"

"I know you'll only be fifteen in February, but I'd like to ask your Papa's permission to marry you in April." His eyes searched my face.

All I could do was stare and breathe in and out—unable to say yes. Not ready to say no. *I'm not ready. Am I?*

"I'm sure I love you and want to make you happy. You are wonderful, brave, strong, and, as I said to everyone, you are the prettiest girl around."

Instead of feeling flattered, I bristled at being part of his collection of beautiful things.

"I … I'm not ready to answer. This is unexpected." I stared at the floor.

He leaned closer. "When I come for Christmas dinner, may I ask your parents?"

I dropped his hands. "You're not listening. We've only been courting for two months." Blood boiled in my veins. "Wait until after my birthday."

His mouth drooped like a scolded child.

I calmed. "I know you love me, and I'm not saying I won't marry you."

Why did I say that?

His slight smile returned. "I'm sorry. I will wait."

He eased closer and reached around me. "I do love you."

He cradled my head and pressed a gentle kiss on my lips, but somehow it still felt wrong.

I cuddled into his cedar-scented chest, wishing I could say yes.

A loud throat clearing startled us apart.

"Papa's ready to go." George glared, then stomped away.

He's never accepted Hans nor has Cody. What is it?

Hans kissed my cheek. "I won't see you until Christmas morning. I have a lot to finish in sixteen days."

I gazed at him and smiled. "Have a blessed week."

Tears formed as I strolled away—not from leaving Hans but from knowing I would have said yes to William.

I blew out a breath and dried my face. *I don't love Hans.*

William

December 23

Benny tired but didn't complain as we traveled the rough trails. He seemed delighted to learn the sounds of the forest and identify footprints and broken twigs near narrow, uncleared paths. He learned which plants and roots one could eat. I kicked a log over and introduced him to his first slug. My instructions to *swallow don't chew* resulted in a gag followed by a bite down. The oozing mess caused his puking. The next day I gave him an earthworm. That time he understood "swallow." Four days later, he gulped them down for breakfast and beamed with pride.

Concern for Benny's safety grew throughout the morning as I mulled over crossing the Kanawha River later in the day. When we stopped to rest the horses and eat lunch, I left him with a hunk of jerky and joined Charles and Thomas, checking the area for Indian signs.

"When we reach the river, should Benny learn to cross or ride with me? Either way, I think we should make camp with a fire once we cross."

Thomas nodded. "We were just discussin' the matter." He stepped to a large oak.

"Aye, and we're agreein'." Charles dusted his hands off on his shirt. "Let the lad decide when he sees the river. Concerning a fire. Well, we're no longer on scout duty, and I don't want to hear the lad whimperin' from the cold all night. But, indeed, the mite's stronger and braver than his age. I'm mighty grateful."

After checking the trees' bark for Indian markings, my brother approached. "No signs of trouble, but let's hurry on to the Kanawha."

I returned to a napping Benny already stretched out on the ground, sleeping while he could.

"Time to go, little scout." I wiggled him awake. "Fetch your horse."

He rubbed his eyes, pushed to his feet, then trudged over to his gentle steed and lifted the lead rope. "We walkin' or ridin'?"

"Ridin'," Charles's voice boomed.

"Huzzah," I whispered when we reached the dark gray-green river. "Looks low and lazy."

But my stomach knotted with everything that could go wrong if the boy wanted to cross on his own.

I turned to Benny. "Ready to learn river crossing?"

His face paled as he stared at the river.

He shook his head. "Can I ride on the horse with you?"

I confirmed with a relieved, "Yes."

After a few more glances, he marched toward Babcock and climbed in the saddle.

Charles mounted, and as he headed across the current we assessed the depth and force. I mounted behind Benny. We eased into the river, and the lad tensed. The water level reached our horses' backs as they walked.

Once we climbed the bank, the child shouted, "That was fun."

I dismounted and lifted him to the ground. "Gather kindling for a fire as we walk."

He frowned. "I'm not cold. I want to scout."

"Come on with me, lad." Charles chuckled. "Won't take long, then we'll spark a fire."

His acceptance of the boy came as a relief. Benny followed his lead through the mud, parting shrubs along the way until we reached a clearing in the woods.

Thomas and I unsaddled and groomed the horses, then led them to a grassy area and hobbled their legs.

When we returned, Benny dropped an armload of sticks on the ground and Charles arranged them for a fire. The boy knelt down and struck the flint. He produced sparks, but Charles took over and started the fire.

I collected branches for a lean-to shelter to block the wind, figuring the lad would warm up faster.

Charles stood brushing off his pants. "Thomas and I will hunt small game for supper. Your turn watchin' the lad."

Benny kept the fire fed with sticks while I chopped branches into logs with the hatchet. We had plenty of coals by the time our mates returned with squirrels.

I approached Thomas. "I didn't hear gunshots."

"We used rocks," He said and leaned toward my ear. "A few Indian signs, a day or two old."

Charles placed the skewered bodies on the coals. "Soon as these finish charrin', and the lad is warm, we need to douse it all." He looked at Benny. "Sorry, but you'll have another frosty night. No whimperin' though. Could be Indians nearby."

Benny nodded. "I won't cry, sir. I'm a real scout now."

My chest swelled with pride at the brave child and my hope for one like him grew.

After we ate, he helped construct his shelter. He collected leaves, and once his bed suited him, he lay down and didn't move.

My brother and I left to check the perimeter. We hunkered down, listening for voices, footfalls, or anything that would reveal a human presence other than our own.

We returned in fifteen minutes, and Thomas reported all clear. "Who's taking the first watch?"

"William's turn," Charles said. "You're next and I'm last. Turnin' in now. Keep down the noise." He wrapped his blanket around his shoulders and laid his head on his saddle.

I slipped the hatchet back in my shoulder sash with the knife and stocked my pockets with jerky. Then I loaded the muzzle of my rifle with gunpowder, rammed a patched ball down, and readied the flash pan.

In the clear starlit sky, I slinked around the camp. There wouldn't be a moon sliver again for five days—about the time we'd pass Fort Randolph. I listened for unnatural sounds and stared into the darkness. I longed for home in the Greenbrier Valley so I could tell Mary I'd give up Kentucky until it was tame and safe—focus on breeding horses, repairing the small shanty on my land, and planting corn until she can marry. *Best focus on guard duty for now.*

Chapter Fourteen

December 24

The cool, sunny morning drew me to the front porch to finish stitching together a shirt I started making for Hans after the Harvest Dance. Back then, I entertained the idea of becoming his wife and hoped to impress him with my sewing skills. Tomorrow I'd give it as a parting gift and wish him well while breaking off our courtship. For two weeks, I prayed for a way to reject his proposal but keep him as a friend.

I sewed the last stitches in the linen shirt, then raised it up in the gusty breeze, tugging at the seams to check my work. I pulled my shawl around my shoulders as worrisome clouds blew across the darkening sky.

Cody limped onto the porch and lay beside me. I leaned down and rubbed his fur as my brothers entered the yard.

George lifted a large bird overhead. "Cody flushed out this turkey for us."

"And rabbits." Charlie showed his catch.

I clapped my hands and stood. "Wonderful. And I'm glad you're back before the storm."

My brother focused on the sky. "Come on, Charlie, we need to clean these for Momma."

Our dog stood sniffing the air before growling, then he glanced at me and hobbled into the woods. His sad reaction to Hans's approach alerted me, and I rushed back inside.

"Land sakes." Momma startled from her mending.

I ran up the stairs two at a time. "Sorry. I can't let Hans see the shirt I'm making."

Lizzy's voice trailed behind me. "How do you know it's him?"

I peered over the railing. "Cody runs off."

Once in my room, I folded and laid the garment on my nightstand. But as I turned to leave, a sudden concern for William caused a flutter of guilt in my chest and I sat on the bed. I had stopped marking the days since he left and stopped praying for him.

Please bring him through the trouble and home safely, God.

"Mary, Hans is here." Katie's voice boomed from our doorway. "What's wrong?"

She entered, and I rose to my feet, still panting, but forced a smile. "Nothing."

"Didn't look like nothing." She came close and took my hand. "You're cold."

I sucked in a deep breath. "Just needed to pray."

She squinted at my eyes, then released me.

I'm not alright. The desire to saddle Jasper and ride out yelling William's name until I found him wouldn't let go. But I didn't know where to start and I'd freeze to death.

When the jitters in my belly stopped, I descended the stairs ahead of Katie as sleet hit the porch.

Hans stared up, grinning. "Surprise. I finished all my deliveries and wanted to spend the rest of the afternoon with you."

I forced a smile but still hurt for William.

Momma gazed at him from the hearth. "By the looks of the weather, you best stay the night."

I reached the floor. "Yes, please stay. We are worried enough about ..." I pressed my lips together and turned to Momma. "When will Papa be home?"

The door opened to George. "The turkey and rabbits are ready. There's snow mixing with the sleet now." He raised his chin at Hans in a greeting, but it seemed forced as if still out of duty.

Charlie carried an armload of firewood to the hearth.

"Thank you, Sons." Momma raked coals to the sides of the fireplace. "Set the bird on the table for skewering. Bring the rabbits here." She stood and released a sigh. "Papa thought he'd be back before supper. He went to Fort Culbertson."

My breath caught with the memory of the place I first encountered Isaiah Brown, the man I shot in the knee—the one Cody dispatched at the Shawnee village before I would have.

I blew out a breath and stepped closer. "Why?"

"Delivering news." She added a head bob. "Please ready the turkey." She turned to Hans. "Make yourself at home."

My head throbbed with worry over William and now Papa for risking his life as a spy again.

William

Scaling the steep trails took longer with a child in tow, but after the first week Benny stopped asking how much longer and accepted the need to walk to spare our horses. Over the last two weeks, he'd fallen into our routine with little complaint, but I noticed he'd grown more exhausted and quiet of late.

He perked up this morning when I told him he'd be with his family by the end of the day and enjoy a Christmas feast the next.

Mid-morning, we topped a ridge with a gusty cold wind that caused Benny to stumble a bit.

"When can we ride again?" A childish whine replaced his bravery.

I pointed down. "After we descend and examine trees for paint or scarring. Remember to stay quiet."

I didn't tell him the signs had been sparse for days, and the Indians would be in their villages by now. He needed to keep his mind on survival. He hushed and trod forward.

A few minutes after entering the forest again, he stood still, pointed, and looked back at me wide-eyed. He whispered, "I ... see ... something."

I motioned for him to squat.

My mates also peered at the nice-sized buck staring from the shrubs a few feet away. I gestured my intent to let Benny have the shot. Thomas gave a nod, but Charles scowled.

"Move slow and quiet, but come here."

When the boy reached me, I propped my rifle for his height in the fork of a hickory tree and whispered. "It's a buck. You're going to shoot him for meat and hide. I'll help."

I lined up the shot, let him look down the barrel, and positioned his finger on the trigger and whispered, "Squeeze."

"Got him." Thomas confirmed.

When smoke from the blast dissipated, I pointed through the bare branches. "See him there on the ground?"

Benny stared, then grinned. "I'm a hunter."

"Yes, you are. Now it's time to learn how to pack it out."

After we dressed and salted the meat, I loaded it on his horse, Johnny. "You'll share with your family at Arbuckles for supper."

I'm going to miss him.

After we crossed the Greenbrier River, the wind gusted, and the sky dropped cold rain.

Thomas pointed ahead. "Those look like snow clouds. We better fly if we're going to make the five miles to Arbuckle's Fort."

Our quick pace up the next ridge slowed as the trail slicked with mud. I made Benny dismount and climb on with me. Johnny followed Babcock.

When northerly winds hit our faces full force, I secured my hat with a scarf and endured the stinging sleet blowing past my upturned collar before melting down my neck. The forearm of my coat dampened by wiping snot off my upper lip. The boy tightened his grip around my waist several times and snuggled against my back, sniffling.

We veered off the main road about midafternoon, then followed the southerly path through the frosty haze toward Arbuckles, soaked, starving, and exhausted.

Upon sighting the palisades, I shook Benny awake. "We've arrived."

He moaned and shifted in the saddle.

The gate opened and a dozen men greeted us.

Charles addressed them. "We rescued a lad name Benjamin Nichols. Was told he has family here."

"That he does." A gray-haired man came closer, peering at Benny's face.

I dismounted and lowered the lad.

"Uncle Robert?" Benny asked, easing forward.

They embraced, and the man shouted, "Martha, come. Benjamin is alive."

Seconds later, a woman squealed from a cabin, ran across the yard, and rushed Benny into her arms.

Ten others gathered around him. I assumed family members. They all spoke at once, asking him questions.

I stepped out of the way before things became more emotional. It happened too fast, and I felt gutted. I led Babcock and Johnny toward the barn within a corral.

Running footfalls grew closer. I turned. The wet-eyed boy held out his hand. I knelt on one knee and reached, but instead of a handshake he threw his arms around my neck and kissed my cheek.

"Thank you, Mr. ... McGuire. Are you staying?"

I gulped hard, as if swallowing a large slug. "No. I—"

"But ... I want you to live here." He pointed to the ground.

I took his hand and shook it. "It's Christmas Eve, and I have family wanting me home. We've two more miles to go. You understand?"

His lips pooched out. "Yes, sir."

"Someday I may see you again. Grow up to be a good man, lad." I stood.

He nodded and straightened. "Strong and brave like you."

"Merry Christmas, Benny." I swallowed and blinked, then stepped toward the barn.

Leaving him with his family released my attachment, but his tearful "I love you" twisted my gut.

I shivered upon entering the warmth of the barn where our saddled horses munched from grain bags. A stableboy had Benny's horse in a stall.

Thomas pointed at the sky. "We've gotta rush ta beat that storm."

I squinted at the northern clouds, then hurried to Babcock. "I know we're exhausted, boy." I removed his feed. "But I'm determined to see Mary in the morning." I examined him for travel. "Another hour, boy." I rubbed his neck and led him out into the blowing sleet. "Or two, if the weather worsens."

Snow dropped on us in wet splats for the first mile then accumulated fast and heavy as the wind kicked up with fury. The clothes on our bodies flapped like the sails on a sloop in the ocean. Panic clenched my jaw, but Babcock remained calm and slowed his pace to a trudge as the drifts deepened around his hooves and then up to his knees. When we lost the ability to see our landmarks in the sudden howling blizzard, we dismounted. I felt along my saddle for a rope then reached for my brother who once stood at my side.

I cupped my hands around my mouth and shouted, "We need to connect our ropes."

"Follow me down the trail." Thomas's voice sounded distant, but I saw his arms waving ahead.

My teeth chattered as I checked Babcock's nostrils and cleared them of ice. I resumed tramping down the steep mountain until my feet slipped. I hit the ground, sliding on my shoulder all the way down, then tumbled twice.

I grabbed a pine sapling, hoisted myself to my feet, and glanced around. Nothing but whiteness.

"Haloo," I yelled into the howling wind. No one answered. I attempted a whistle from frozen lips then shouted, "Babcock," with outstretched arms, but failed to find him. I couldn't see his form anywhere.

I'm in big trouble.

Tree branches creaked overhead. I inched forward, gazing ahead and from side to side but couldn't determine a direction. My face stung from ice and my eyes burned. I stumbled over a fallen log. I felt around it and found a long stick, then managed to stand.

My next step dropped me into shallow rocky water. I used the stick to check the width and depth. *A creek, but which one?*

I yelled for Babcock, then for my brother and Charles, but only the wind howled back.

Panic surged when my body stopped shivering. My sight went from white to a shadowy gray. *No, don't pass out.*

When I stumbled forward, vision returned to blizzard white, and my foot sank through snow but found ground. I stood still and blinked upward where the sky should be, pleading, "God, let me see a marker or lantern light from a cabin. Something."

With my stick tapping the bank of the creek, I stayed with it the best I could, knowing I'd end up somewhere. *Dead or alive, but it will be somewhere.*

My mind numbed, but my body ached. Energy waned. I forced steps for what seemed like hours, then I heard a whistle, but not from a human. Something large, hollow, and with an echo—a cave? *Yes, a cave!*

I glimpsed a dark archway low on a cliff face.

"Hallelujah," I shouted and moved toward the sound.

The only whistling cave I knew was on Laurel Creek, less than a mile from my parents'.

I'm not going to die.

When a horse-shaped shadow moved in front of the entrance, I thought it a hallucination until it whinnied.

"Babcock?"

The horse rushed toward me. "Good instincts, boy." I wrapped my arms around his neck. Heat from his body warmed and thawed me. I thanked God and rested with Babcock until the wind and snow tapered off and my body shivered again.

"We're close." My teeth chattered. "You'll like the warm barn." I mounted the horse and continued the push homeward.

Within a quarter of a mile, I glimpsed flickering lantern light inside the cabin window. Aromas of oak and hickory smoke stirred a savage hunger in my belly.

I entered the warm and dusty barn, slid from the horse, and unsaddled. Da's horses whinnied. I groomed Babcock, covered his back with a blanket, and gave him grain. My legs wobbled, and my body trembled all the way to the cabin door. I knocked twice.

"There ya are." Da grabbed me before I fell and led me to a bed in the corner.

I sank into the warm feather bed—relieved and thankful.

Ma rushed toward me and removed my boots before burying me in quilts.

"Praise to God, the devil lost again, so he has. I'll get broth."

Da turned my legs on the bed so I could prop my back against the wall. "There, now. Your brother and Charles stopped here an hour ago, concerned for ya. They've gone on to the fort. Plannin' to lead a search in the mornin'."

He left me sinking into a grateful bliss, but I heard his words to Ma. "Aye, and I have to tell them not to go searchin' for one not missin'."

Ma sat in a chair beside me. "I'm thankful God brought you here safely." She spooned warm beef broth past my quavering lips until my eyes closed.

A moment later, I'm sure I heard her whisper, "And ya might consider winnin' back the heart of that Mary Shirley."

I forced open my eyes. "What?"

"Well, I thought you were sleepin', but 'twould be a shame to lose the lass you've been pinin' over for a year." She stroked my temple. "A furniture maker is bein' allowed to court. And herself, not fifteen yet."

Hans. I moaned inside. *Worse than freezing to death.* I touched Ma's hand. "I'll sleep off the bad dream now."

Ma kissed my cheek. "Merry Christmas, Son."

The pile of blankets stopped my trembling body but not my quavering heart. *I'll go see Mary tomorrow on my way back to the fort. Maybe it's not too late.*

Mary

I worried about Papa stranded in the snowstorm until he shouted, "I'm home." His boots stomped on the porch, and Momma hurried to the door as he entered.

The rest of us scooted from the table, but Momma hugged him first.

"Praise be to God. I thought the blizzard buried you somewhere."

"It came on just as I arrived at the fort." He held and kissed her, but his face remained serious.

What is it? Maybe just exhaustion.

When she stepped back, he hung up his hat and rifle, then removed his wet coat. We took turns hugging him.

He shook Hans's hand. "I waited out the storm in your shop. Glad you're here and not lost somewhere."

His flat tone and serious face sped my heart.

"*Jah,* good you sheltered." Hans returned to the table.

I studied Papa's pressed lips as he eased closer and reached for my hands.

My throat tightened.

"Charles and Thomas came into the fort during the blizzard. They need volunteers searching for William in the morning."

I gasped. "My William is lost?"

Hans heard my words, but I don't care.

Papa wrapped me in his arms, then sat me in the nearest chair and squatted before me.

"Take a deep breath."

I inhaled but felt dizzy and nauseated.

Papa held my hands. "William knows how to survive a snowstorm. He knows the caves between here and the Greenbrier River."

Hans draped a blanket over my shoulders and sat beside me. Silent.

Papa moved to the fireplace, and Momma handed him a cup of coffee, I cuddled against him, sniffling, but I couldn't make out their words.

George eased up to them. "I want to help find William in the morning."

"I'll go back to my cabin now," Hans whispered and touched my arm. "I'm sorry about Mr. McGuire." He stood. "I will also help find him." He leaned down and kissed my cheek. "Good night."

He doesn't understand.

I pushed to my feet and grabbed his arm. "No. Don't leave. It's Christmas Eve. Please ... I don't want you to be alone. William is our friend."

"Stay, Hans." Momma pointed to the bench. "I insist."

She handed a plate to Papa.

Hans complied and dried his eyes. "I'm ... sorry."

"You are missing your family." Momma placed a plate before him. "You will always be welcome in ours."

My sisters sniffled and held one another. Charlie sat near the fireplace, tossing chunks of bark into the fire. George plopped down in a corner, hunched forward with his hands pressed together and his eyes closed. His mouth moved but without sound, as if praying.

Papa leaned back in his chair. His face brightened. "Bring my Bible. It's time to read the Bethlehem Story. Then we are going to pray and go to bed."

As he read, peace came like a warm blanket—a knowing from God. *William is safe.*

A tear dribbled down my cheek, and after I wiped it away, Hans held my hand.

He hasn't replaced William in my heart, but he makes me feel loved.

A loud knock on the door made us all jump.

"Blessin's to this house." A man's voice boomed.

Papa opened the door to William's da. "Come in, Mr. McGuire."

I squeezed Hans's hand, breathless.

The man stepped inside and closed the door. "Praise be, our lad is home safe. A bit froze, but recoverin'."

I clasped my chest as tears of joy flowed.

Papa said, "Very good news."

Hans slipped his arm around my waist, but I resisted laying my head on his shoulder.

"Care for coffee, Cornelius?" Momma asked.

He grinned. "Aye, but I must share the news at the fort." He pulled his coat collar tighter around his neck and stepped into the cold, calling, "Merry Christmas."

"And to you." Papa secured the door.

Hans dried a tear from my cheek. "All is well now?"

I nodded, but my gut twisted with the truth.

I'd rather be in William's arms.

Chapter Fifteen

December 25

The smoky aroma of roasting turkey woke me as Katie stuffed a note under her pillow, then turned, smiling. "Merry Christmas."

"And to you." I flipped back my covers and sat up, expecting a cheerful good morning from Lizzy. Her vacant bed and smoothed quilts explained her silence.

Katie slipped into her tan petticoat and sage-green blouse.

I lit the candle on my bedside table and waited for Katie to finish dressing and glance my way.

I pointed to her pillow. "Is the note from John? I hope you're not defying Papa."

She lowered her eyes. "Leave me alone."

She retrieved the folded paper and shoved it into her apron pocket, gathered her gifts for the family, and scurried out the door. I shrugged and supposed she'd work out her own troubles.

In the flickering light, I shimmied into my brown wool skirt and pale-blue blouse, nervous about ending the courtship with Hans, but I couldn't pretend anymore. His hurt would heal in time.

I gathered my packages and descended the stairs. After greeting Momma and my sisters, I placed my gifts with others in the corner, then helped Lizzy finish the pancakes.

Papa and Hans came in from feeding the livestock. George and Charlie carried logs to the hearth.

"Merry Christmas, family. Snow isn't as deep, but clouds are threatening." Papa hung up his hat and coat. "I'm starving."

Not another storm. I wanted Hans to leave after our breakfast feast and gift exchange so I could saddle my horse and go visit William.

I gathered with the family around the table and sat on the bench, staring at my plate. Hans scooted beside me and clasped my hand. I eased it from his icy one and laid it back in my lap. He shifted.

Papa bowed his head. "With grateful hearts, we come together and share this meal. You have provided food, shelter, protection, and the blessing of one another in our new home. Thank you for the gifts of life and mercy and especially for remembering we are dust."

Giggles traveled around the table. "I read Psalms 103 this morning." He chuckled.

Charlie rushed from the table and swiped his finger across the windowsill. He stared at the collection of dirt, then blew it off. "How does God make people from dust?"

"He spits on it," George said. "Makes mud and shapes it into us."

Momma snickered. "He only made one man from mud. Then he made a woman from bone. The rest of us come from parents. Now, eat, so we can bless one another with gifts."

I grinned and forked a succulent slice of turkey onto Hans's plate, then mine.

He stared down, mouth drooping. I leaned into his ear.

"Are you thinking of your family?"

He swallowed and gave a nod.

I held his hand in sympathy. If I hadn't escaped from the Shawnee five months ago, I'd be weeping now. *How quickly life can blow away like Charlie's dust.*

While my family chatted, I scanned their faces and dabbed my eyes with the napkin, confirming my unwillingness to leave them again so soon.

I lifted my knife and cut a small bite of tender meat.

"Everything is delicious, Momma," Hans said, a timid grin on his face.

I sat back, shocked by his sudden claim.

My siblings' reactions varied from wrinkled foreheads to frowns from Katie and George.

"Thank you." A pleasant tone accompanied her smile.

Why didn't she correct him? Pity for his loneliness? Papa's somber face troubled me as he leaned forward and resumed eating.

Does he assume I've agreed to marry without his blessing?

Utensils clanked as everyone ate.

My younger siblings folded their hands on the table as each finished and stared at Papa. He raised his last bite, held it near his mouth, then grinned and tossed it into his mouth.

"Clear the table." Momma stood and gathered plates while we giggled and removed cups, utensils, and food.

Hans and Papa moved the table back, while my brothers carried a bench to the gift corner.

Once seated, we took turns passing out our cloth-bundled surprises. Hans received a leather pouch with bullets and flints from George, a reed whistle from Charlie, a carved leather rifle sash from Papa, wool socks from Momma, tallow candles from Katie, and handkerchiefs from the rest of my sisters with his initials embroidered. I gave him my gift last. His eyes widened at the shirt. He held it to his chest. "Thank you, *liebchen*."

My face grew hot from my family's stares.

He addressed Momma. "May I try it on in that room?" He pointed to the girls' room.

"You may."

He darted inside and closed the door.

"*Liebchen*?" Papa frowned and tilted his head.

I gulped. "I told him not to call me sweetheart."

He nodded and pressed his lips together as Hans stepped out, stroking the shirtsleeves and smiling.

"Fine quality. I'm proud of this." Hans beamed at all of us. "Thank you for these special gifts and making my life happy again ... since losing my family." He moved to the outside door. "Now, my turn. I brought gifts for everyone." He rushed toward the barn.

"I didn't see him bring anything yesterday." George shrugged and peered out the window. "But Charlie and I were gutting rabbits when he rode in."

Papa laughed. "Safe to say it's not furniture."

"Whatever he gives,"—Momma scanned our faces—"remember to be kind and thankful."

George opened the door. "He's coming with a large burlap bag."

Cold air blew in with him, and the door had to be shouldered closed. Gratitude swelled for William being safe and warm.

Hans lowered the clinking bundle in the middle of the room. "Mary's first."

He untied the bag as I neared and lifted out a pair of white leather shoes with eyelets.

I gasped at the beautiful but impractical footwear.

"Try them on." He placed them in my hands.

I stared at them and sat in a chair. *I can't keep these but no harm trying them on.* I slipped off the moccasins and slid my feet into the perfect-fitting shoes. "They are beautiful, but I shouldn't accept. I can't—"

"Well, perhaps you won't mind after you make a new dress from these." He pulled two bolts of cloth from the bag, one bleached cotton and the other of pale-blue calico. "I hope it's enough for you, Momma, and the sisters."

Speechless, I gawked from the shoes to the cloth, then at him, at a loss for what to say and if I should refuse them.

He placed the bolts in my arms, and I carried them to the table with panic speeding my breaths.

William could never afford things like this.

Momma came beside me and fingered the cloth. "I've never felt material so soft."

My sisters took turns touching. I imagined a fine skirt and blouse with the shoes.

Momma's ginseng lesson came to mind. *How quickly riches tempt—but not enough to steal my heart. I must return these items in private when I reject his courting.*

I turned to Hans, feigning a smile. "Thank you for these wonderful gifts."

He grinned. "Now, gifts for everyone."

In turn, Momma received a bag of coffee beans, a wooden box full of tea, and a copper pot. Papa stared at the barrel-making tools and a new handsaw.

Katie held up a lace collar for blouses, and the rest of my sisters squealed over brightly colored yarns and new needles.

George opened and closed a folding knife and grinned at him for the first time.

"Land sakes," Momma said as Charlie raised a hatchet in the air. "Lay that on the floor and be still."

Papa approached Hans. "Thank you for all of this. But I must ask how you afforded such items in so short a time? Are you still leaving for Williamsburg in April?"

I sat as my breath caught. *He's told him? Did he mention his marriage proposal?*

"Everything came from barters, except Mary's shoes. I ordered them." He smiled down at me. "You didn't notice me measuring your footprint in the sawdust of my shop one day." He turned back to Papa. "I wish to leave in April."

My family took turns watching me as if expecting a reaction. I averted my eyes and sat on the floor with my youngest sisters, admiring the yarn colors as everyone thanked him.

"And thank you all for caring for me. You have made this first Christmas without my family easier to bear. I'm leaving now so I can rest." He gathered his items. "Please. May Mary walk with me to the barn?"

An instant headache pounded, and my heart sped.

I must end this lie.

After a nod from Papa, I stood, pulled on my coat, wrapped a scarf around my head, and resisted taking Hans's arm.

When we stepped onto the porch, Cody growled.

"It's alright, boy."

Cody stayed back.

I gazed up at Hans. "I'm sorry he reacts to you this way."

"I don't care for him either." His tone deepened. "I don't care for animals as pets."

No wonder there is tension.

He offered his hand, but I stomped past him. As we trudged through the snow to the barn, I continued processing his attitude.

"I remember your family having two dogs and puppies. You never pet them?"

"No. They were annoying and yapping all the time." He sighed. "My momma loved them, though."

When we entered the barn, I faced him. "Before you continue, I must tell you I can't marry you."

He frowned and stepped back. "I thought you agreed." His breaths sped. "You said I could ask in February." He shook his head. "How could you lead me on so?" His brow furrowed. "I bought the material so you can have a nice dress and shoes to wear in April."

"I asked you to wait, but you continued planning things. I won't rush into marriage." I stayed calm. "You're a kind, generous friend. But I don't love you." I gulped. "Your gifts are wonderful, but you gave them with marriage in mind. I can't accept."

He sighed and stared at the ground. "No. I'm sorry I misunderstood. Keep the gifts." His tone sweetened as he raised his glistening eyes. "I want you to have nice things—always." He swallowed and took my hands. "I wanted you for a wife the first time I met you. When Mr.

McGuire said you were no longer in Kentucky, I thought God led me here."

No wonder he assumed so much.

He released me, and a deep breath. "I will always care for you. I'll leave now." He stepped back, frowning. "Please let me know if you change your mind."

His harsh tone concerned me.

When he stormed out of the barn, I followed. "I'm sorry too. Please remain friends with me and the family. Continue to visit us."

He mounted his horse, Tilly, and after a loud sigh added, "Merry Christmas." Then he rushed away.

I did the right thing. Hans loves me, but my heart longs for William and he deserves another chance to choose me over Kentucky.

The desire to ride out to the McGuires' place grew until squelched by the reality of not knowing the way. Nor could I find the trail in the deep snow with another storm coming.

Cody hobbled toward me and sat at my feet. I knelt and rubbed his damp, smelly fur.

"Thank you, boy. What a stressful morning."

As I stood, Cody stared and sniffed toward the woods behind our cabin.

"What is it? A deer?"

When birds flushed from a distant clump of shrubs, I squatted down in a panic.

"Who's there?"

Cody's tail wagged as a bundled man on a bay horse emerged from the frosty haze.

He yelled, "Your Christmas present, if you still want me."

Joy burst out of my mouth. "William?"

I focused on the gray-wool scarf wrapped around a nodding head and hidden face. He halted and unwound himself like a gift.

My heart thumped like an impatient child. *The best present I've ever received.*

I rushed forward, wanting to embrace him. "I've been so worried. I thought you were recovering at your parents' place."

He stepped back and raised his hand. His teeth chattered.

"Come inside and warm by the fire," I said.

He shook his head. "Headed to the fort ... but need answers ... in the barn."

His tone pricked my soul.

He led Babcock inside and I followed—concerned by his kinked brows and lack of a smile.

I swallowed and fought a rising need to bawl.

His eyes glistened. "I rode home in the blizzard yesterday ... to be with you for Christmas and agree that Kentucky is too dangerous for families at this time."

I held my chest. *Did I hear correctly?*

"Ma told me you've accepted courting from Hans Mueller, and this morning, Sis added you're marrying him and moving to Williamsburg—in April."

"What?" Anger burned my cheeks as words spewed. "Where did she hear this? It's not true."

He studied my face. "From the man himself, according to Christina. He's been bragging about the fact."

I marched to the door, flung it open, and stood in the cold gust until I calmed, but my eyes watered.

William moved to my side and eased me and the door back into place. "He hasn't asked your pa about marriage?"

"No. I told him to wait until my birthday. I didn't agree to marry him." My head pounded. "He only had permission to visit. He was rushing everything."

He stared at the beams and shook his head. "You told him to ask about marriage ... on your birthday?"

"I ... I ... well, yes. But I had jumbled feelings." I huffed fog into the air. "Today, I told him no. I don't love him."

William held my hands and gazed into my eyes. "Five months ago, I proclaimed my desire to court you on your fifteenth birthday. It's still my wish." He swallowed and tilted his head. "Why did you consider Hans?"

"He adores me. And he isn't going to Kentucky."

His jaw dropped as he released my hands and scowled. "You would marry a man you don't love to keep from going with me to Kentucky?"

I gulped and stared at the ground before gazing up embarrassed and blinking tears.

He sighed, then shook his head, but his face softened.

"I told Hiding Turtle of your fear."

Annoyed that he consulted him about me, I swallowed and asked, "What did he say?"

"Something like 'Remind Shoots in Knee she is a warrior, and her God protects her.'"

Conviction punched me in the stomach. *He understands faith better than I.*

"Someday, when it's safe, I wish to raise horses there. But I desire you by my side."

His soft, penetrating words seeped past my resolve like warmed honey, but I couldn't form words.

He clenched his jaw and moved toward the door, tying the scarf back around his head, then turned.

"I'll stay in the area hunting and scouting, then come visit again at the end of January. If you want someone else courting, I'll move on to Kentucky this spring." He gave a nod. "Merry Christmas."

My heart rattled with the barn shutters against the gusty wind. Thoughts jumbled.

When he opened the door, the bitter wind swirled inside the barn. He leaned out and into the storm ahead of Babcock.

I shouted, "I want you," but the door closed.

I rushed out and watched the horse high-step through the snow and hop over drifts until William faded from my sight.

My eyes stung and watered.

The cabin door opened, and Papa stepped out. "Come inside. What are you doing? Hans rode out ten minutes ago."

I left knee-deep holes in the snow on my way to the porch. Tears frosted my eyelashes.

I'm more afraid of a future without William than of Kentucky.

William

My head and chest pounded as I rode away. I'd always planned to lock in a land claim in Kentucky with streams and rich meadows—but not without Mary.

Babcock's hooves crunched through the packed snow on the bridge as we crossed. "Good boy." I rubbed his sweaty neck. "Almost out of the weather."

I dismounted inside the fort, then led my faithful stallion into the barn, unsaddled, groomed, and offered him a grain bag.

As I draped a blanket over his back, a young woman with braided-blond hair walked into the barn humming.

The lass stepped back, releasing a gasp. "Oh. Bless me. I didn't notice ya there so quiet."

She eased up to a sleek black horse in a stall, offering a cube of sugar. "There, lad. Maybe the weather will clear for a ride tomorrow."

Pretty lass. New since I left.

Nice horse. "He's a thoroughbred?"

Her green eyes widened. "That he is. My da is buyin' land in Kentucky in the spring. We'll be raisin' the breed for racin'. Have you been there?"

"Yes, miss." I stood in a daze, fighting an urge to learn more about her.

From an Irish family, and shares my interest in racehorses.

"Who is your da? I'd like to speak with him."

"Robert O'Donnell. Whom shall I tell him is inquirin'?"

"William McGuire. I'm a fort scout. Arrived with the blizzard last night. He needs to know the situation in Kentucky before he risks his fine horses and family."

Her eyes grew larger and hypnotizing.

"Sorry, miss. Didn't mean to scare you. I need sleep. I'll seek him out in a day or two once I'm rested. Are y'all staying in the fort?"

She nodded and stepped aside.

I moved toward the doorway. "Good day."

"Mr. McGuire, sir."

Her calm, sweet voice turned my head.

"Sorry to be so bold." She glanced at the ground, then back to my face. "We've heard of the danger. My da said soldiers will arrive by spring and build sturdy blockhouses and large stables. He's hiring men like you as guides. If you are interested."

Last thing I want to do.

"Sorry, Miss O'Donnell. I'm not." I tipped my hat. "Merry Christmas."

I hurried away through the biting wind.

I'm only interested in Mary.

Chapter Sixteen

January 27, 1777

Intermittent freezing rain and snow ended after four weeks, and Papa and my brothers dashed out the door to hunt. Their steps to the barn left holes in the deep, soft snow, much like the holes William left in my heart. He hadn't come back to visit yet, and I grew more anxious to speak with him.

I stuffed my mended stocking back in my sewing basket and stood from the bench at the table. "I'd like to ride Jasper to the fort."

Momma turned from the stew pot. "You may."

Katie shot from the bench at the table. "I want to go."

"No, please." I moved to the door, slipped on my coat, and turned to my scowling sister. "I need to visit—"

She huffed and plopped back down. "Tell William you'll marry him already. How hard can it be? We all know you love him."

I stared at her, stunned. "I ..."

"Katie. Hush that kind of talk," Momma said. "Land sakes. You have no idea how hard it is to make such a lifelong decision."

I let her rudeness drop and hurried to the barn.

I saddled my horse and led him out. The frigid air stung my face but settled my nervous stomach.

I kept the horse at a slow pace along the white trail, surrounded by creaking barren oaks and greens of pines and cedars drooping from the weight of snow. A stark-red cardinal landed with a bounce on a thin cedar branch and dislodged a pile of snow onto Jasper's head. He jerked but calmed to my "Whoa, boy."

At the bridge, ice crackled under his hooves, but he didn't slip. The snowy meadow shimmered from sunbeams breaking through the last of the clouds. The slight lift in my mood sank again as I entered the fort. I scanned the area for William, needing to draw strength from the sight of him.

I halted in front of Christina's cabin and dismounted, hoping he'd notice and come inside. After securing Jasper to the porch post, I knocked.

"Come in."

I opened the creaky door. "It's me."

"Bless me. This is a fine surprise. Sit." She eased up from stirring a hanging kettle.

Reese and James sat in opposite corners, fidgeting as they each marked on a small slab of gray slate with screeching chalk.

Christina's swollen belly shocked me when she turned.

"I'm sorry it's been so long since I've visited. How are you feeling?"

She caressed the bulge. "Mighty tired and ready to carry this babe on the outside in April." She waddled to her rocking chair. "Aye, and the furniture maker occupied your mind for a bit. I'm glad he's not whiskin' you away to Williamsburg."

She clasped her hands in her lap. "Now, what's your mind about William?"

I smiled. "Confused. I need to speak with him concerning ... well, a few things need to be settled." I plopped down on the bench. "Why did you choose Charles?"

Her eyes widened as I grinned and then sat back in her chair. "Before my family left the Shenandoah Valley, I had my mind set on a tame farmer. One day, Charles stopped by our place to visit my da. His tales of huntin', explorin', and scoutin' stole my heart." Christina turned to Reese. "Go gather a large pile of kindling to the porch, and don't let your brother eat bugs."

"Yes, ma'am." He beat James to the door, flung it open, and waited until the toddler passed before easing it closed.

Christina chuckled. "Now I can explain. Charles drifted by every day visitin' and talkin' sweet until he lured me out a fishin' and stirrin' my passion with kisses. 'Fore long, he stated his intent of marryin' when he returned from trekkin' a group of families over the Alleghenies. Only, he didn't come back nor send word." She shook her head. "My previous suitor married another. I felt mighty low and loathsome."

"What happened?" I leaned closer. "How long before he came back?"

"Two years and a few days after my eighteenth birthday, I looked up from hoein' corn, and he came canterin' up the trail beaming a smile. My heart leaped for joy upon seein' him alive, but I went to gougin' out weeds with malice in my heart."

I pictured her hacking the ground.

"He stayed back a ways and said hello. I told him not to expect a happy greetin' from me. He explained the Indian trouble and being wounded—figured I'd married by then. He took my hands, and his charmin' blue eyes drew me against his chest. He asked if I'd still marry him, and here I am."

I laughed with her as she shook her head and continued. "We wed two days later, and the following week the whole family moved here, obtained land, and built a shanty. Capt. Bowman wants him to return to Kentucky when his duty here ends in a year. Maj. Clark is planning a campaign against British garrisons that are encouraging the northern tribes to raid." She frowned and touched my arm. "What happened to turn your heart from my brother?"

"Kentucky." I stared out the window, determined not to cry. "He wants to end up there, but I don't." I bit my lip.

Christina sighed. "Aye. I'm sorry. It's not an easy decision."

"I need him to clarify something he said about waiting until I'm ready. But what if I never agree? Will he resent me? I need to find him."

Christina pushed from her chair and embraced me. "'Tis a hard time now, like birth pains, but one day you'll embrace the one you love."

"I need it to be today." After a deep breath, I stepped outside and led Jasper into the yard, scanning.

I glimpsed William speaking to a young woman I hadn't seen before. A pretty blonde, older than me, who giggled and held his arm as if they were courting.

My head pounded. *He's given up on me?* I climbed on Jasper and rushed into a gallop, allowing angry tears.

William

While I made my way to the corral, Ellen O'Donnell called my name and approached. I waited—not wanting to be rude, but I planned a ride out to the Shirleys.

When she tripped, I took her arm to steady her, and she giggled about being clumsy, then reported her da wishing to speak with me. After freeing my arm, I saw Mary riding away and my gut twisted in a panic over what she might have observed and why she came.

Miss O'Donnell shook my shirtsleeve. "Are you alright? You've stopped breathin'."

Her eyes shimmered from a concerned face. "Is the lass someone you care for? I'm sorry, I shouldn't be so nosy. But the color drained from your face."

"Not feeling well. I'll talk to your da later."

She sauntered toward her family's cabin, and I headed to Christina's for advice.

I knocked and entered as she said, "Come in. Did Mary find you?"

"No. But she might have seen Ellen speaking to me." I closed the door.

She frowned. "She left here, seekin' you. Fears losin' your love over Kentucky."

My stomach knotted. "I'll go see her."

As I stepped outside, Thomas drew near.

"What's got you so riled?"

I glared and sucked in icy air. "Don't have time to say."

"Mr. Bradford sent for us." He yelled at my back. "We're leaving for Fort Culbertson in an hour. Some kind of activity north of the Bluestone River."

I stopped and turned on the heel of my boot. "I'm on furlough through spring."

"Not when we're requested. Courtin' has to wait."

Anger seethed. "If I'm not back within the hour, I'll catch up."

Thomas raised his chin.

I jogged to the barn, groomed and saddled Babcock for the trip, but left him waiting while I walked toward the Shirleys' home, hoping she'd believe me about Miss O'Donnell.

When I neared the yard, the dog stood, barked once, and wagged his tail. Mary peeked from the window but didn't come out to greet me. *Aye, she's mad.*

I knelt and ruffled the dog's fur. Mrs. Shirley stepped out.

"Welcome. So glad you're well."

"Yes, ma'am. Thank you. I'd like to speak with Mary. There's a misunderstanding I need to explain."

She smiled. "I'll tell her."

Little girls peered out the window, grinning.

The door creaked open, and Mary marched past me to the barn.

I followed, expecting an unpleasant sting.

She turned with narrowed, puffy eyes and a red nose.

I resisted hugging her. *Can't comfort a bumble bee.*

I cleared my throat. "I'm sorry if you think I'm sweet on that woman you saw. I'm not. She passed on a message from her da and tripped. I caught her, is all." I stayed steady and gauged her narrowed eyes. "I'm sorry if you think I desire Kentucky land more than I desire you. I don't." I shifted and swallowed.

Her gaze remained fixed and worrisome. "What if I never want to leave the Greenbrier Valley? Can you give up your desire to raise horses in Kentucky?"

Didn't expect "never."

"You hesitate." She remained stoic, but her eyes watered. "If you're hoping I'll relent after we're married—I won't. I'll never be safe from Loud Hawk." A tear slid down her rosy cheek, but she swiped it off.

Shocked but wholeheartedly sure of my love for this strong-willed woman, I grinned and said, "I'll come courting on your birthday, and we'll make plans. I'm sorry to say, I'm ordered to the Bluestone for a week. Please don't accept courting from anyone else while I'm gone."

I reached for her hand, but she crossed her arms and stepped back. I remained resolute and after a minute more, she sighed.

Her face softened with a slight smile as she said, "I won't."

I dared an approach. "I'm coming over there to kiss you."

She gulped and eased closer, speaking in soft but confident tones, "I'm going to kiss you back."

"Was Hans a good kisser?"

She stopped mid-stride and smirked. "Go kiss him and find out."

"Naw." My neck burned. "Rather not know."

Her breaths sped like mine as I held her face and tilted my head. Her lips touched mine, light and sweet, then again, firmer. I supported the back of her head with one hand and slid the other to her mid-back. Her arms wrapped around my waist, and a soft moan preceded deeper kisses.

I pushed away and caught my breath. "Whoa. Can't do that kind of kissing."

She panted. "Hans's kisses didn't ... do that."

"I'm pleased and sorry to leave again. But I have no choice."

She rushed against my chest, and I wrapped my arms around her.

The barn door squeaked, and her da's calm voice rumbled. "Don't remember giving you this kind of permission, Mr. McGuire."

Mary jumped backward. "My fault, Papa. I hugged him."

Michael continued inside with his horse and grinning sons.

"My apologies, sir. I intend to speak to you formally when I return from the Bluestone. Charles, Thomas, and I have orders."

His lips pressed, then twitched into a grin as he gazed at her. "No more feelings for Hans?"

"None."

George hooted. "'Bout time."

"See you when I return." I winked, kissed her hand, and moved forward.

She whispered, "Stay safe."

Michael followed me out. "Katherine and I prayed she would be honest with Hans. Glad she refused his proposal of marriage at Christmas. He told everyone but failed to ask us."

"I admit my shock upon learning of it." I pressed my lips. *Especially after I committed to wait until her fifteenth birthday to court.*

When she came out from the barn, Michael whispered, "You have our blessing to court when you return." He waited for her to wave and go inside, then clasped my arm. "Watch your back out there. Chief Pluggy's death in Kentucky has stirred retaliation, and Blue Jacket's men are on the prowl, but no one knows why."

"Thank you, sir. Keep your family safe." I shook his hand and turned toward the fort. Despite the sun overhead, a chilly breeze made me shudder and pull my coat collar snug. I dreaded another long, cold trip, but Mary's kiss lingered warm and sweet all the way back to the fort.

Chapter Seventeen

February 17, 1777

The rumors of pending raids near the Bluestone River proved false, but scouts at Fort Randolph requested our help for ten days. Updates from the war effort against the British came in daily, as well as reports of Indian activity from Fort Detroit and all points south of the Ohio River. Our service ended on Mary's birthday. Irritation clung to me like burrs for not being there.

Thomas, Charles, and I chose a shortcut back to the New River—a worn, vine-tangled deer trail discovered by ancient Seneca Indians and used by fleeing Shawnee in the spring. Within a mile of Fort Culbertson, a twig snapped two feet to my left. Hairs on my neck prickled until three taps on a tree revealed Hiding Turtle.

I waved him in. "Glad it's you."

He frowned and stood before me. "Not good news. I search many days for you." He placed his hand on my shoulder. "Warriors sent to capture Shoots in Knee. Bring her to Blue Jacket Town. Answer for death of Chief Lone Duck." He took a breath and frowned. "Turkey Claw says she gave him poison. But he is guilty. Wanted chief and your Mary gone."

Rage burned in my gut as I mounted Babcock. "Do they know where she is?"

His chin raise confirmed. "Spy at fort. One moon passed."

I rushed my horse into a gallop, determined to make the eight-hour trip back to Cooks Fort by morning. Shouts of "Wait for us you dang fool" faded quickly behind.

The need to save Mary drove me like a rabid animal until I eased Babcock down the bank and into the swift, icy river. After swimming across, he climbed the bank, breathing hard and snorting.

"Sorry, boy. We'll rest every hour. Can't lose you. But I'm not making camp for the night. Our Mary is in trouble."

Mary

I stood in front of the tub of rinse water, rubbing the tin plate dry with the linen towel. All morning I expected William to come for my birthday lunch, but Papa returned from the fort reporting news of them detained at Fort Randolph.

"Are you trying to make a hole in the center?" Momma touched my arm. "Breathe."

I gazed at her and set the item down.

She took my hand. "Leave the man you love in God's hands and find enjoyment in your day."

I kissed her cheek. "Thank you. I'm disappointed he's not back. The sky is clear and perfect for a walk or horseback ride."

"You can still enjoy an outing gathering dandelion greens for a spring tonic once you finish drying the dishes." She chuckled and returned to the hearth.

Staying busy is best.

Cody barked and hope soared. I hurriedly draped the wet cloth on the peg and wiped my hands. Papa scooted his chair back, but George craned his neck and peered out the window from the table.

"Uhh. It's Hans." My brother glared and plopped back down.

I released a disappointed sigh.

"I thought you ended it with him," George said.

Papa opened the door. "Welcome."

Hans entered, holding his hat. "Thank you." His blue eyes shimmered as he glanced at each of us. "I've come to ..." He settled on my face. "Please accept my apology. I rushed you into courtship and mistook your kindness and friendship as an interest in marriage. My behavior was wrong."

I swallowed my pride like a slug. "Thank you, but it wasn't all your fault. I'm sorry too."

He stepped back. "Before I go, please ... accept my wish for a happy birthday and a future full of blessings." His brief smile fell flat. "I should go now."

He moved to the door, but I couldn't let him leave looking so dejected.

"Wait."

When he turned back, I smiled. "I still consider you a friend. Would you like to accompany me as a guard while I gather dandelion greens? We won't go far. I saw a patch growing a mile up the north trail, and we can talk more." I gazed at my parents. "Unless you think it is inappropriate?"

Momma spoke. "It is acceptable and good to have someone on watch."

George stood from his chair, frowning. "But he ..."

My sideways glare hushed him from pointing out Hans's inability to fire the rifle.

He plopped back down, crossing his arms.

Papa addressed Hans. "Understand her friendship boundaries?"

He nodded. "Yes, sir. She cares for Mr. McGuire. But I didn't think to bring my rifle. I was too nervous."

His admission sent a flush of heat to my face. *Not helping George's opinion.*

I raised a rifle and the bullet pouch from the rack and handed it to him. "Carry ours."

"Want me to come too?" George asked.

Hans faced him. "I'm capable of guarding your sister." He peered at me. "Want me to saddle your horse?"

"No." I smiled, delighted by his firm stance against my brother's doubt. "We'll walk with yours."

His face brightened before he closed the door behind him.

I donned my scarf and addressed my family. "We'll be back in a couple of hours. I just want him to feel accepted."

"Watch for Indian signs." George made his opinion heard from the table. "'Cause he won't."

I pressed my lips together and exited the cabin, shaking my head. *Scouts would have warned of signs in the area, and Papa checks every day.*

As I closed the door, Hans drew his horse, Tilly, close. I handed him the flintlock rifle, and he slid it into the sheath.

"This way." I pointed and led.

Squirrels chattered and scurried up trees as we passed, while songbirds flew from tree to tree, repeating their sweet songs.

He came beside me and gazed with a grin. "I'm glad we can remain friends. I'm still going to Williamsburg in April if you change your mind about Mr. McGuire."

I stood still, not sure of his intent. *Maybe this was a bad idea.*

He laughed. "I know your feelings, but I had to tell you. I'm enjoying this walk as your friend."

I resumed the stroll in the crisp breeze and thought of a new topic. "How will you establish a shop when you arrive in Williamsburg?"

He talked while I watched a hawk float above the meadow in the bright blue sky, wishing I could ask of William's whereabouts. I lost sight of the bird a half-mile later as we reached the sugar maple on Papa's northeast boundary. I spotted a patch of dandelions on the wooded trail ahead and veered toward them.

My eyes caught movement beyond the shadow of an ancient oak. I froze, then grabbed Hans's arm. He silenced and stood still.

"Gun ... now," I shouted as two tan warriors rushed from the bushes, shrieking like barn owls.

Oh, God, no. Please, no.

Hans whipped the rifle from the sheath before the horse bolted.

I ran toward him, but something hard knocked me forward, and I stumbled and fell to my hands and knees. A rank smell accompanied the sharp pain to my ribs as I rolled on the ground. A tan-skinned man kicked my stomach. I rolled into a ball, unable to breathe, but screamed when hands snatched my hair and whisked me to my feet. Sobs gushed. My scalp burned and throbbed. I writhed, trying to kick him, but couldn't break free.

Why didn't Hans fire?

I glimpsed Hans aiming at a man in a wolf fur cap, who inched closer, taunting in a language I didn't understand.

"Shoot," I screamed like a banshee.

My captor swung me around and punched my nose. I fell to my knees, crying and holding my wet, snotty face as a sharp pain wrenched my neck.

The deafening *crack* and *boom* rang in my ears.

Hans fell backward and slammed to the ground.

"No!"

My captor lifted me by the forearms. His lips were as black as midnight.

"I am Piqua," I spewed in Shawnee.

He slapped my jaw and whisked me over his shoulder. My head bobbed as he ran deeper into the woods. The searing pain weakened my body, but I was sure I glimpsed Hans roll over.

He's alive! Where is wolf cap man?

My captor, Black Lips, stopped running but kept to a brisk pace through the wood while tree branches smacked the back of my head. Misery, terror, and anger swirled. Then I retched upside down, praying for Papa to find me, crying and wanting William.

I struggled to stay alert and forced my stiff neck to stretch upward to release the pressure in my head. But without seeing the sky, I had no way of knowing the time.

The man turned down a hidden path and moved northwest, toward the Greenbrier River. I counted the creek crossings and noted the terrain until my mind grew fuzzy.

When we crossed a shallow creek, the forward movement stopped. I flew up and over the man before landing on my feet, but my legs buckled. I plopped down hard on my rear and held my bruised belly while my head pounded.

Another man, darker-skinned, pulled a forearm length of what looked like sinew from the creek and approached. When he grabbed my wrists, I fisted my hands. He bound them in front of me with the slimy cord. I resisted his tightening as much as I dared, hoping to stretch the substance before it dried to allow my hands to slip free later.

Wolf Cap helped hoist me onto the horse, then Black Lips slid on behind. Dark Man shouted in the unfamiliar language as we rushed into a gallop. Tears poured down my cheeks and fear deepened. I had no way of knowing their plans for me or if they were taking me to Blue Jacket. Bile still burned in my throat from being upside down and jostled, but I regained control of my will and stopped crying. I took a deep breath and risked a few quick scans to stay alert. Wolf Cap rode Tilly, and another horse followed but there were still only three men.

Whispering Leaf's story of slitting the throat of her white captors came to mind. *I must do it before reaching the Greenbrier River crossing. I won't be a captive again.*

Despite the ache in my neck and shoulders, I wiggled and stretched the binding around my hands every few minutes, feeling it loosen more each time.

My heart beat like a war drum. I allowed anger to build a fire in my belly and sear my conscience.

We crossed four more creeks before the men slowed the horses and stopped at a spring. I looked for the sun's position above the treetops.

Three or four in the afternoon.

Black Lips dismounted, then shoved my leg over the horse's neck and pushed me off.

My feet stung when I landed. He raised his chin toward a clump of shrubs and made a squatting movement.

I understood and eased in. He followed but waited a yard behind and I avoided his gaze. When I finished straightening my garments, he clutched my arm and pulled me back to the other men, speaking in their language.

Wolf Cap patted himself on the chest. Dark Man shoved him and yelled something. Black Lips shook his head, grunted, then pointed to me, then himself.

My breaths shallowed as I realized they fought over who would violate me first. I couldn't outrun them.

They continued shouting, then quieted, nodded, and untied their sheathes and tomahawks from their leggings—piling them on the ground. Each gawked at my chest with wild eyes.

Fear pounded the war drum in my head as Wolf Cap and Dark Man approached from opposite sides while Black Lips unfastened his pants.

Wolf Cap raised his hunting knife and stepped closer.

See you in a minute, God. They're not taking me alive.

An unexplainable force hurled me forward, and I jerked my hands free from the binding.

My knee struck Wolf Cap's groin. When he bent forward groaning, I grabbed the knife and plunged it into Dark Man's chest, then his neck. I shoved him backward into Black Lips, who almost grabbed my arm.

I thought my heart might burst, but I couldn't rest. Something savage and vicious took over.

Wolf Cap struggled to stand, but I rushed him and slit his throat in a half-moon cut. Blood spurted everywhere as he fell and startled my senses.

I didn't see Black Lips until he shoved me to the ground, face-first. I dropped the knife but squirmed to reach it. He held me down with one hand and raised my skirt with the other. In a surge of anger, I tossed a handful of stones over my head. He paused his fumbling.

I lunged and grabbed the knife, twisted to my side, and slashed his arm. While he grasped the wound, I squirmed under his weight and stabbed his chest. He tumbled over. I climbed onto my knees and plunged the blade into his throat until the gurgling sounds ended with a final moan.

I sat on the ground trembling and breathing hard, then the sight of the motionless bodies covered in blood became a blur.

I'm not sure how long I lay on the ground, but loud croaks from tree frogs alerted me to the late afternoon. Horses whinnied.

What am I doing here?

I pushed up on wobbly legs and spotted the motionless bodies sprawled on the ground, then the blood on my hands.

I did that? Bile rose and my body trembled.

I swallowed hard and turned away, wiping my hands down my skirt as the terrible images replayed. I staggered toward a horse I recognized but couldn't name. I led it to a fallen log and mounted. My body ached everywhere.

Wispy clouds to my right swirled with pale yellow, indicating west. I remembered the horse as Tilly.

Is Hans alive? I saw him move. I must make it home. I rubbed the horse's neck. "I'm trusting you to know the way back. I think we crossed five creeks. We might be ten miles from home."

As the horse plodded along a faint trail, images flashed in and out—the Indian attack, Hans on the ground, images of me stabbing men, out-of-my-mind.

How do I reconcile this, God? Tears fell. *They were going to hurt me.*

Darkness came upon the forest and swallowed me inside. I felt far away, hidden and safe, but I knew it wasn't true. I lifted my head and fought to stay awake and upright. Only the occasional splashes of water brought awareness of Tilly crossing creeks. I listened to the forest, expecting, hoping, to hear a rescue party.

I'm close enough to be found now.

Then I heard Papa calling my name, and I woke in a bed with him standing over me, pleading, "Come back to us."

I whispered, "I don't want to."

Chapter Eighteen

February 18

Sunrise climbed the ridge behind me as I descended toward Cooks Fort and resumed a gallop.

Guards shouted, "Incoming."

"William McGuire," I yelled. "Let me through."

Once the gate creaked open, I rode to the corral and dismounted. I stumbled into the barn on numb feet, trembling from the cold. My hands ached as I lifted off the saddle and gave Babcock grain.

As I took the brush from a peg, light footfalls turned my attention to the entrance.

Miss O'Donnell approached with a worried face.

"What's happened?"

I swept the brush down the horse's back. My teeth chattered. "Hopefully nothing. I must warn Mr. Shirley."

"You didn't hear of the raid yesterday?" Her eyes searched my face.

I swung my head in her direction too fast and swayed. "What?"

"Indians captured his daughter right off their land. Mr. Shirley brought poor Mr. Mueller in wounded and gathered a search party. They found her before dark."

A sensation of floating above the ground ended with a ringing in my ears.

Her gloved hand touched my arm. "You don't look well. You should rest and have warm broth."

I crumpled to the ground as she yelled, "Someone come help Mr. McGuire."

I woke to Christina hovering over me—not letting me up.

"Stay down. Mary is safe and recovering."

I wiped my cheek on my shoulder before a tear reached my ear. I pushed to sitting, despite Christina's effort to prevent it.

Thomas pulled a chair beside me.

"We found her five miles up that old overgrown deer trail. Covered with blood, slumped forward on the horse, and barely holding on. When she heard Michael call her name, she sat up, cryin' and babblin' words we couldn't understand." He nodded. "I couldn't discover the details, but sounds like the lass fought like a bear to escape."

I flung off the covers, then hid my bare self again. "Bring my clothes, Sis. I need to go to her."

Christina retrieved the garments from a rack by the fireplace and tossed them across the room. I dressed, then she handed me a mug of coffee. I sipped the soothing brew and stuffed corn cakes into the pocket of my steaming coat.

Charles entered. "Whoa, there. Where are ya goin'?"

"To the Shirleys'."

He shook his head and removed his hat and coat. "I just talked to Michael. He doesn't want anyone comin' out for a few days. Says his daughter's in a terrible state." He sat at the table, and Christina handed him a cup of coffee.

"I followed that trail with two scouts all the way to the Greenbrier River and found the carnage at dawn. The lass dispatched three warriors. Slit throats and multiple stabs."

I plopped back down on the bed, shocked and nauseated.

He peered at me as if gauging my mental state. Hesitating to tell me more.

"What else?"

He sighed. "Appears the men were preparin' to violate the lass."

Anger sped my heart and burned my eyes. I couldn't blink away the pain of not making it back in time to save her.

Charles continued his report. "Their sheaths and tomahawks lay in one pile. One man had unfastened pants. But I don't think he was successful by the amount of dirt on his face."

I clutched my chest as it squeezed out a relieved breath like a bellow.

Charles grinned and nodded. "We skedaddled from there as buzzards gathered. I reckon those waitin' for 'em on the other side of the Greenbrier discovered what's left by now. So you understand why Michael gave her a small dose of laudanum and said let her be."

I stared at him as panic rose. "She's in greater danger now. I must warn Michael. They won't stop coming after her and might retaliate."

He stood. "I'll inform the captain and the scouts here and about."

"I'll check on Babcock and see how Mr. Mueller is before heading out." *Maybe I need some laudanum.*

"I heard they shot the lad in the shoulder. He's weak—but livin'." Christina hugged my neck. "Mary will recover. Be patient."

"Thank you, Sis." I stepped out and off the porch, tilting my hat down from the biting wind.

I quickened my pace to the barn, still kicking myself for leaving her. But I couldn't disobey orders.

Inside, I found Babcock well-groomed and his legs wrapped with strong onion poultices.

"Thank you for the hard ride." I rubbed his neck. "I'll let you rest today."

I pulled my coat tighter and trudged to Hans's shop wondering why he was with Mary.

After I knocked, a deep voice said, "Enter."

As I ambled inside the cedar-scented place, Dr. Coats looked up from Hans's bed on the opposite side of the shop. I noted the tidiness and all the tools along the wall and stepped closer.

"He's groggy from the laudanum. But you can say hello."

I stayed back. "How's he doing? I'm headed out to the Shirleys and will give an update."

Hans mumbled something.

The fort doctor leaned down. "What's that you say?" Dr. Coats stood straight and shrugged. "He's asleep again." The doc stepped toward me. "As long as Mr. Mueller doesn't develop an infection, his wound will heal. The bullet entered at close range, below his left collarbone, and exited clean. He won't be making furniture for a couple of months."

'Twas God allowed him to live and keep his scalp.

I shook the doc's hand and opened the door. "I'll come again later. Thank you."

My chest pounded as I scowled and scanned the men of the fort for anyone I didn't know on my way out. *Someone is an informant for Blue Jacket. Woe to the man when I discover him.*

I seethed all the way to the Shirleys' home. Cody barked from the porch as I came into the yard. Michael and his two sons stopped splitting firewood and glanced up from the woodpile.

I must see her. If only for a moment.

Michael brushed his hands down his shirt and neared. "Charles said you rode all night to give warning. Thank you. He told me of your conversation with Hiding Turtle this morning."

"Wish I hadn't been too late. Have you identified the spy?"

"Not yet," he said. "Come sit on the porch."

I plopped down, and Cody lay beside me. I scratched him under the neck, then the cabin door flew open and I jumped to my feet.

Mary rushed out wide-eyed, barefooted, and wrapped in a blanket.

I stood gasping at the sight of her red puffy cheeks, swollen nose, and a right eye swirled in shades of a ripening plum.

Reprobates. I gnashed my teeth to keep from cursing.

"Come in out of the cold." She spoke fast and darted back inside.

I looked at Michael.

He shrugged and stood. "She's had a small dose of laudanum, so I think she's able to visit for a minute. Might not remember it later. But if she gets out of her head, she'd want me to have you leave."

"I understand. I won't stay long. Charles told me to wait, but I needed to alert you to possible retaliation and additional attempts to capture her."

He nodded and led the way inside.

I entered on stiff legs and greeted Mrs. Shirley and her daughters. They curtsied and went back to chopping nuts.

Mary sat on a bench in front of the hearth, holding a steaming mug.

I took a seat beside her, rubbing my hands toward the flames, and whispered, "They weren't Shawnee."

Her bloodshot eyes widened at me like a wildcat, then back to the fire, nodding and saying,

"Strange speech." She faced me again, this time frowning. Her eyes darted. "Did Loud Hawk send them? He said, 'Stay out of Kentucky.' Why did they come here? Tell me." She stomped her foot and ranted, "Why must I live in fear? Will I ever be safe?"

Her emotional state unnerved me.

I eased to my feet and whispered, "I'll leave now and let you rest."

She threw the blanket off and stood in a chemise. "Don't leave me. I love you." She lunged against me and wrapped her arms around my chest, bawling, "I want you—forever."

I held her despite her family's stares. My whole body burned, but I didn't care. I didn't want to let go. My soul screamed, *I love you too.*

Michael freed me from her embrace. "Best pretend you didn't hear all that. She'll be embarrassed."

"She'll be mortified!" Katie wrapped the blanket back around her sister, then stood and whispered to me. "She meant those words, though. She never loved Hans." Katie rushed back to cooking.

Peace settled in my mind, and the tension in my shoulders released.

"Thank you for allowing my visit. I'll be able to rest now."

Mrs. Shirley stood from the hearth. "Please, stay for lunch."

"Thank you, but I'm more sleepy than hungry. I'll come again." I turned to leave. "Good day."

Michael walked me out.

"No need to worry about Hans. He came on her birthday as a friend and apologized for being angry when she refused him. She invited him to forage." He sighed. "We heard a gunshot. By the time I arrived, Hans lay on the ground moaning, 'Indians,' and Mary is gone."

I shook my head and released a hard sigh. "I'm glad they didn't scalp him. I'll talk to him in a few days."

"Katherine and I are thankful for your return and care for Mary." He patted my shoulder. "Now, get some rest. You look like something Cody dragged up. I'll give you an update in a few days."

I shook his hand. "Yes, sir. Thank you for allowing my visit. I wish Cody could drag me home."

He chuckled and strolled toward the barn.

My whole body ached as I made the five-minute brisk walk back to the fort, giving God thanks and asking for Mary and Hans to heal.

I froze.

Is the informer someone of rank?

Capt. Bradford ordered us to the Bluestone River, but no one knew why. Then a rider came with orders for us to help run relays at Fort Randolph.

Someone wanted us out of the way, and I'm going to find out. I'll talk it over with Thomas and Charles later. I need to sleep before I pass out.

A rush of anger quickened my steps back to the fort.

I entered my cabin, stirred the coals for a fire, and remembered the hoecakes in my pocket. I placed them on the table, sat on my bed, and removed my boots.

Chapter Nineteen

February 25. 1777

My head pounded and my body trembled as I rose from the bed needing a dose of laudanum.

I shuffled to the railing and eased downstairs. Hot one minute and cold the next, desperate for just one drop.

After two days of taking the medicine, Papa said, "No more." I'd become too fidgety and didn't sleep. But the memories of the attack, along with the rage, returned.

Why won't the Shawnee leave me alone?

While my family sat at the table chatting, I wanted to scream and cry all at once.

"Good morning," Momma said.

But her sweet greeting clashed with my demons. I plopped onto the bench beside Lizzy. "Might I have one drop of laudanum?" My voice crackled. "To settle my nerves?"

"I'm sorry." Momma placed a cup before me and touched my trembling hand. "Drink this willow bark tea and eat at least one bite of porridge. The effects will last a few more days, but you'll feel better."

I huffed and folded my arms. "It's cruel to make me suffer."

"Look at me, polliwog." Papa's deep, firm voice lifted my gaze to his. "Take a drink."

After a shuddered breath, I sat up straight, grasped the wooden cup with shaking hands, and sipped the warm honey-sweetened tea.

"Now another." He watched me comply and repeat the process until the last drop.

In a moment, the headache eased but not the deep anguish that simmered and swirled.

I can't talk about it. Do they already know? I can't remember telling Papa, but I remember his face when he found me.

Images flashed. *Nearing the Greenbrier River. Dismounting. Holding a bloody knife.*

"Eat a bite of porridge," Papa said.

He gave me a spoon, but I dropped it and showed my hands. "No, I can't. There's blood ... on the knife ... everywhere."

He swooped me into his arms and carried me like a child. "Where are you taking me?"

When we came to the spring, he sat me down and slashed icy water on my face.

I screamed.

He lifted me to my feet. "Open your eyes and look. The blood is gone now."

I lifted my hands. *No blood. It's over.*

"It was horrible." I cuddled against him for a minute or two, then stepped back and stared at the water. "What are we doing outside?"

"You had a memory." He held my arm as we walked back to the cabin, then he wrapped his warm arms around me. "These visions will come, but you no longer need laudanum." He backed up but held on to my forearms and peered. "Coming back to peace takes time. Even I have battled memories at times. Talking to others helps, as does facing what happened and working through the fear."

I inhaled the crisp air and my head cleared more, but his words jumbled. "I don't understand. Talking about what happened brings back the pain and fear. I don't want to talk about it." A vision of Hans's terrified eyes came. "How is Hans doing?"

He offered his arm and I held on, wobbling like a rocking canoe.

"He's off laudanum and able to get around. Been begging to come see you."

I shook my head. "No, I'm not ready." More memories flashed. "He aimed the rifle but didn't fire." I stepped back and wiped a stray tear.

"Hans told me he froze, like during the attack on his family. He is still upset."

We moved onto the porch, and I stopped as another image came. "Was William here, or was that the medicine?"

He grinned. "He came that midmorning. Rode all night hoping to give a warning before anything happened. Hiding Turtle told him of the plan to capture you and take you to Blue Jacket Town."

A new wave of panic weakened my knees. "What have I done to cause the wrath of this warrior?"

Papa held me up. "Take deep breaths. I'm sorry. I shouldn't have told you."

After swallowing a gulp of air, I shook my head. "Did he say why?"

"He believes you poisoned the chief, but you can ask William the details. Time to warm up and eat our porridge."

Turkey Claw is to blame!

"I need a moment alone. Then I'll come. I promise."

He nodded and moved inside.

I remained seated on the porch and pulled my knees to my chest. Cody plopped down beside me, and I tickled his neck and calmed.

The cabin door creaked. A quilt draped over my shoulders.

Katie came around and scooted under it with me. "I'm sorry you're not feeling well. Papa said your mind is better." Her warm hand slipped through my folded arm. "I need to tell you something." Her voice was low and soft.

I gathered a handful of the quilt with both hands and squeezed. "Is it going to make me cry?" I looked sideways. "I don't want to cry."

She shrugged. "Maybe. But it might make you happy." Her eyes brightened.

Happy? How?

"You were still out of your head when Mr. McGuire came by." She paused and watched my face.

I straightened and held my chest. "What did I say?"

"Something about an Indian and staying out of Kentucky. Then, in front of us and God, you threw yourself on William and said, 'I want you forever.' It shocked us all, and he turned as red as a cooked beet. You were in your chemise.”

I laid my head on my knees. “Laudanum is terrible. How embarrassing.”

“Don't worry. After Papa peeled you off the man, he told him to pretend it didn't happen. I'm telling you because he didn't push you away. That's why Papa stepped in.”

Katie slid out from under the quilt and covered me back up before standing.

I rocked forward and eased to my feet. “Help me inside, please.”

Upon entering the cabin, I found Papa standing in front of the fireplace, eating his porridge. I padded to the table, retrieved my bowl, then joined him in the flickering light.

“After we eat, will you please take me to the fort? I must see Hans, and then William, if he's there.” I addressed my family. “I'm sorry for my behavior with him. Katie told me.”

Giggles echoed from the table.

Momma rushed to me and studied my eyes. “You should wait another week.”

“I'd rather speak with them while a remnant of laudanum remains.”

She grinned. "I'll help you change into fresh clothes. Finish eating and drinking the willow tea." She kissed my forehead and said, "It will all come out in the wash," as she climbed the stairs.

"Thank you."

Papa handed his empty bowl to Lizzy. "I'll go saddle and meet you on the porch. You'll ride with me on Sherwood."

I finished my porridge as he donned his hat and lifted the rifle I brought back with Tilly.

"Did you already take Hans's horse back? I can ride her if not."

He opened the door. "I took her. And you're not as steady as you think." He stepped outside and closed the door.

Momma returned with a chemise, cornflower-blue blouse, and a sage-green wool petticoat. I followed her to her room and undressed. She slipped the bleached white linen chemise over my head and then the gown. I smiled at the notion of her helping me dress for my wedding someday.

"How did you decide to marry Papa?" I adjusted the drawstrings on both garments to fit my shoulders.

She grinned and held the petticoat ready. I expected her usual reply of "That's a story for another day" as I stepped in.

"It was silly." She raised the garment and tied it around my waist, then handed me my gray wool stockings.

"Please tell me." I sat on her bed and slid them on my feet and up to my thighs and tied them.

She helped me up. "My uncle chose a wealthy landowner, twice my age. I met with him once. He was kind and handsome, so I agreed to consider him."

She tucked my stray hair behind my ears. "One day, I gathered with my friends to watch a group of soldiers march into our township. When they halted, a dark-haired private gazed sideways, grinning and fixing his wide eyes on me."

"Papa." I giggled.

She chuckled. "Until that moment, I hadn't experienced such a wild heart flutter. I rushed away. Needless to say, he discovered my dwelling place and tried many times to gain my uncle's approval to visit."

"Why didn't he like him?" *I knew nothing of her parents except they had died of an illness.*

She sighed. "Because he was a soldier and not a rich man. I told my uncle of my interest in Michael Shirley, but he insisted I do the sensible thing and refuse him. Instead, I did the rash."

"Eloped?" My mouth stayed open a moment. *The story for another time!*

She walked toward the door, then turned. Her eyes sparkled. "We sneaked into the next township in the middle of the night, crossed into Virginia, and married. Life has been hard, but I love him. He reminds me of my papa, and I know he would have approved of him the same way your papa and I approve of your choice." She smiled. "I'm glad you're not sensible either."

Her words shocked. "What do you mean?"

"You've given up a comfortable life with Hans to marry the one who makes your heart beat wildly." Her smile raised.

I rushed into her arms. "I'm sorry I've caused so much trouble and hurt."

"Papa is waiting." She stepped back, blinking her eyes. "Tell Hans to visit again before he leaves."

She opened the door, and I stepped out addressing my worried-faced siblings.

"Everything is going to be alright. I have to talk to Hans." I passed them and held Papa's arm.

He helped me outside, then lifted me. I swung my leg over his horse. He climbed behind me and told Cody to stay.

I watched birds flitting among the trees carrying brown pine straw and leaves while they chirped love songs. As we drew closer to the fort, sweat beaded on my face as I remembered the gun blast and Hans falling to the ground. My stomach knotted. *I need a drop of laudanum.*

"I'll visit Hans first," I said.

We halted in front of his shop, and Papa dismounted. I put my foot in the stirrup and swung my leg back over.

"You're trembling. Want me to go in with you?" He lowered me to the ground.

I moved back. "No. I'll be fine."

"I'm going to the blockhouse for news." He leaned down and kissed my cheek.

I trudged toward the furniture shop, stepped onto the porch, and knocked.

"Enter," Hans said.

I released a puff of air and stepped inside.

He beamed and eased up from his workbench. The bandage on his left shoulder shone through his shirt, and his arm rested in a cloth slung around his neck as he approached.

"I wish to hug you, but my shoulder is too sore." His eyes watered. "I'm sorry I froze and failed to protect you. The memory makes me ill." He sighed. "I'm glad to see you at last. Your papa asked me to wait. Do you want to sit?" He took a step toward the table.

My eyes burned. "No, I won't be long. You mustn't blame yourself. If you had done anything, they would have killed and scalped you." Knots twisted tighter in my stomach. "I'm glad they only wounded you."

He drew a deep breath and returned. "In case you don't remember my words, before the Indians surprised us, I say again. If you change your mind about Mr. McGuire, write to me." He grinned. "But he loves you. I've known since meeting him at Woods Fort when he didn't want to tell me how to find you. All is well."

"I'm sorry I hurt you. Thank you for forgiving me. You're a fine man and my friend."

He gave me a light hug with his good arm and pecked my cheek. "If you ever come to Williamsburg, look for my shop." He walked me to the door.

"Thank you." I grinned and stepped onto the porch.

When his door closed, the heaviness lifted from my shoulders. I held onto a post and gazed into the sky. *Thank you, God. Bless him with a happy life and a woman who loves him.*

William

As I left the corral, I glimpsed Michael Shirley's brisk walk away from the blockhouse. I rushed to meet him. "What's wrong?"

He motioned for me to follow and pointed to Mary hugging a post on Hans's porch. The muscles in my shoulders and neck seized as Michael spoke.

"I stepped in for a quick news update while she visited with Hans." He flashed a quick grin my way. "Wanted to set his mind at ease. Still struggling with the laudanum but tired of being couped up."

I danced a jig in my head, and my body relaxed.

He shook my hand. "What have you found out?"

"I spoke with scouts from Fort Arbuckle yesterday. They conferred with Shawnee sources who said Blue Jacket sent three warriors from an unknown tribe."

He halted with his horse and frowned. "Why is he so sure she poisoned that chief?"

I peered at Mary, who stepped from the porch and turned toward us. "She is coming our way. Should I visit with you later?"

He held his palm out toward her to stop. She frowned and sat on a stump far enough from hearing.

"A shaman accused her, so Blue Jacket wants her to answer for it." I growled, then glimpsed Mary peering at my mouth as if trying to make out my words. I turned my back to her. "She is still troubled by Loud Hawk's threat—now she has this. I want to lead a campaign against the lot of them."

Michael glared. "Have you discovered the scoundrel who gave our location?"

"Aye, could have been me by accident, but I hope I'm wrong."

I hesitated, not sure how he'd react.

He tilted his head. "Go on."

"I learned this from the same scouts. Blue Jacket hired Indian spies mid-August to watch for men traveling with her lame dog. That Mr. Jones might be the informer who led the spies here after I told Hans Mary's whereabouts."

I took a breath, not wanting to say the rest, but I'd never been a coward. "So, I'm guessing the spies carried the news back to Blue Jacket."

His head bobbed slowly. "But why did they wait so long?"

"Timing." I sighed. "Could be the reason for the false reports made to Capt. Bradford. They lured Charles, Thomas, and I away. I'm double-checking my sources and scrutinizing even the trusted scouts on the back trails. With your permission, I'll patrol your land, but tell George not to shoot me."

"I'll tell the family to stay nearby. My boys won't like the restraint, but I'm not willing to move back to the fort yet. Thank you for the updates. She wanted to speak with you also, but I best take my daughter home. Wait another month before coming out to visit. She's still out of sorts and needs her family to comfort her now."

His request stabbed my chest like a dagger.

"Yes, sir."

We shook hands, then I waved to Mary, who frowned.

I strolled toward the barn to fetch my horse, intending to be Michael's rear guard and patrol the area.

"Mr. McGuire, can I have a word with ya?"

I glimpsed Mr. O'Donnell approaching from my left.

"I'm needin' a scout. Can you take my party to Kentucky in April?"

My glance back revealed Mary on her papa's horse, with him leading.

"No, sir." I shook Mr. O'Donnell's hand. "Thank you for the offer, but I'm needed here for defense, and I wish you would change your mind. Scouts are relaying increased raids already, and it's going to be worse."

The man frowned. "Aye, we're leaving just the same. I'll take my leave."

"Yes, sir." I bowed. *God be with ya.*

I waited for him to depart first, then jogged to the barn, mounted my horse bareback, and cantered out of the gate. I slowed at the sight of Michael, not wanting to be obvious.

Mary gave a slight head turn as if she heard Babcock's lips ripple but kept forward.

I stayed at the perimeter of the yard as they entered the barn. Their dog barked and sniffed the air in my direction before sitting.

Glad I told Michael I'd be out here. That's one smart dog to know me by scent and accept me as a friendly.

Mary emerged from the barn holding her papa's arm. When they stepped onto the porch, she peeked around him and waved before entering the cabin.

Yep, the dog gave me away.

I mounted and rode up to the ridge for a wider view. There were no tracks or signs to justify making a cold camp. I headed back down the trail opposite the Shirleys' place, still regretting the agreement with her da and wishing to hold her in my arms.

After dismounting, I walked the outer edges of their yard and planned a picnic in April. *Christina will have had her babe by then and will be at Ma's.*

Pleased with myself, I led Babcock back to the fort and worked through the details of the surprise. *She won't expect me to propose marriage so soon.*

Chapter Twenty

April 7, 1777

Momma released me from six weeks of light chores this morning after I begged to help the family clear the northern field for our garden. My scalp, nose, and jaw remained tender from the attack, but my back, shoulders, and arms regained strength.

I followed Papa into the barn this morning, before the family came.

"Please tell me the updates and why William is scouting our land, but you haven't let him come to visit yet?"

Papa grinned and loaded the wheelbarrow with garden tools. "All is well. I asked William to wait until you were more recovered. He insists on helping me and George check our land every day. Area scouts also report the all clear. Perhaps they have abandoned their quest for you. William will visit soon. Are you ready to work?"

Still frustrated for him delaying my visits with William, I huffed and grabbed a rake. He handed me a rifle, and after shouldering it, I stormed toward the garden.

I had some understanding based on the bits and pieces I overheard and the small amount spoken by William that day I watched his mouth, but I already knew. *Blue Jacket believes Turkey Claw's lies and sent men to capture me. I don't know if Loud Hawk is involved.*

I set to work thrashing the ground for an hour, raking brush into the fire until my body ached. I didn't want to let on about the pain. Staying busy helped curtail bad memories, and exhaustion would aid sleep.

I straightened and rubbed my lower back. Momma turned toward me at the wrong time.

Caught.

"Go on to the cabin and rest. We'll come for lunch in another hour."

I shouldered the rifle and rake and enjoyed the stroll home in the cool midmorning breeze scented with honeysuckle blossoms and wisteria vines.

Cody limped up beside me and dutifully escorted me into the yard but suddenly stepped in front of me. He raised his head to the north and sniffed the air drifting from the woods behind our cabin.

My head pounded with panic, and the rake crashed to the ground. I dropped to my knee, cocked the gun, and aimed where the dog stared.

Then he wagged his tail and sat.

I clutched my chest and stood.

William again. "Thank you for the warning, boy."

I set off to verify my hunch and crept toward someone humming, then recognize William's voice singing, "Now who's been here since I've been gone? The pretty little girl with the blue dress on."

After taking cover behind a wide oak, I peeked around, watching his buck dance in the leaves while his horse grazed.

No Indian signs, obviously. I bit my lips to keep from giggling.

When he finished dancing, he strolled to the horse and reached for the stirrup. Before his boot lifted from the ground to mount, I growled like a wildcat to scare him on purpose.

He jumped down into a crouch—rifle ready.

"It's me. Don't shoot," I shouted, but waited behind the tree until he uncocked and stood scowling.

"Tarnation. Mary come out from there. Sorry for my curse, but you know better than that."

His jaw clenched, and his eyes remained narrowed.

I ambled closer but stayed back. "You needed a lesson about paying attention. I hope you're not distracted like that while scouting. I'm supposed to be in danger—remember?" I smirked.

His face relaxed. "How did you know it was me? Your dog?"

"He lets me know you're out here, and I've come to ask you to stop scouting round our place. It makes me nervous about the bounty on my head. Have there been signs?"

He stood straighter and crossed his arms. "No signs. It's clear from here to Laurel Creek. I'm sorry you're still a mite nervous, but I'll keep to my task, so I will."

"Papa and George scout our perimeter every morning while checking traps. They haven't seen signs either."

He tilted his chin up and smiled. "Doubly safe then. Christina birthed a son eleven days ago, and they're resting at my parents'. I've come for you if you've a mind to visit. Asked your parents' permission yesterday."

"Yesterday? They didn't tell me this morning."

His sheepish grin grew. "It's a surprise. But you were supposed to be in the field. Shall we go?"

"Yes, but I have a gift for the baby. I'll meet you back here."

Despite aching muscles and a touch of weakness, I ran to the cabin, too excited to slow down.

I grabbed the bleached linen baby gown from my basket and opened the door, startled to see William there petting Cody.

He stood, then led Babcock to me. "You're still sore and needing to ride."

"Thank you. I suppose I do."

He helped me climb aboard Babcock, slid on behind me, and reached through my arms for the reins. His muscular arms cuddled mine and his warm, spice-scented chest pressed on my back as he urged the horse forward.

Memories of the closeness we shared on the trail back to my family at Boonesborough flooded my mind with longings meant for marriage. *Why can't I marry him now, God?*

The memory of Katie's words about the laudanum's effect returned. I turned my head so William could hear me over the songbirds.

"I'm sorry for my behavior the day you came to check on me. Katie told me what I said. I wanted to speak to you that day at the fort."

His breath on my neck raised prickles. "It was the laudanum, but I didn't mind hearing it."

I imagined the smile behind his playful tone.

He touched my face as he leaned forward and kissed my cheek. I faced forward and gulped. *He's not making it easy to bring up Kentucky again.*

He cleared his throat. "I'm sorry you had need of the medicine at all. And I know you're still troubled by terrors. But I'm proud of your survival and pray you'll come to peace with it all."

Flashes of stabbing those men triggered a shudder. "Me too ... but I would do it again. How do you cope after killing someone?"

He sighed. "Over time, my mind grew numb. If they're determined to kill me, I'm set on living."

My eyes watered. "Have you allowed some to live? How do you decide?"

"Some, but it's hard to describe. A certain look in their eyes. Sorrow over anger maybe, but it happens without thinking." He cleared his throat and shifted his weight in the saddle. "Once we climb this hill, it's another mile to my parents."

Thankful for the change in topic, I nodded. "I've met your ma but only spoke with your da in greeting. What is he like?"

He chuckled. "A lot like me and Thomas. Are you nervous?"

"Yes." I laughed. "At least now I'm prepared for the torment. Sing me that song you were humming earlier."

"Aloud? I'm better at singing while a fiddle plays."

"I don't mind. It helps pass the time and settles my nerves. Papa always sings the frog courting song."

"I know. I've traveled with him." He laughed. "We can sing it together."

I nodded. "Good. You lead."

William sang the verses, and I added the "humble dum, humble dum," and "tweedle, tweedle, twino" refrains. We finished the last verse, giggling as a blockhouse came into view.

William helped me down.

My heart raced as a gray-haired man stepped from the barn. He looked tired but brightened when he saw us.

William helped me from the horse. "Da, this is Michael Shirley's daughter Mary."

"Ah, yes." He drew closer, grinned, and nodded. "Pleased ta see ya again, lass."

I curtsied. "And me you, Mr. McGuire."

"Go on inside if you've a mind to. Best be holdin' your ears first. This babe's still riled about bein' born, so he is." He chuckled and glanced at William. "Come help me in the barn while you're here, lad. Hope that

Charlie's comin' to fetch his family back today. I've taken to sleepin' in the barn."

William stepped onto the porch with me and knocked.

The door opened to Mrs. McGuire. "Oh, come in, lass." She opened the door wide enough for me to enter. "Have a fun visit." William backed. "I'll be in the barn with Da when you're ready to leave."

I nodded and ambled inside. "Thank you, Mrs. McGuire."

The two-room cabin was spacious. Christina and the new baby occupied a small bed against the wall near the hearth, where Mrs. McGuire returned to chopping a root of some kind.

Christina glowed in the lantern light as she sat propped up on pillows.

"Glad ya came," she shouted over the squalling, flailing infant in her arms, then shifted him to her other breast and pulled the quilt up as she wiggled into a more comfortable position. "There now."

The babe suckled as she waved for me to come beside her. "God continues blessing me with sons. I've named him Cornelius, after my da. And he's already an unruly lad, so he is."

My eyes teared at the sight of mother and infant. She smiled down at the round head of the now content bundle at her breast. She released his suction from her nipple with her finger and eased him away, showing me his sweet chubby cheeks and spikes of red hair.

"He's beautiful." I smiled and handed her the smock. "I hope it's not too small. This was my first baby garment. Momma helped me with it some."

Christina held it up to him. "Thank you! It will fit for a month or two. You did well. Now, tell me how you're doin'."

"And we're pleased you've come to your senses," Mrs. McGuire said. "Shame it took such a terrible event to reveal—"

"Ma, hush." Christina's tone stirred the baby's whimper. "Leave her be." She leaned over a small cradle and laid Cornelius inside.

I stared at the floor. *What does she mean? What was she about to say?*

Mrs. McGuire sat in a cushioned chair beside her daughter and folded her hands in her lap.

"I'm sorry, lass. Don't mean to be testy. Ya seem like family, and I tend toward speakin' my mind when things need spoke, but it's not my place."

Her words stung, but I felt the genuine concern in her tone.

I straightened my back and nodded. "Please, continue, Mrs. McGuire. I don't like things hanging in the air." Deep breaths steadied me for more.

"My William oft' risks his life for ya, but that Mr. Mueller was chicken-hearted. Not a good match for ya at all." Her eyes lowered.

Mine stung as I pressed my lips together at this truth.

She shook her head. "Heard he had a clear shot but cowered. Watched those rogues ride off with ya. Aye, and I hope ya know now which man's more deservin' of ya."

I gasped as her statement stabbed my soul. *If she only knew how much I care for him.*

She shifted in her chair. "I'm sayin' ya are a strong woman and a good match for our William. Hope ya won't be long in acceptin' him."

She pushed to her feet, peering from teary green eyes sparkling with the same love, care, and hurt as my momma.

I stepped back to break the spell, weighing how much to say, not wishing to cause her more disappointment.

"You give me too much worth for your son. I care for him, but the experience with Hans proves I'm not ready to be anyone's wife. I need to heal, and I'm not yet sixteen."

And there's still the lingering question about Kentucky.

Mrs. McGuire wrapped her arms around me, and I laid my head on her shoulder.

"There now, lass. I'm sorry to add to your burden. May it be God alone who guides ya and not a protective old crow like me." She stepped toward the hearth, drying her eyes.

Christina smiled at me and mouthed the words, "Well done."

She raised up and addressed her ma, "Please help me up. I'll relieve myself before this babe wails again. Charles should arrive soon ta fetch us home."

"I should go now. I'll visit you at the fort in a few days." I kissed her cheek.

She whispered, "Sorry about my ma."

I nodded despite feeling overwhelmed.

Someone knocked.

"Come in. I'm covered," Christina said.

William entered. The floor creaked under his boots as he neared the cradle and gazed at the sleeping baby, then at his sister. "Another fine son, Sis." He leaned to her cheek and kissed it. He tried to whisper, but I heard, "May I take Mary now?"

She chuckled. "I suppose. I did promise not to keep her all day."

"Yes, it's time for me to return home. My family will have lunch ready if you'd like to stay."

Christina peeked around William at me and grinned. "Come see me Friday. I'll have my brood settled in by then."

"I will, and congratulations on the healthy baby."

My head turn caught Mrs. McGuire handing her son a cloth-covered basket.

He met my gaze with a shy grin. "I planned a surprise picnic if you're not too tired. Your parents know about this too. I'd love to show you the new horses I acquired, and maybe I have one you'll like."

I stared at him speechless and excited, but confused by the secrecy.

William frowned and took my hand. "Should I take you home instead?"

Six pairs of unblinking eyes watched me shake my head.

"No, I'd love to see your horses. I'm just shocked Momma didn't tell me."

Their collective sighs raised a giggle.

"He's right fond of ya, lass. But make him keep his distance." Mrs. McGuire grinned.

While my mouth dropped open, William stepped closer to her.

"How will I find a wife if you don't behave, Ma?" He kissed her cheek.

I took a deep breath as my heart thumped. *Wife?*

William whisked by me, leaving the door open. I forced a smile at Mrs. McGuire and curtsied.

"Thank you for the visit. I promise to keep my distance."

The words were wrong, but I laughed with his ma and sister and stepped onto the porch with my cheeks burning, unsure if the floating sensation came from excitement or fear. *Is he going to propose?*

Chapter Twenty-One

William stood beside a wagon and smiled as I approached.

"Thought you'd be more comfortable this way. There's a nice place five minutes from here." As he helped me up, I caught the fresh scent of lye soap and witch hazel, then noticed his recently shaved face.

He climbed aboard, jiggled the reins, and the horses walked. "Did you enjoy your visit?"

"I did. And the garment I made will fit the baby."

Sitting beside him stirred butterflies in my stomach. Our previous conversations stayed light and silly, but traveling to see his land and sharing a picnic required discussing topics not broached in three months.

My life remains in danger from Shawnee desiring to capture me. I hope he understands my unwillingness to move closer to them.

The wagon bumped along, and we sat in silence until I asked, "What have you been doing these past weeks? Do you have to scout soon?"

His pleasant smile increased the flutters.

"I've stayed local mostly, relaying information and other things I can't speak of. And something funny."

I turned my head when he paused.

"Hans asked me to guide him over the mountains to Fincastle in the morning. He'll join a party going to Williamsburg. It's been eight weeks, and Doc removed his stitches."

In the morning? I hope he comes to say good-bye.

I felt his eyes on me as I stared at the wide trail before us. He touched my hand.

"How are you about him leaving?" His caring tone soothed the awkward moment.

"At peace. We parted as friends."

His gaze brightened. "No regrets?"

"None. He'll be happy and have a wonderful life. I'm just surprised he hasn't visited the family and told us this news."

William's eyes sparkled. "He plans to do so before we leave. Are you ready to eat? We're here."

He halted next to the creek, then pointed to a quilt spread out under a large shady oak tree. Puffs of smoke rose from the ground under a small circle of stones.

"How long have you been planning all this?" I chuckled.

He winked and helped me down but continued to hold my hand as we walked, then he bowed. "Have a seat, milady."

I laughed. "This is fun."

"You deserve much more."

His smile widened as he took a wide-bladed shovel he had propped against a tree and removed the stones. He raked back the dirt and ashes and lifted four charred items to a wooden plank cut to the size of a serving tray. William carried the board back toward me and set it down. "Hope you like pheasant and roasted potato."

"Very much, thank you. I thought you were working in the barn with your da all this time."

"Good. My plan worked."

He chuckled and peeled the charred skin back from two birds with a knife and fork. He sliced the juicy, tender meat, wiped off the knife, then sliced the potatoes into wedges. My stomach growled from the aroma of wild onion and sage.

I relished the succulent scents as he wiped his hands on a linen towel and sat beside me on the quilt.

"Thank you." I gazed at his adoring-me eyes. "You've put a lot of time and work into this picnic. What if I'd said no?"

A sly grin rose. "You didn't."

"But you enticed with the offer of a horse. How did you know I'd fall for it?"

"I was hoping." He took my hands and bowed his head. "Thank you for your blessings and bounty, Almighty God."

He forked a slice of meat and handed it to me, then waited. I took a small bite.

"Have I told you how I acquired Babcock's Boy?"

I shook my head, savoring the pheasant.

"I worked for Mr. Hershel Babcock for five years. I asked him to pay me with a foal from one of his fastest sires. Babcock's Boy is a seven-year-old but still one of the fastest quarter horses around. I'm mighty proud of him. I've bred him to a few mares. Rebel was his progeny." He ate a few slices of meat.

"Babcock is a fine stallion, and Rebel was wonderful," I said. "Strong, sleek, and fast."

My chest ached remembering my favorite horse being led away by one of the Indians who ambushed my family three years ago. We were a few miles from the Boonesborough settlement. They also killed my precious childhood dog, Drummer.

I focused on William's face to keep my eyes from watering. "It would have been fun to race him against you."

He chuckled. "Well, Babcock wins more than he loses."

"How far is your land from here?"

"Sitting on it. My shanty is farther down Laurel Creek. Never made time to build a cabin."

I glanced around. "This is a nice location for one. The land is every bit as beautiful as Kentucky. Don't you agree?"

His eyebrows raised as if he'd caught my hint, but he cast his gaze to the food. "Let's finish eating, then I'll show you where the horses are grazing."

"Well, it's a pretty spot for a picnic. Thank you." I smiled when he looked up.

He lifted my hand to his lips and planted a sweet kiss. "I'm pleased you accepted. Care for a sweet cake Ma made for us?"

"I don't think I can. I'm stuffed and ready to see your horses now."

I helped him gather everything back into the wagon, then he offered his hand.

"The herd is this way."

As we strolled through bright spring grasses and tiny purple wildflowers, I enjoyed the width and warmness of his calloused but comfortable hand. We walked along a narrow trail shaded by elm trees and serenaded by songbirds until he stopped before the clearing and put one arm around my shoulder. I melted against him as he pointed to a muscular red horse with the same markings as Rebel and whistled.

The steed raised his head, then trotted in our direction.

"Look familiar?" He grinned and watched my face.

I clutched my pounding chest. "Looks like Rebel."

"Because it is."

I turned my face to his. "Oh, William. How did you find him?"

"Came across him a few days ago." His smile widened. "Amazed me too. I walked by a group of tethered horses at Fort Randolph and one whinnied. I glanced its way—curious."

"You said you were staying local."

"I said *mostly*." He grinned and continued. "After confirming his markings, I found the owner, who claimed to have raised him as a foal. I reported his lie to the captain. Questioning exposed him as a spy for the King's

8th Regiment in Detroit. I took charge of Rebel and planned this surprise."

I wiped my eyes, anticipating the feel and smell of Rebel. "He looks wonderful." I held out my hand. "Hi, boy, so happy to see you."

Rebel stretched his neck, sniffed, then eased forward. I rubbed his chest while tears slid from my eyes. I moved closer and hugged him, sniffing his coat. "I've missed you so much. I'm sorry we lost you." I wiped my wet cheek.

William touched my arm. "Want to ride him bareback with my help?"

"No. I want to wait until my body heals so I can ride fast and far."

"You can take him home today. I have a rope in the wagon."

I turned and wrapped my arms around William's chest. "Thank you so much."

Instead of moving away, he drew me closer. His head rested against mine and his soft moan deepened my longing.

Rebel nudged us and whinnied.

William stepped back, breathing fast. He pushed Rebel's nose, and the gelding backed, then stood still.

"I have to say this." His face paled. "I love you. I've loved you a long time. I'm willing to wait until you're sixteen, but you're the woman I want. Forever and a day. Not just my friend but lover and mother of our children."

My heart fell to my stomach at his sudden proposal.

His eyes glistened. He sighed and swallowed. "Truth is, I want to marry you today. I'm talking like a fool, I know. But I can't hold you like this anymore without knowing I can count on a marriage bed in ten months."

"I do love you and want to marry you, but with all that is happening and the threat on my life, I don't think I'm ready. I know I'll never be safe in Kentucky, and it's not fair of me to hold you back. I know you've always wanted Kentucky land."

He frowned.

My eyes watered again. "I'm sorry. Can't we build our cabin and lives here?"

"We've time to discuss everything when I'm back from the trip to Fincastle. I should take you home for now. Maybe I'll go find that warrior and end the problem altogether."

I gasped. "Please don't tease. Promise you won't go looking for him. I do want to marry you in ten months."

He sighed and nodded. "I promise I won't go looking for him, but if he shows himself in my territory, he's finished."

But I'm under a threat from Blue Jacket now. I shuddered and moved to the wagon.

He helped me up and tethered Rebel behind. I threaded my arm through his and cuddled against him until he drove the wagon forward.

I relished being beside him and remembered the day's sweet moments, even the conversation with his ma and wished we didn't have to wait ten months.

An eagle floated among the wispy clouds above us and I remembered the Shawnee believing in an eagle messenger and the Bible mentioning soaring on wings of eagles when one hopes in God.

I'm soaring for sure.

We arrived in my backyard, and my family stepped outside, greeting William and glancing at me as if waiting for news of something.

"You found Rebel?" George asked. "What about General? I'd like him back someday."

William climbed down and turned to him. "Sorry. Can't remember what he looks like. I raised Rebel and noticed him right off. Saw him at Fort Randolph and reclaimed him. I'll raise a fast one for you."

"Thank you." George held out his hand.

William shook it, then offered his hand and helped me down.

Momma neared and asked, "How are Christina and the new baby?"

I grinned. "She's well and has another son, but he is beautiful."

"And loud." William chuckled and turned to my family. "I'll visit again when I return from guiding Hans over Peters Mountain to Fincastle."

George laughed. "You're taking him?"

I cut my eyes at my brother.

He shrugged. "It's just funny they ended up friends."

William gave George a playful shove. "Good afternoon, all."

Papa untied Rebel, stepped around with him in tow, and shook William's hand. "Thank you for returning the horse. Safe travels. I'm off to set traps with George and Charlie before fishing."

"And the girls and I have work." Momma herded everyone back inside, leaving William and me alone.

I didn't care if my sisters were still taking peeks; I hugged William. "Have I said I love you?"

He planted a sweet kiss on my cheek, then smiled. "You are my forever. See you in three or four days. Don't worry, I won't harm Hans."

I chuckled. "He's a good man, just not suited for the frontier. It's kind of you to keep him safe. He's become like a brother. Thank you for the visit today—and for Rebel."

"You're welcome." He leaned to my ear. "I love you too, puny girl."

His breath on my neck sent a shiver down my back.

"Now, I've a long trip tomorrow. We'll talk again when I return." He climbed up in the wagon.

I watched him until he disappeared up the northwest trail to return his da's wagon, and my longing for him deepened, but so did the uncertainty in my troubled head.

Kentucky still scares me. But he's not ready to give it up. I dried my cheek and went inside.

William

I arrived at my parents' barn and unhitched the horses from the wagon. Pa entered and helped me put the gear away.

"Is the lass agreeable to your courtin'?

"Aye, but asking me to change my plan of settling Kentucky and remaining in the Greenbrier. She's still troubled by that war chief's threat. So, I've ten months to eliminate the threat or change my plans."

Da chuckled. "The lass has a strong hold of ya, for sure and certain."

"That she does. But I'm still hoping she'll change her mind when the country is free of British interference and the Indians settle down." I shook Da's hand. "Thank you for the wagon and your help today. Give Ma the update. I'm in a hurry to return to the fort and turn in."

"Takin' that furniture maker ta Fincastle?" He shook his head.

I nodded and hoisted the pad over Babcock's back, then the saddle. "I feel for the lad and figure I'd look for a new mare while I'm there."

"Safe travels to ya, Son. I'll go inside and distract yor ma from cornerin' ya." He moved outside and toward the cabin.

I waited until he entered, then led my horse out, mounted, and urged him into a canter all the way to the fort.

When I strolled him into the barn, Thomas met me.

"There ya are." He drew closer. "What took so long, and what'd she say?"

"Took Mary back to her family then returned Pa's wagon. She's thinking on it. Now let me be." I shoved past him. "I'm tending to Babcock and going to bed. Long day tomorrow. Heading out after Hans says his good-byes to the Shirleys."

He laughed. "Aye, makin' sure the lad leaves so Mary's not distracted?"

I sighed, unsaddled, and took a brush in hand.

Thomas snatched the object and handed me a jug of whiskey. "Have a few swigs ta help ya sleep. I'll take care of groomin'."

"Thanks. I took the jug and trudged across the yard. I entered the cabin we shared.

I sat on my bed, freed my feet of boots, and uncorked the jug. After wiping the rim, I lowered it to the table.

My mind is numb enough. I stuffed in the cork and placed the container on the shelf.

Chapter Twenty-Two

Friday, April 8, 1777

When my bed shook, and I opened my eyes to Thomas grinning down at me in the candlelight.

"Be dawn soon. Ya hung over?" he asked. "Sis has breakfast ready. Me and Charles are pulling out with the O'Donnell party in half an hour. Saw Hans hiking toward the Shirleys' place."

I squinted at him. "I didn't drink. Save me some bacon."

He scuttled toward the door.

I stood on the cold wood floor, ignored my razor and shaving soap, and dressed in my worn out traveling clothes.

After rolling my bedding for the trip, I finished packing my haversack and bags from the list in my head. Years of scouting and readiness made the task quick. Jerky, shave kit, tinder box, shot pouch, flints, moccasins, and spare clothes.

I pulled on my boots and tied on my leather leggings, then gathered lead and bullet-making supplies into my saddlebags. My butcher knife, hatchet, and old musket were in my sash. I shouldered my rifle and hurried out the door, leaving everything in a pile for packing on Babcock.

As I shuffled toward Christina's, I caught sight of Hans returning slumped-shouldered and sad-faced. My heart pricked in sympathy knowing leaving without Mary forever could have been my fate too. *Only I'm returning.*

"Morning," I called out. "We'll leave soon as you're ready."

He looked my way and raised his chin in response. "I'll be back." He plodded on to his shop.

I knocked on Sis's door, then entered to the sound of her infant's flatulence. Her sons' giggling lightened my mood.

"Morning, Sis."

"Aye, and I'm glad you're in time for these." She lifted the platter, revealing four remaining thick slices of bacon. "And I'm waitin' to hear if Mary agreed to marryin' ya."

I wrapped the crispy meat in a linen napkin for later and grinned. "Aye, but we've plenty of time to work out the details. 'Twill be a torturous ten-month wait for sure, but she's worthy."

She gathered items for diaper-changing and stood before me again. "Aye, and may God bless her with peace."

"And me with patience. If not embarking on a journey with Hans, I'd be lingering at the Shirleys' table, sipping coffee and gazing into my Mary's eyes."

Sis tilted up her cheek, and I kissed it.

"Thank you for breakfast." I stepped outside and reached the crowded barnyard as Charles shouted instructions to the O'Donnell party.

Ellen waved.

I gave her a nod and entered the barn, feeling grief in the pit of my stomach, knowing the danger she still faced.

Four young slave boys of George's age walked the O'Donnells' sleek thoroughbreds out, then stood still, waiting for me to pass.

I stopped and addressed them. "Safe trip to Kentucky, lads. Stay strong."

One raised his eyes briefly and acknowledged, "Yessuh. Thank ye."

At least they'll enjoy living free with the Shawnee if raided. Not so for Ellen and her family.

I greeted Babcock, prepared him for the trip, then led him to the cabin for loading.

As I finished securing my bundles, Hans arrived with his horse and a mule burdened with packs and carpentry tools.

"I appreciate you taking me, Mr. McGuire." He lowered his gaze.

I held out my hand. "You're welcome, but call me Will."

Instead of reaching back, he turned away and led his horse toward the gate as if I'd slighted him in some way. I scratched the horse's neck and clucked my tongue. "Let's go, boy, I'm eager to return."

Once beyond the palisades, the O'Donnell party headed westward. I waved to Thomas and stepped in front of Hans.

"We'll ride most of the day. You ready?" I mounted and waited for him to settle on his horse with his mule in tow. "Need to make a hard thirty miles to my campsite before sunset."

He gave a silent nod.

I urged my horse into a trot away from Hans then kept an ample distance between us.

Maybe I should let him punch me in the face so he'll feel better. I chuckled and urged Babcock into a canter down the old buffalo path followed by Seneca in this valley years before the French war ended.

We followed Indian Creek along the Shirleys' southern border until their cabin came into view through the woods. Cody yapped, and I spotted Mary waving from the porch.

I raised and waved my hat over my head, unconcerned with Hans.

Seconds later, the dog released ferocious barks and Hans urged his horse and mule up beside me before slowing.

He sighed and grumbled. "Glad I didn't have to make friends with that coyote. I didn't realize he was tame the first time I saw him. I kicked him, remembering the night at the grave of my family." His voice cracked. "I could never tell Mary the reason her dog hated me so."

"She would have understood," I said. "But you're fortunate the lame coyote didn't tear your leg off."

I heard his whispered, "*Jah.*"

When we passed the Shirleys' maple trees, I shouted back. "We'll dismount every hour and allow the animals to rest and graze."

I felt sorry for the fearful lad but thankful for Mary cutting him loose.

At noon, we stopped for a long break to eat and check the horses and mules for sores and cuts. Hans looked exhausted and walked bowlegged while rubbing his shoulder.

"Your wound hurting?" I asked.

He nodded, then rubbed his backside. "Mostly saddle sore. I haven't been on a horse this long since leaving my family on the Bluestone River."

"We can walk the horses awhile, but it's another hour and a half to the foot of Peter's Mountain. We'll camp there and tackle the rocky climb tomorrow. How's your horse's back and legs?"

Hans loosened the cinch and lifted the blanket. "Good."

I judged the lad as immature but not without merit. Definitely suited for business and city life, not the rugged frontier.

He removed a bundle from his haversack and unwrapped a long brown loaf. "Would you like to try my rye bread? I used to watch my momma when I was a child.

It took me several tries." He tore it in two and handed me half. "Melted butter would make it better."

I broke off a bite. It smelled like weeds but had a tangy, nutty flavor. "It's strong but not terrible. Thank you for sharing. All I have is jerky and hoecakes."

He laughed. "I also have dried meats, but will you hunt on the way? Can we cook?"

"Not unless we make it to my campsite tonight. The Shawnee use this trail. That's why it's important we veer off in an hour and head south."

Hans's eyes widened. "I would like to ride."

"Wise choice. Not interested in fighting a skirmish today."

It pleased me to have a relaxed conversation with him.

Once refreshed, we continued on the path for thirty-minutes until I recognized a large pile of stones marking the southerly trail. I halted before a meadow where a dozen grazing does noticed me but didn't run.

I dismounted and turned to Hans.

"Bring your rifle."

He climbed from his horse with the gun and approached, then spied the deer. He stood still and pale.

I backed toward him a few steps and placed my hand on his shoulder before looking at his dazed eyes.

"Did you grow up hunting?"

He nodded. "But since the raid on my family … I, well, the gun blast makes me ill."

"Remember the excitement of hunting with your papa when you were a boy. Hear his voice instructing you again."

He sighed.

I shuffled to his side. "Is the muzzle loaded and the flint ready?"

He nodded, then swallowed.

"Get in position and breathe—this isn't life or death. No hurry. Take aim and fire."

He eased down to one knee and grimaced as he propped up his right elbow. The gun swayed, then steadied.

I held my breath until the shot rang out. The doe fell and Hans sat on the ground, trembling and sniffling.

"You did it. We'll have venison steaks for supper." I leaned toward him. "Breathe. Did it jar your shoulder much?"

He blew out a deep breath. "*Jah,* but not as bad as expected."

He raised his right hand, and I pulled him to his feet.

"Shooting game will be easier for you the next time. I'll retrieve salt from my pack so we can preserve the meat and pack it out."

I left him staring at his kill, smiling.

We tied its legs and hoisted it up a tree branch.

"May I?" He held his butcher knife ready at its neck.

I moved back. "I'll check the area and help salt the meat."

In an hour, we had the salted venison carved up and rolled in the hide for transport away from the blood and guts.

He stood, then shook my hand. "Thank you. I'm not afraid now. You've restored my dignity. I only wish it had been in time to help Mary that day."

"You're welcome." I moved toward my horse.

I didn't tell him that firing one shot wouldn't have stopped the other warrior from planting a tomahawk in his forehead. His lack of action probably saved his life. He wouldn't have known to duck and lunge forward with a butcher knife in hand.

"Let's move from here before the buzzards alert the Indians of our location."

I wasn't keen on the idea of defending us both if raided.

When we arrived at the foot of Peters Mountain, I led the way behind a grove of trees where a white table rock made a lean-to roof. "My campsite is through here."

I peered through low-hanging branches to make sure there were no other occupants, and Hans followed me inside while I gave instructions.

"All that's needed is a bit of clearing and a fire for roasting the venison on a spit. We'll carve off some slices for supper and pack the rest for tomorrow.

We unburdened the horses and his mule, and he agreed to groom them while I struck the flints, lit the kindling, and skewered the meat.

I brushed it with the fat, then placed the pole between two forked sticks over the fire and gave it a turn before sitting. I looked up at Hans. "We'll be able to eat some in three to four hours if we keep a hot fire."

He sat opposite me and stared. "This is a perfect camping place."

Before I could agree, he cleared his throat.

"You are a capable man—brave and strong. I understand why Mary prefers you." His eyes narrowed. "But you are a fool."

Shocked by his jab, I scowled, then grinned at his sudden courage.

Finally fired his rifle and now he's feeling cocky?

His face relaxed. "Mary's eyes were red and swollen this morning when she came outside to tell me good-bye. I thought she had changed her mind and wanted to leave with me. But after wishing me a safe trip and happiness, she rushed back inside."

I frowned, confused, and hoped he'd explain.

"Katie waited for her family to enter and followed me to my horse. She explained Mary cried all night because you still want to live in Kentucky."

What?

Hans shook his head. "*Jah,* you are worse than a fool. If Mary had loved me the way she does you ... I would have done anything she wanted. She would be by my side now—going to a safe town far from Indian raids." He stood. "I want to slap you for hurting her. But I will walk away and let you explain later."

He marched toward his horse before I could respond.

I told her I'd stay—didn't I?

I watched a log sizzle and smoke from dripping meat juices for a minute, then stood and rotated the venison. *He hasn't heard my side. She misunderstood.*

I lifted my rifle and strolled from the camp to check the perimeter. The only marked tree was a birch, baring a faded buffalo symbol. I tramped back, careful not to scuff the ground.

Hans stood near the fire and acknowledged my return with shifting eyes, as if unsure of my mood.

"No fresh signs around, but we should sleep in shifts tonight." I propped my rifle nearby. "Once we top the mountain and start the descent, we'll be in the clear."

Hans faced me. "I will guard early. Too worried for sleep. Thank you for checking the area."

I nodded, kicked a log closer, and sat. "I told Mary I'd give up living in Kentucky until it was safe and was ready." I flicked a beetle off my leg. "It's hard giving up a long-held dream for a new one. My horse perks up considerably after eating the fertile blue-green grasses of Kentucky and I'd rather raise horses there instead of on the depleted soil of the Greenbrier Valley."

He remained quiet, so I added, "You're a fine craftsman. Would you stop making beautiful furniture in Williamsburg if Mary was afraid of living in a town, or give up your dream and stay here, farming?"

His mouth twitched as if fighting a smile. "She doesn't love me. I heard soldiers talking this morning. They know she will remain near Cooks Fort and her family. One spoke loudly of his intention to court her if you leave for Kentucky again."

My legs went numb. "What's his name?"

He shook his head and spun the meat. "I'm hungry. Shall we eat?"

I unsheathed my butcher knife and placed the blade in the fire to burn off the residue from whatever I'd butchered last. "I'm buying a new mare in Fincastle and speaking to Mary again when I return."

"Farm and make Mary happy. You would be miserable in Kentucky without her. Want me to slice the venison?"

I cleaned the knife and handed it to him. "You'd make a good statesman."

Hans raised his chin. "If she hasn't married you or someone else by the time I write to the Shirleys, I'll ask her again." He sat on a stump, laughing, while cutting the meat with the knife.

Riles me like a politician can.

I squinted. "You're going to be too busy securing a home, shop, and business to think about us. I bet a Spanish dollar you'll be a city official within a year."

He studied me for a moment. "I accept your bet, and I sincerely wish you and Mary much happiness."

"Appreciate that." I plated a slice of venison.

After eating, I walked to my bedroll. "I'm used to sleeping four or five hours while scouting. But wake me earlier if needed."

He held the gun and nodded. "Sleep well."

I lay down but pondered asking Michael's permission to wed Mary before her sixteenth birthday like Hans had hoped.

Chapter Twenty-Three

April 15, 1777

Cody's single bark from the yard released a swarm of butterflies in my stomach.

Lizzy stopped chopping walnuts and glanced out the window, then at me, grinning.

"Your Mr. McGuire is talking to Papa."

I stirred butter and sweet maple syrup into the steaming pan of thickening cornmeal, then peered out at the man Cody trusted and I adored.

My brothers shook his hand, then strolled inside. Charlie carried an armload of kindling to the woodbox.

"Um. Smells yummy. I'm hungry."

George smiled at me and hung his hat on the rack. "He's staying for breakfast."

My cheeks cramped from smiling.

Momma set a bowl and spoon next to Papa's place and pointed to the corner. "Bring the extra chair."

Katie added a bowl of chopped plums. "He's never come for breakfast." She faced me with a wry grin.

Heat rushed up my neck as I dashed to the cupboard for a mug. I remembered him insisting on drinking his coffee before escorting me back to Boonesborough. *He likes it black.*

George smiled at Momma. "Mr. McGuire mentioned a bear hunt. May I go with them if Papa agrees?"

Her eyes widened, but she turned toward the entering men.

"Welcome. Would you like coffee?"

Before William answered, I set the steaming cup at his place beside George then scurried around to the bench and stood beside Katie.

"Thank you." He focused his smile on me and sat, making a wonderful sight at our table. Clean-shaved, tidy black hair bound in a short ponytail, and a quiet, unhurried manner.

Katie sat and tugged on my sleeve. I eased down on the bench instead of plopping.

Papa prayed, but I didn't hear his words because *William is sitting at our table* repeated in my mind, and I pinched my arm to prove it true. My cheeks ached.

"Amen," I added with the others and dared a peek at my love while he sipped his coffee.

George straightened in his chair. "May I go on the bear hunt? I'm almost ten."

Papa placed his mug on the table and studied my brother's hopeful stare.

"I'm not opposed. But you must prove yourself responsible by completing your chores without reminders—until we decide the time."

"Thank you, sir. I will."

When did he become old enough? His deep, confident voice prickled the hairs on the back of my neck. I stared at my untouched breakfast, realizing again how much time I'd lost living with the Shawnee for almost a year, and then being distracted by the courtship with Hans.

"Killed my first bear at your age." William's statement drew me back.

I ate and listened to the lighthearted conversations from my siblings. My occasional glimpses at William caught his and became more frequent until I laid down my spoon.

He finished his last bite and glanced at Papa, who gave a nod.

William stood, gripping the back of his chair, but the corners of his lips raised with his gaze. "May I speak to Mary outside alone?"

The sudden thrill of his words caught my breath.

Papa grinned.

Momma grasped my hand and smiled as her eyes glistened. "You may if you wish."

I pushed to my feet, trembling inside, floating toward him as if caught in a fast current leading to an unseen waterfall.

The only man I want forever.

William

Mary's footfalls across the floor kept time with the hard, steady beat in my chest as my mind wrestled with giving up freedom. *Are you sure you want to do this?*

I opened the door as she neared. Smoky, sweet maple scents heightened my desire to hold her in my arms as she passed and won the fight. *Yes, I'm sure.*

When I stepped out, she slipped her arm through mine and snuggled. I struggled to breathe and led her toward the barn, out of the chilly air—away from the curious eyes of her family.

I freed my arm and stood back.

She studied my face.

Words stuck in my dry throat, and swallowing didn't help. I wiped my sweaty palms down the legs of my pants and forced out the words. "I've been awake all night thinking through this."

She frowned when I paused to gulp and regroup.

"I've made a decision concerning Kentucky," I said.

Her sudden gasp and watering eyes broke my train of thought. I reached for her hands before she could flee.

"I'd rather live in the Greenbrier Valley for the rest of my life than live in Kentucky without you."

Her luscious mouth dropped open, then a slight smile rose. I felt drunk and detached from my body.

"I want to marry you. But if you want me as a husband, I need you to trust my word. I promise not to ask you to move to Kentucky."

Her eyes widened and shimmered like river stones as she stared.

I nodded. "You heard me clearly, lass. I'll. Never. Ask. You. To. Move. To. Kentucky."

She eased closer, slipped her hands around my waist, and laid her head on my chest.

I breathed her in, longing for more, but forced a step back. "Shall we go inside and officially ask your parents?"

Her breaths shuddered. "I've wanted you all along. Are you sure you won't regret giving up your dream of Kentucky?"

"You are my dream." I held her hand and led her from the barn.

She broke free and hopped into stomping steps around me. Her seductive looks slashed at me like knives. My skin tingled and burned. "What are you doing?"

She laughed. "The Shawnee courtship dance. I can hear the turtle-shell shakers on my ankles beating the rhythm of my heart."

"We should stick to the Virginia Reel for now, but I look forward to seeing your dance again." I took her hands and led her into side-skips toward the porch to break the enchantment.

A few scurrying noises inside the cabin quieted when I opened the door for her and followed, removing my hat to a peg.

The females took turns giving sheepish grins while drying dishes and tidying the room. Michael and his sons counted bullet pouches in an already stuffed ammunition box. The boys took turns giggling.

Yep, they saw us.

I released a sigh before saying, "She said yes."

Her family surged forward all at once.

"Yippee," George shouted. "It's about time."

Laughter followed, then Mrs. Shirley hugged us together.

Michael shook my hand. "Congratulations. I'll send a request to Minister Alderson for his services in February."

I took a step back, as if pushed by a gust of wind but remembered my plan to ask for sooner in private.

"I'll start building a cabin soon. Should only take a month or two." I hoped the hint would prepare him for my request.

He turned from me and embraced Mary. "We are pleased, Daughter."

"Thank you." She sniffled, then stepped back to me and cuddled my arm. "Shall we ride out to your parents?"

While I considered disclosing the news to my family, she turned to her ma.

"Can you spare me for a few hours?"

Mrs. Shirley chuckled. "I can picture Tessie dancing a jig at this news."

I nodded at the image. "Yes, ma'am. She will for certain." I grinned at Mary. "Riding with me or on your own horse?"

Her smile widened. "I've often wondered if Rebel could beat Babcock in a race."

I laughed. "What's the wager?"

"Loser cooks our first breakfast after we're married."

She held out her hand for me to shake.

I kissed it instead, confident of a win. "Deal."

She held my arm on the way to the barn. "Don't hold back either. I want Rebel to beat his sire in a fair race."

"And that he will, lass."

After grooming and saddling her horse, I checked Babcock's hooves and legs. "You ready to race, lad?"

George scraped a starting line with the heel of his boot. Michael rode a quarter of a mile ahead to mark our finish. He'd proclaim the winner.

Babcock whinnied and Rebel snorted.

I peered at Mary. "Ride safe."

She raised her chin. "I like my eggs scrambled and my bacon crispy but not burned."

George shouted, "Are you ready? Are you set? Go."

Babcock's customary quick start left Rebel behind, but seconds later, she shouted, "Hi-ya" as the younger horse dashed past me and finished first.

I shook off a daze as Michael ran toward us.

"Rebel, it is—at twenty-one seconds."

Mary stood on the ground and hugged the horse before walking him back. "I knew it. He is faster."

I dismounted, still stunned, but rubbed Babcock's neck and whispered, "I won't tell anyone." I bowed. "How do you like your coffee, milady?"

"Strong but sweet like you." She laughed, then rubbed Babcock's neck and spoke. "Your son is faster, but you're still the champion."

Pride swelled in my chest and strengthened my resolve to continue raising horses. "Aye, and our new mare will breed more winners. We'll keep a record of all sold and not race against our own."

She swiveled my way with a grin. "I like the sound of *ours.*"

Michael mounted. "Good race, you two. See you home by supper, Daughter."

We waved as he left us, then I took her hand.

"My parents will approve of our news, especially Ma."

She took my arm. "Yes, she made her opinion clear before we left for the picnic."

I led her toward the narrow trail. "Aye. She doesn't withhold her opinion or a scolding if she feels it's due. She does mean well. There'd not be a war with King George if my ma had his ear."

"I expect not." She laughed. "Or it would be over by now."

I mused at how soon Ma and Mary could end the conflict if sent to negotiate peace.

As we walked along the leaf-strewn path, I watched for scuffing and broken branches as a trained scout. But listening to the forest sounds proved impossible while Mary prattled about the beautiful maples and pointed to different patches of plants she wanted to forage in the spring.

No more quiet, solitary ways once married.

When we left her da's last boundary tree, her conversation waned, then she fell silent as we crossed Laurel Creek and approached my parents' cabin.

"Ma likes you. Don't worry."

She sighed before saying, "I hope so." Her grip on my arm tightened. "She's rightly protective of you."

Ma stepped onto the porch, squinting at us. "Is that the Shirley lass hangin' on your arm?"

"It is. And she's accepted my proposal."

A smile lit up her face. "Best go fetch a preacher and have the weddin' tonight, 'fore she changes her mind."

"No, ma'am." Mary chuckled and fired back. "He's building a proper cabin before we marry in February."

My ma burst into a hearty laugh, holding her stomach. "Well, then, come here so I can hug ya both. Your pa's gone fishin', but I'll tell him."

Ma mashed us together with one hug, then plastered our cheeks with kisses. "I'm pleased for a new daughter. You've told Christina?"

"Not yet."

Mary shook my sleeve. "Let's go tell her. Then I must return home and help with chores."

"Alright." I kissed Ma's cheek.

Mary stepped around me and did the same. "Thank you for accepting me. I love your son."

"The bond between ya is strong. Bless ya, lass." She ambled back inside.

I loved the sparks of fire in their banter and the mutual respect.

We rode to the fort but strolled toward my sister, who sat in a chair on her porch. As we approached, she laid down her knitting and stood.

"Aye, and I saw ya leavin' toward the Shirleys' this mornin', and here ya are together."

Mary rushed into her arms. "I've agreed to marry your brother. We've just come from telling your ma."

I eased closer, and Sis hugged me.

"Mighty glad. How long ya goin' to make us wait?"

Mary said, "February. Papa will request the minister."

Sis nodded. "Long wait, but I'm happy for you two."

"I'm taking leave from scouting for a bit and hiring cabin builders."

"Oh." She looked my way. "Charles and Thomas want you at the blockhouse." She lifted her project and sat back down. "Talkin' to the captain concernin' a mandatory muster in May."

My stomach knotted, and Mary turned pale and frowned.

I wrapped my arms around her. "I'm sorry to leave you here. I might be awhile. Try not to worry over the muster. It's part of an updated militia act."

She sighed and stepped back, nodding and forcing a slight smile. "Come see me when you can. I look forward to planning the cabin."

I kissed her cheek. "Soon, I promise."

She turned, dabbing her eyes.

I wobbled like a drunkard. *Decisions I make now affect Mary. I'll ask for a pardon from the upcoming muster.*

Mary

William's stride toward the blockhouse changed from stooped and slower paced, to staggering. I turned to Christina.

"What's wrong with him?"

She chuckled. "Reality of getting married in a few months."

"Do you think he regrets asking me?" My chest hurt.

"Not at all." She winked. "'Tis the news from his mind reachin' the body."

I stretched my arm out toward her. "Pinch me so I'll know it's happening. My mind is fuzzy, and I can't stop smiling."

She tweaked my skin and laughed. "I'm happy for you both, and the waitin' will pass quickly. Plenty of spinnin', weavin', and sewin' along with gatherin' household goods."

"Put that way, I'm thankful for months instead of weeks." I chuckled.

Christina stood again and stretched. "The babe will wake soon for nursin'. I need to find out what mischief the lads are into. I look forward to seein' the both of you more oft', now you aren't avoidin' each other. I've been slighted by you both."

"I'm sorry. I'll come again soon." I hugged her and called for Rebel to follow.

As I passed through the gate, dizziness hit along with exhaustion and the reality of marrying in a few months with much to do.

I climbed in the saddle to keep from plopping on the ground. *Is this what William felt?*

Along the path home, a list of everything needed ran through my head. I'm finally going to use the material from Hans. I'll need a new petticoat, blouse, and ... *undergarments!*

William's going to see them.

Shocking conversations overheard in the Shawnee women's tent came rushing back, engulfing me in flames of panic, but the sounds of cantering drew my attention ahead. An unfamiliar man rode from the yard and passed, tipping his hat as I moved aside.

When I entered the yard, Papa stuffed a letter into his coat pocket and neared.

Anger seethed as I dismounted. *I hate this war.*

"Did you have a good visit with Will's family?"

I met his grin but didn't return one.

"I did. Everyone is pleased. What is in the dispatch?"

His eyebrows raised. "Confirmation of an updated militia act. We have to meet for a regiment muster at Burnside Fort on top of our monthly drills." He stroked his chin once, then Rebel's neck. "Go on in. I'll groom him. See you inside."

He hurried into the barn and I stormed toward the cabin, staring into the sky venting, "I've had quite enough of the British conflict. Papa's document better not include William."

Chapter Twenty-Four

May 16, 1777

Cody yapped on the porch in the excited pitch reserved for George.

I stopped slicing venison for supper and stared out the window as George cantered his horse into the yard from the east. He dismounted and rushed inside, panting.

"The men are entering the meadow."

Charlie's "Yippie" expressed my relief and joy.

A week ago, every male from sixteen to fifty complied with the order to muster for militia drills at Burnsides Fort, a day's journey northeast. William hated leaving our cabin unfinished but didn't want to pay a five-shilling fine if he didn't show.

The next day, I rode out to see our cabin. The board floor needed additional smoothing and the walls more chinking between the gaps, but a table and two simple log benches sat in the corner near the gray stone hearth. I stood admiring the fine work and imagined us sharing our first breakfast, the one he agreed to cook for losing the race. When I left, I used a leafy branch to cover my footprints and would act surprised when he showed it to me for the first time.

Charlie stood from his stool and dropped his paring knife into the pail of potatoes. "I'm finished peeling these. May George and I go to Papa?"

"You may." Momma smiled and retrieved the knife.

I removed my soiled apron and wiped my hands. After covering the meat with a clean cloth, I faced her. "If you don't mind, I'd like to greet William."

Katie rushed to my side. "May I say hello to Mr. Baughman?"

"Land sakes." Momma grinned. "Some days I forget you're both grown. You may go." She twisted her shoulders and peered at the younger girls. "But I need the four of you tidying up while I finish supper."

I hurried to the barn with Katie. We climbed on Rebel's bare back and caught up with our brothers already across the creek. The Greenbrier men parted company in the meadow. Papa waved at us and strolled in our direction, followed by William and Katie's John.

Papa didn't yet approve of John's wish to court Katie, but he didn't forbid his occasional supervised visits. John showed respect and seemed more patient than my sister.

Katie slid off the horse and stood waiting.

I lifted my hem and jogged toward William. "I'm so happy to have you back."

He turned from Babcock and grinned from a shaved face.

My legs weakened at the sight. I hurried into his arms, expecting the sour odors from several days of travel but breathed in the freshness of lye soap. He moved slightly, cradled my head, and pressed mint-flavored lips against mine.

When I moaned, he stepped back, and I whispered, "You smell good. Kiss me again."

"Not yet." He shifted away. "I'm going to finish the cabin and be your husband before I hold you again. How do you like the cabin so far?"

"It's wonderful."

He grinned and nodded. "I knew you'd peek."

"It's true." I laughed at being caught. "I couldn't resist."

He leaned as if to kiss me again but straightened and sighed. "I look forward to us."

"Me too." I longed to melt against him. "Are you too tired to come for supper?"

His head bobbed. "Yes, sorry. I need sleep."

"Tomorrow, then?" I raised a slight smile as my chest squeezed hard.

Somber, he took my hands. "Yes, tomorrow."

I rushed closer and kissed his cheek, then returned to my waiting family.

When I climbed behind Katie on the horse, she sniffled.

"What's wrong?" I asked.

She sighed. "John is leaving for Fort Boonesborough in the morning."

"I'm sorry." I rubbed her back. "What's happening?"

Katie wiped her eyes. "Shawnee and other tribes are planning raids. Kentucky scouts are begging for volunteers to come. Of course, John heeds the call."

My throat knotted. *Does William wish he could?*

Katie sobbed, "I ... I ... I'm tempted to ... sneak to his cabin tonight and leave for Kentucky with him in the morning. I'm not afraid, and I'm not ashamed of loving him that much."

Horrified, I clutched her arms. "Oh, Katie. Please don't. Please wait. Did John ask you to do this?"

He's never acted impatient.

Her breaths shuddered. "No. He wouldn't. But I'm desperate. He's the man I want. We'll find a minister once we're there."

My stomach churned and tears spilled down my cheeks. "You can't. I want you at my wedding, and Momma needs you now. Please stay home."

Should I alert our parents?

She shrugged and climbed on the horse, remaining silent. My worry over her swirled like a whirlwind.

What should I do?

When we arrived in the yard, Katie dismounted ahead of me and rushed into the cabin. I slid from the horse and glimpsed Momma backing from Papa's embrace, saying, "Supper is waiting when you're ready."

She strolled past me, smiling.

Papa led his horse into the barn with my brothers following at his heels. I led Rebel into the barn and hurried to hug Papa, struggling not to bawl and tattle on Katie, who'd have to resist the temptation on her own.

"Good to see you, Daughter." He shuffled backward and held my forearms. "Are you well?"

My heart pounded. "Overwhelmed, but I'm glad you're home."

He frowned. "What's troubling you?"

"It's nothing that can't wait until you're rested. How are you?"

He clenched his jaw and turned to unsaddle. "Tired and starved."

I glimpsed Papa's furrowed brows.

"I'm sorry I worried you." I rubbed Rebel's neck and prayed for Katie to stay home.

He looked up. "I'm troubled but it's not from you, polliwog. Let's finish up here. I'm beat."

His flat tone and focus on his task made my chest hurt. I didn't want to hear bad news.

My brothers finished the horse grooming, and after Charlie left, George eased close to my ear. "Something's troubling Papa, and he said the bear hunt is called off."

I nodded. "Maybe tired like he said." I washed my hands. "Let's go inside."

We entered the cabin to our sisters' giddy chatter. My stomach soured with all the worry. I glanced at Katie, but she turned her face away.

Momma hummed a sprightly tune while stirring the stew, then stood from the hearth and smiled.

"How is William?"

I plopped onto the bench. "Wonderful but tired. He'll visit tomorrow."

After hanging his hat on the rack, George sat, folding his hands, then Papa stamped his boots on the porch twice before entering.

"Smells wonderful." He slid out his chair, sat, then welcomed the younger children's hugs in turn.

Everyone grinned widely except me, Katie, George, and Papa.

He bowed his head. "Father, thank you for the safe trip, my family, and our home. Continue giving us wisdom and strength for the days ahead. Amen."

Momma's smile faded.

I ladled stew into my bowl but stared at a floating carrot, too worried about Katie's state of mind and Papa's foreboding mood to eat.

I sipped on broth until Papa finished devouring his stew and corn cakes. He sat back and pulled a letter from his pocket.

I swallowed my last bite, dreading the news.

"The post rider found me at Burnside Fort. It's from Hans."

My breath caught.

He unfolded the paper and read.

May 1, 1777, Williamsburg, Virginia

Dear Shirley family,

I'm safe in Williamsburg at last, after a long and adventurous trip down the James River. Thank you again for your kindness in taking me in and wishing me well. I have secured lodging, and a generous businessman has loaned me the funds to acquire a small shop. I will write again in the coming days. I hope this letter finds you all well and happy.

With loving regard,

Hans Mueller

A relieved sigh escaped. "I'm glad he made it safely."

"Yes, indeed." Papa nodded, then folded his hands on the table and scanned our faces. When he pressed his lips and blinked, my breaths shallowed and dread returned.

His gaze settled on Momma. "I'm sorry to ruin the evening." He reached for her hands.

Her eyes widened as she placed her palms on his.

I gulped and squeezed my fists in my lap.

He released a hard sigh and squirmed. "I received orders to join a Virginia regiment in Winchester."

Momma sat back in her chair.

I fought the bile rising in my throat. *Called into the war?*

"A regiment?" George sat up straighter in his chair. "You're ... Why?"

Papa drew a deep breath and held Momma's hand. "I'm sorry. I can't refuse the order. I've been personally requested by Capt. Briscoe."

Momma whispered, "When?"

"I must leave before dawn on Monday and make the trip in eight days."

Papa's voice echoed in my head as if in a dream. *It can't be true.*

I bolted from the bench. "Oh, Papa. Will you be back in February for my wedding?"

The room spun as he stood and eased me back down beside Katie.

My sister sniffled, placed her arm around my waist, and laid her head on my shoulder.

"Will you be a spy or a soldier?" George's solemn question drew all eyes to Papa.

He blinked at the ceiling before speaking. "The regiment marches to Pennsylvania on the twenty-sixth. I'll work with others infiltrating a Hessian company under British command—can't say where, but we'll relay information to Continental contacts."

The younger children scanned between our parents with confused faces.

I buried my wet face in my hands, wanting to scream, unable to think.

Papa sighed. "Col. Washington begs for volunteers to no avail. Therefore, Governor Henry ordered local militia drafts. Pray the war turns in the Continentals' favor before my three years are up."

"Three years?" Momma groaned as if delivering a baby and wiped her eyes with a dish towel.

Papa rushed to her side and embraced her while she wept. "Now, *liebchen*, I can stay alive that long, and they'll release me at age forty-nine."

My head and heart pounded. "Will William be called too?"

"No. He'll remain here as a scout."

He held Momma while I released a relieved breath.

George whispered, "Wish I could go as a drummer."

I bumped him with my foot. He glanced up, frowning, and I mouthed, *hush*. Tears fell from sorrow over Papa leaving but gratitude for William remaining.

Papa consoled Momma with reminders of God's care and watchfulness.

In a few minutes, he whispered something in her ear. She nodded, composed, then blew her nose and came to me with Papa, motioning for me to stand.

My legs wobbled.

"Now, happy news." His face brightened. "I asked William to marry you on Sunday, and he agreed."

I gasped. "This Sunday?" Confused and on the verge of dropping onto the floor, I sat on the end of the bench. "But the cabin isn't finished."

"You are my firstborn daughter." He knelt before me and took my hands. "I desire to pronounce my blessings over you both while I can." His eyes glistened in the lantern light.

"How can I be joyous with you leaving the next day and for so long? But ... I am happy to wed with your blessing."

Papa stood, lifting me to my feet.

"As for the cabin ..." His eyes gleamed. "William kept my secret and told you he'd be resting tonight. Truth is, he and two teams of men are trading off working on the cabin from daylight to dark for the next two days."

Papa took a breath and gazed at Momma's blinking eyes. "Don't worry. Minister Alderman is coming."

Momma nodded and fell against him, weeping.

My siblings were glancing between me and our parents. Katie wiped her eyes and ran upstairs.

I stepped out into the warm evening breeze, closed the door, and rushed to the barn with Cody following. I lay down on clean loose hay and bawled. Worrying over Katie running off with John in the middle of the night and Papa's leaving for three years of war mired the joy of marrying William before my birthday.

In a moment I heard *Be thankful.*

The thought ended my cries, but I sat up fussing. "Be thankful for what?"

Understanding came like a jolt. *I'm no longer with the Shawnee. Papa won't leave before my wedding or without my good-bye. But what about Katie?*

I brushed off and took a deep breath, bobbing my head at Cody. "I'm here to keep her from leaving with John and breaking Momma's heart. William and I will help Momma handle things until Papa returns."

Katie entered the barn at that moment, wiping her eyes, and I stood and met her in the middle. We embraced and sniffled until she stepped back.

"I know I can't leave Momma now," she said. "But I hope John comes back for me someday."

I hugged her again. "I'm sorry you're hurting for John, but I'm glad you're not leaving."

"What are we going to do without Papa?" Katie sniffled.

A strange strength came as I spoke. "We'll pray hard for him and John and stay brave for Momma's sake."

She dried her face in her apron. "I hate all of this war trouble, but I'm happy for you and William."

I draped my arm around her shoulder. "Thank you. I'm sorry about John. Hard to sort it all out. We should go inside and up to bed."

When we entered the quiet candlelit cabin, our parents and siblings had retired to bedrooms.

The stairs creaked as Katie and I embarked on the journey together and my head pounded. *Why must life turn topsy-turvy all in one day?*

Lizzy lay in her bed, already asleep. I crept to my side of the room and removed my garments and slipped into my bed gown, hearing Katie's stifled sobs.

I joined her on her bed and we cried quietly, hugging each other like little girls when we were in trouble. There were no words, only the shared understanding of too many sudden life changes in one day.

"Thank you," she whispered and let go first.

I dried my eyes and sat up, holding her hands. "May strength, courage, and faith rise with us in the morning."

I kissed her cheek and padded back to my bed praying she'd stay home.

Chapter Twenty-Five

May 17, 1777

Katie's sobs woke me from a troubled sleep, concerned, but I was relieved by her presence. My bed creaked as I rose in the pale gray light and padded barefooted across the floor.

"Sorry you heard me," she said and stood. "Lizzy just went downstairs, and I needed to cry again."

I wrapped her in my arms. "Terrible night for sleeping, anyway, but I'm glad you're still here."

She sniffled, stepped back, and wiped her nose. "I sneaked out an hour ago to meet John before he left. Told him I'd go with him."

I shook my head. "But you said you wouldn't. What a terrible lie."

"I'm sorry. I didn't mean to, but I woke early and panicked. Went to say good-bye, but when I saw him, the words slipped out." Her eyes widened. "Please don't tell Momma. John scolded me and walked me home. Said he wants me as his wife but not by eloping."

"I'm glad he has good sense. What if he'd taken you? How would our family recover?"

She frowned. "Well, don't continue fussing. I'm here. Let's dress and help with breakfast. No need to mention this again."

Katie turned away, leaving me surprised by her maternal tone and the finality of the subject, as if claiming my place as the eldest child in the home. I gulped and clasped my chest at the slight squeeze, then sauntered back to my side of the room, relinquishing the role to her.

For the second time in my life, I was separating from my family. But this time by choice. Tomorrow, the McGuire clan would adopt me as Mary McGuire. The new name floated around in my head, sounding odd as I stepped into my skirt and smoothed my hair. I mused, *Better than Shoots in Knee.*

I approached Katie as she wiped her eyes.

"I'm thankful you're here for Momma when I leave tomorrow. John will come back for you."

She hugged me. "I know, but my heart hurts. Happy I'll see you wed to William tomorrow. Are you nervous?"

"Not until you mentioned it." I chuckled.

We crept downstairs as the first beams of dawn lit the room and highlighted Momma flipping pancakes at the hearth. A single candle flickered on the table where Papa sat cuddling three-year-old Sally. "You'll be a big girl of six when I return."

The words twisted my heart. We endured many years of his absences on survey jobs, but never three long years. My eyes watered with my prayer, *Please, God. Keep him safe, and let there be peace soon. May the king accept our independent nation.*

He kissed Sally's forehead and stood her on the floor before pulling on his boots.

"Good morning, beautiful daughters." His grin widened. "Heading out with the boys, checking traps, and hoping to bring back venison for tomorrow's wedding celebration."

He stood, then motioned for Katie. He took her hands and gazed at her with firm but glistening eyes. "Proud you came back. Heard you creeping out the door in the dark, and I watched you head toward the fort. I refrained from following you."

My heart raced, watching Katie pale.

She gulped, then stuttered, "I ... I ..."

Papa nodded and released her. "Glad John brought you back. You need our blessing, but I approve of him as your husband. I prefer you wait another year, if not until I return."

"I'm sorry." Katie glanced between Momma and Papa. "I'll wait a year, but I can't wait three. We won't elope. I promise."

Momma turned away, rescued a pancake, then dried her eyes and handed Papa a cloth-wrapped bundle.

He tucked it into his haversack and kissed her cheek. "Thank you, *liebchen*." After removing his rifle from the rack, he stepped outside.

I shuffled toward my stoic, silent sister, intending to hold her, but she shuffled to Momma.

The spatula dropped to the floor as the two embraced, sobbing.

Lizzy entered the cabin with a pail of fresh milk. Susie and Nancy followed with a bucket of water and a basket of eggs. All frowned and glanced at me as if waiting for answers.

At a loss for how to explain the whirlwind changing our lives, I shrugged and retrieved the spatula, cleaned it, and finished cooking.

Momma stepped back from Katie, straightened, and wiped her eyes before facing us.

"Our lives will be different without Papa, but we'll live life to the best of our abilities as we do now." She scanned our faces and raised a smile. "Mary will move in with Mr. McGuire tomorrow and tend to her own house, but she won't be too far away for visits. We will all miss Papa and Mary in our home, but we have one another and will remain strong."

"I hope I can be as strong as you one day." My voice quavered.

She waved her hand as if swatting a fly. "You are all stronger than me, and I'm thankful we can comfort one another through these lonely times. Shall we eat breakfast and begin this busy day?"

"Yes, ma'am." *I bested those men who attacked me due to fear, but I don't feel stronger.*

My head pounded, knowing the day included finishing my new clothes, packing my things, and helping Papa gather his supplies and mending his clothes. I hunched before the hearth and lifted our steaming teakettle from the heat.

"Who else needs chamomile?"

Momma clutched a mug and held it toward me. "Sounds wonderful."

I poured the flowery scented beverage and asked, "How have you managed all these years when Papa's called away?"

She sipped the tea and sat at the table with the others, patting Papa's chair for me to sit.

I complied but felt awkward at the head of the table.

"Cried a lot at first." She lowered the cup. "Then I learned to trust in providence and focus on my tasks. This is why I say staying busy is best. When babies come along to keep you company, the separations are easier."

She took my and Katie's hands and bowed her head. "God, we thank you for all things. Please keep us strong and healthy while the men we love are in danger. Keep them in your care, and return them to us without affliction."

Everyone repeated "amen," and Momma passed the platter of pancakes to Lizzy but continued speaking to me and Katie.

"Give God thanks when the men you love return and enjoy doting on them for a few days so they know they're loved and appreciated. Life is full of uncertainty."

She placed a hand on my shoulder. "Thank you for the tea. We shall conquer this day, and tomorrow, you and William will marry. You both have much to look forward to in life, and your papa will have many stories to tell his first grandchild when he returns." She chuckled and passed the maple syrup around.

Grandchild?

The thought hovered until it thumped me on the head. *Ooh.* Heat rushed up my neck.

Marrying tomorrow is shocking enough.

I smiled at an image of Papa returning with his arm outstretched as I hand him a ... *one-year-old?*

William

Full daylight shining on my face jolted me awake. *Didn't mean to sleep this long.* I scrambled into clean work clothes and shaved.

I slept at the fort cabin at the insistence of my da, who pulled me aside about midnight and told me to let the other men finish the work and to go get sleep or I wouldn't be fit to be a groom come Sunday. I rode Babcock to the fort but wondered how I didn't fall off when his whinny woke me in front of the barn.

I splashed witch hazel on my cheeks and waited for the burn to cool. But I grinned knowing how much Mary enjoyed the fresh rain smell, *or something like that.* I smiled, anticipating our quick last visit before our ceremony tomorrow at noon.

I rushed to the barn, saddled, and rode toward the gate. The remembrance of Michael's news slowed my pace. *What if Mary is too upset and wants to wait?*

When I reached the Shirleys' yard, Michael and his sons were busy butchering a good-sized buck. Mr. Shirley glanced up, grinning—a good sign.

"Welcome. Pardon my need to keep working. Didn't expect you today. The cabin finished?"

I climbed down and removed my hat. "Hoping so. On my way back there but wanted to see about Mary."

"She's accepting the news and staying busy." He pointed. "Making bullets around back."

I nodded. "Oh, reminds me. Thomas heard reports of short supplies in everything for the troops, so take extra shoes and rations. Stay on the perimeter of the camps if you can, and avoid the dysentery and pox—it's causing heavy losses."

"Heard this too." Michael turned toward his sons. "Don't mention any of this to your momma."

George and Charlie held up their right hands, echoing each other. "We won't."

"I'll visit my bride-to-be and see you all tomorrow." I waved and strolled toward the stench of hot lead.

Katie saw me first and spoke to Mary, who smiled and continued pouring melted lead into the bullet mold. She straightened, and Katie took the spoon.

Mary removed her apron and approached, tucking loose hairs behind her ears.

I held out my arms, despite my former vow to wait, and she wrapped hers around my waist and laid her head against my chest, releasing a sweet, "Mmm. I'm glad you came."

"I needed to make sure you're all right and still wanting to marry me tomorrow."

She squeezed me tighter. "I am. And I'm happy you agreed so Papa can bless us. I'm nervous but excited about beginning our lives together."

She moved back and sighed. "Making all these bullets for Papa. It's hard being strong."

I swiped a tear off her cheek. "I know. It won't be easy. I'll hold you when you need comforting. You can easily make the two-mile ride back and visit anytime." She nodded and cuddled again.

I enjoyed the feel of her in my arms, her light sweet-sour scent from working outside, and the smokiness in her hair. I lowered my head, found her lips, and pressed her closer. Lost in the melting sensation until she pushed me away, panting and wide-eyed.

I grinned as my face and neck burned. "Tomorrow, we can hold each other without interruption. I love you, Mary."

A shy smile rose. "I ... love you too. See you tomorrow and then forever."

I bowed and kissed her hand. "I'm off to see about our cabin and give input for the celebration."

She curtsied and rushed back to her grinning sister.

I staggered away like a drunkard, unable to calm my pounding heart. *Good thing we're marrying tomorrow, or I'd have to go bear hunting until February.*

Chapter Twenty-Six

While I watched William's stride, George pointed behind us and shouted, "A rider's coming."

I turned as shouts of "fort up" rang out from the man galloping past us and up the north trail toward the McGuires' home. My breath caught.

William rushed back to me and grabbed my arms. "Look at me." His wide-eyed gaze steadied me. "Ride to the fort with your ma and the children. I'll help your da and George here."

Momma, my sisters, and Charlie filed out of the cabin and mounted the horses bareback, with Papa and George helping them.

William held Rebel still as I raised my skirt and draped my bare leg over the gelding's sweaty back. William's warm touch on the side of my upper thigh tingled. I gasped. His hand quickly pulled the hem toward my knee. He looked up and sighed. "Go."

I gripped Rebel's mane and leaned forward, following the others in a canter until a volley of gunfire knotted my stomach. Anger rose. I veered my horse around, ignoring the nudge to get to the fort, tired of my family being in danger because of Turkey Claw's lies. *I will confront them with the truth.*

"Get to the blockhouse, gal," a gruff-voiced man yelled from his horse on the other side of the bridge. "Pvt. Baughman reported a hundred Indians at the Big Sandy River yesterday, but Charles Gatliff found three sets of tracks this morning coming up from the southwest near your place."

I dismounted and shouted, "Please take my horse to the fort." I slapped Rebel's butt, and he lunged toward the man.

"Where you going, gal?"

I ignored his shout and ran into the woods for cover, listening and watching for movement before creeping toward the cabin. When I glimpsed William, my heart hurt for one last kiss.

Somewhere, I'll see you again.

Cody barked, then whimpered from a leash on the porch. *Good, he's secure. But I must make it inside.*

When gunshots echoed southwest of the cabin, I rushed to the door and entered the home. I ran upstairs and retrieved my eagle feather from the box under my bed and hurried back down, thanking God for my time among the Shawnee. *Now help me remember the language.*

I tied the feather with its two white beads to my braid and quickly made a yellow paste from Momma's sulfur powder. I smeared two horizontal lines on each of my cheeks, praying for the courage it represented.

The image of Chief Lone Duck surfaced when he painted my cheeks when he adopted me into his clan. *But his yellow came from goose bile.* I had nothing for red, symbolizing the blood I shed when I shot Isaiah Brown in the knee.

Hopefully, they'll respect my feather, paint, and broken language.

I stepped outside and rubbed Cody's fur. "Shh, boy. It's all right. I'll be back." I crept through the woods and spotted Papa, William, and George aiming guns toward our northwest boundary.

When I signaled them with a whistle, Papa double-glanced and waved me forward. William gaped and frowned.

Papa whispered, "What are you doing? Stay down. We have three pinned down behind those oaks."

George stared. "Why are you wearing that?"

Ignoring him, I hunched over and came beside Papa. "I need you all to trust me. I must speak to them in Shawnee. Perhaps they will honor my feather and paint."

"We'll shoot them if they don't," George said.

William clutched my arm and glared. "No. Stay down."

I nodded and lowered.

Still frowning, William released me and focused his gun on his target in the distance.

In one quick motion, I removed the feather from my hair and sprang forward, waving it over my head while shouting in Shawnee, "Listen to me. I am Shoots in Knee of the Piqua clan."

I gulped. *God, shield me and remind them of their belief in an Eagle Messenger and my right to evoke its words.*

I eased forward and chided, "You dishonor your god, Kokumthena, by coming here. It is your Corn Dance time. May she let Moneto curse your homes and your land."

A deep, guttural voice yelled back in Shawnee. "I will speak to Shoots in Knee."

"Come in peace."

I turned my head to my men and switched to English. "Don't shoot him. He's coming out."

A man emerged from the trees—his face painted white with black vertical lines to show his power. "You speak boldly of Kokumthena cursing us."

His voice sent a chill to my bones.

Loud Hawk!

He glared. "It is you that brought shame to the Piqua clan. Blue Jacket demands you answer for the chief's death and your lies against Turkey Claw."

"I did not lie." I kept my tone calm despite my knotted stomach. "Hear the truth now. I saw Turkey Claw gather poisonous mushrooms. His evil medicine sickened ..." *Can't name the dead...* "The kind chief."

Loud Hawk stared at my eyes. "How is your truth greater than his?"

My heart pounded as I searched for the correct words and continued. "Chief did not want to trade me to the white devil for rum and guns. Turkey Claw did. The chief's family will tell you this if you ask them."

He gave a slow nod. "My mother mentioned Turkey Claw's evil toward you. But he says you killed Chief to cause trouble and place blame on him."

A sudden understanding came as I paused and then spoke again. "If I did this evil thing, I would not have favor with the Creator. A Piqua dog killed the white devil and allowed me to escape to my family."

He stood a moment, thoughtful. "I accept your answers and will speak to Blue Jacket on your behalf—if you allow us to leave." He took a sidestep back toward the tree.

My heart pounded in my chest, but I held up the feather again. "Wait. I have something against you."

He turned, frowning.

In my most respectful tone, I said, "You spoke a curse to me about Kentucky—but you have come to my land."

He raised his chin and slowly pulled an arrow from his quiver and handed it to me. "No more curse. There will be peace between us."

My eyes watered as I felt the fear let go of my mind and peace flood in with a surge of joy.

I released a sigh of relief and smiled. "Go in peace and greet your mother, Moon Flower, for me. She was a kind friend."

I turned to the frowns and blank stares of Papa, William, and George. "Let them go. They'll leave me alone now."

Loud Hawk ducked behind the trees. I breathed a long-pent-up breath in relief.

I've just confronted my enemy and lived. My legs wobbled from the realization.

I sat on the ground, trembling and sucking in air.

William darted to my side, kneeling and wrapping me in his arms. "What am I going to do with you? That warrior could have killed you."

I blew out a breath. "I had to end the threat even if I perished. I couldn't allow it to continue against me or my family. That was Loud Hawk."

William moved back, squinting.

Our heads turned at a twig snap. Papa staggered toward us with pressed lips. His eyes were wide and his cheeks ashen. I reached for his hand, and he whisked me to my feet and into his arms.

"What just happened? Who was that? What were you thinking? I thought my heart would burst. It hurts to breathe."

William stood shaking his head, then waved to several men in the shadows.

"She's all right. The Indians are leaving. Let them go. The lass just negotiated peace."

They must have heard the gunfire.

My voice shuddered as I spoke to Papa. "Loud Hawk will tell Blue Jacket my side of the story. He believes me concerning Turkey Claw."

George stepped beside me with wide eyes. "I thought you lost your mind." His voice became raspy. "It scared me. What does the arrow mean?"

I squeezed him in a side hug and handed it to him. "He proclaimed peace between us."

Turning to William, I smiled. "He withdrew his threat concerning Kentucky."

William sighed and turned toward the soldiers. He spoke to them in low tones, and they headed back to the fort. He reached for me as I drew closer.

"Let's go, son." Papa waved for George and headed back to the cabin.

I lay my head on William's chest, and he cuddled closer.

Tears streamed down my face. "I had to confront Loud Hawk for coming here. Has my defiance changed your mind about marriage tomorrow?"

He stepped back, shaking his head but holding my trembling hands. "I'm exhausted and drained from everything, that's all. I can't believe what happened. I'll love you forever, little fairy creature. You're frightening, but beautiful." He planted a kiss on my cheek, "I'm returning to the fort, then gathering my workers. I'm determined to wed ya tomorrow, lass."

He galloped toward the fort, and I staggered to Papa, who waited on the porch puffing smoke from his pipe.

"You should go upstairs and rest until the family returns," he said. His free arm wrapped around my shoulders. He kissed the top of my head. "I can't begin to understand what happened. I'm still struggling to breathe and thought I'd die from a heart attack when you lunged into danger."

"I'm sorry, Papa." My eyes watered, unable to bear him leaving at all. "I'm free of that man's threat now. William and I will make a good life together, and you will return from duty with a grandchild to spoil. I refuse to believe otherwise."

I stepped away, drying my eyes, then entered the cabin, too drained to pull my exhausted body up the stairs. I plopped into a chair near the hearth instead and stared at the simmering coals. I blew them back to life and added kindling so Momma wouldn't have to when she returned.

Joy came when I remembered the first time William called me a fairy creature and something about being beautiful, powerful, and frightening. It was the day I had threatened to head to Boonesborough on my own. A surge of strength flooded in with the realization of not being afraid of Kentucky anymore. *Everything came out in the wash, just like Momma always says.*

William

I slowed my pace once out of Mary's sight with my gut still knotted. The image of her fearless defiance of my order to stay down had made me insane as she surged in front of those warriors.

My head still pounded from the helpless panic of watching her confront the very warrior who threatened our future with his words.

How did she go from being fearful to having no regard for her life? She rushed toward him shouting and waving a feather, and he showed her respect.

Did her fierce eyes bewitch him and win his favor?

As I neared the gate, the doors creaked open. I rode in and dismounted as men gathered around as if needing an explanation for the account they heard.

"'Tis true lads. My future wife is a banshee warrior. She painted her face, let out a hair-raising scream, and waved a feather in the air."

I searched their awed faces as additional residents gathered, then I embellished my tale some more. "Aye, and the Shawnee warrior turned pale as linen and fell under her spell, before fleeing before her."

Cheers rang out, and I straightened with pride. "Now, help me prepare to wed the magical creature tomorrow and our place of celebration, while I rest and recover my wits."

I handed off Babcock to an eager young man and entered my cabin.

Away from the crowd, I collapsed on my bed, depleted of strength and emotional restraint while I processed my failure to notice the signs of intruders. *There were none yesterday. Did they sneak in after scouts left the area and stay hidden all night?*

The image of Mary rushing into danger with a feather renewed the rapid pounding in my chest. I rose and splashed my face with water from the bucket, then grabbed my hat on my way out, eager to finish the cabin and build a new bed for my bride.

Once out of the fort, I nudged Babcock west into a gallop along the south bank of Indian Creek until crossing at the Laurel Creek fork and heading north along the tree-lined trail to my land. Sounds of hammering and sawing sped my pace.

A group of men worked on a platform in the yard for the fiddlers to stand on. The other men tied canopies over tables made from planks across several sawhorses.

I strolled inside the cabin, examining the chinked walls, then I knelt and rubbed my hand across a smoothed floor, pleased. *Sure would ruin the evening if my bride caught a splinter in her foot.*

As I stood, Thomas and Da carried in a polished oak headboard and one for the foot of the bed.

"Bring the sideboards and ropes," Thomas said. "We'll help you set the frame, but you're in charge of stringing the ropes." He laughed. "That way, if the mattress crashes onto the floor with the both of ya, we're not to blame."

Da leaned close to my ear. "Best on the floor anyway, if ya ask me." He snickered.

I shook my head, embarrassed, and hurried to the barn for the rest of the bed. Ma and Christina glanced up from stuffing straw into the mattress tick and waved. I grabbed the boards and rope and rushed away before they could tease, hoping Mary wouldn't regret being part of my family.

Once framed, we centered the bed on the wall, and when Thomas and Da tired of ribbing me, I worked the ropes in a weave pattern to hold the mattress. My hands hurt, but the taut ropes would hold.

I stepped back and admired my work as Ma and Christina came inside and placed the mattress on the frame.

"You did well," Christina said. "Now leave and stay out. Ma and I will add the female touches."

I strolled to the door. "But shouldn't I bring my things from the fort?"

"Tomorrow." She rested a hand on her hip. "You may bring your belongings but set them on the porch."

I left a bit out of sorts from being kicked out of my new home.

Well, not just mine. Tomorrow I'd share space with a woman and learn to be patient. She'll want to say where things go and what I can keep or not. What's mine is hers, and what's hers will probably stay hers.

Chapter Twenty-Seven

May 18, 1777

After breakfast, Papa and my brothers carried their wedding clothes out to the barn, leaving the rest of us in the cabin.

Momma pointed me to her bedroom, where a large bucket of steaming water sat on the floor for washing.

"Call for me when you're finished."

I nodded and closed the door but heard her tell my sisters she'd be next, then the usual birth order would apply. A pinch of melancholia came with the reality of another last time. No more sharing wash water with my momma and siblings. But I'd be first in my home and that made me giggle.

Once finished, I wrapped in the towel and called for her. She eased inside with my new chemise, and I raised my arms. Crisp scents of lye soap and sweet jasmine tickled my nose as the garment slid down over my head and unfurled toward my feet. "Thank you for the flower water rinse. Smells so nice."

Momma smiled and produced a brush. "Now, I will twist your hair into a special bun and give you this." She reached up and pulled out one of her hairpins and placed it in my palm.

"It may not appear special, but it belonged to my momma. I removed it from her head before the ship crew tossed her body into the ocean on the terrible journey from Rotterdam. I needed something of her as a keepsake. When I look at it, I remember her bravery."

My eyes watered as I touched her shoulder. "Oh, Momma. Thank you, but you should keep it."

She never spoke of her family. I asked about them when I was eight, but she shook her head and turned away. It was Papa who explained to each child in turn that her family died from sickness.

"I've always planned to pass it on to you at your wedding. You may give it to your firstborn daughter on her wedding day." She studied my face as I swallowed hard, fighting the emotions. "You favor her. Did I ever tell you?"

"No, ma'am." My gut knotted as I wiped my eyes.

Momma grew solemn as she spoke. "Her name was Mary Katherina. She was soft-spoken, but resolute and confident. We left the persecution in Germany when my Uncle Franz wrote from the Pennsylvania Colony." She stepped behind me and placed the pin in my bun before walking to her bed. She sat and pulled a handkerchief from her pocket and dabbed her eyes.

"We sailed from the filthy city of Rotterdam, where many people carried a sickness aboard. A few weeks later, my baby brother died. Then Momma, Papa, and my sister, Elizabeth."

She peered up at the ceiling and took a deep breath, and I eased down beside her. I sniffled with her, sorry she witnessed her family thrown overboard like rubbish. *How lonely and frightening.*

"My uncle found me two days later among the orphans." She blew her nose and stood, drying her face. "Now you understand why I don't speak of this." She helped me up and smiled. "You are beautiful."

I hugged her. "Thank you for this special gift. I will treasure it forever. I'm sorry for the loss of your family, but I'm so thankful you survived to be my momma."

She pushed away smiling, as a tear ran down her cheek. "When did you become such a grown-up girl? I'm going to miss you in our cabin, but thankful you'll be nearby.

William is a worthy man, and Papa and I are proud of your choice."

She hurried to bring my new blouse and skirt. I continued drying my eyes and slipped on the pretty white shoes from Hans. A slight prick of guilt surfaced knowing he expected to see me wearing them. *Thank you Hans.* I grinned and faced Momma.

She examined the completed outfit and smiled.

"You are ready." She kissed my cheek and opened the door to Papa, who was waiting to escort me to the wagon.

I rushed into his arms, struggling to be strong. "There won't be time to speak after the ceremony. I'll pray for your safety every day and look forward to your return."

He stepped back, solemn. "Thank you. Today, I leave you in the arms of a good man."

I kissed his cheek. "He's almost your equal, Papa. But you'll always be first in my heart."

His eyes watered. "And you will always be my little polliwog. I'm proud of the strong woman you've become." He blinked, then sighed. "Now, we must hurry to the fort before you're kidnapped by the Scott-Irishmen." He offered his elbow while his face feigned concern under a twitching smile.

We knew of this tradition, and William promised his family would pay the ransom. George and Charlie flanked me, holding their guns in a symbolic gesture of protection as we went outside.

As our wagon reached the blockhouse, a group of armed men led by Charles Gatliff intercepted us. George and Charlie stepped aside, winking.

I screamed, pretending fear as the captors escorted me to a nearby cabin.

I watched from the window as the crowd cheered and parted.

A million butterflies swarmed in my stomach as William strolled forward wearing a sky-blue shirt with a traditional Scott-Irish scarf and kilt, plaid in red, green, and blue. Blue and red tassels dangled from his white knee-high stockings, and he wore black shoes with silver buckles.

He was a wonderful sight and better than I could have imagined.

He carried a jug in one hand and offered it to his brother-in-law. After uncorking and tasting the content, Charles shouted, "It'll do. The lass is free."

When the door opened, I refrained from grabbing William's hand and running away from everyone, wishing we could skip the ceremony and celebrating part.

I grinned and peered into his eyes as he wrapped his scarf around my shoulders and held out his arm. My legs wobbled, but he steadied me. Family and friends crowded inside the blockhouse ahead of us.

As we neared Reverend Alderson, Papa stepped in front of William. "I'm blessing you with my daughter for life, and I expect you to treat her as a special gift. If you mistreat her, I'll shoot you like a rabid dog."

The crowd snickered as Papa took my hand and placed it in William's. Then he bound our wrists together with an embroidered strip of linen according to our German tradition. He moved back and placed his hands on our heads.

"May the Lord bless you and keep you, may he make his face shine upon you and show you his favor. May he lift his face toward you and give you peace—and may he bless you with my grandbaby by the time I come back."

We stepped before the reverend.

I tried to pay attention to what he read from his book, but his dry recitation drew long, and I wanted to exchange vows and dance with my husband.

When the reverend looked at me, I stood straight.

"Do you promise to obey William as your husband?"

I frowned at him and shook my head. "No, sir."

His mouth fell open, and the crowd gasped.

I gazed into William's eyes. "But I will love, honor, and respect you all the days of my life."

He chuckled and took my free hand with his. "I promise to love, honor, and respect you all the days of my life too."

The reverend shook his head, then shrugged his shoulders. "I pronounce you husband and wife."

I leaned toward William, and he drew me into his arms. His lips pressed firm and long.

When the crowd whooped and whistled, heat traveled up my neck.

William stepped back, leaving my heart pounding as he offered his arm and led me to the wagon, now decorated with wildflowers.

Everyone loaded into wagons or rode horses and followed us to our cabin for the celebration.

Fiddlers gathered on a wooden platform and played the "Virginia Reel." William and I led the dance.

When this dance ended, the senior Mr. McGuire stood. "Please join us at the tables for a lunch of stew and corn dodgers."

William escorted us under a family canopy.

Throughout eating, neighbors offered toasts with blessings and funny Irish limericks.

The fiddlers struck their bows, and we hopped into a new reel. After four more dances, the fiddlers slowed to a soft waltz for William and me. In a moment, he lifted me into his arms and carried me toward the cabin amid shouts and jeers from the crowd following us.

I couldn't contain my giggles when William suddenly stood still.

"What in tarnation?"

He lowered me to my feet and pointed to the small log resting atop two sawhorses blocking our door.

I smiled at my husband's shocked faced. "It's a German tradition."

The people roared with laughter.

Papa silenced everyone and held up a rusted crosscut saw, then motioned for us to take opposite ends.

"Now, we witness how well you work through your first trial as husband and wife."

George helped position the blade on the log, backed, and said, "Ready? Go."

William gazed at me like a helpless child that's been told no. But we made the sawing motions to no avail.

The Scott-Irish crowd seemed delighted by this new game as they hooted and cheered.

William shook his head and finally laughed.

Papa held up a shiny saw. "Who will make contributions for this new one?"

The crowd dispersed as we giggled and worked.

In a few minutes, family, friends, and area settlers returned from their horses and wagons with small bags of corn and other gifts of provisions and household items.

Papa looked at us both. "Now, remember, sometimes life is hard, and you must ask for help from those with more wisdom than yourselves."

George took away the old saw, and Papa placed the new one on the log.

"Thank you, friends and family," William shouted, then faced me on the other end of the log. "Ready?"

"Yes."

We cut through the log in five minutes.

Everyone cheered and came forward to say good-bye while our families carried the gifts into our cabin.

I made quick good-byes to Momma and my siblings but lingered in Papa's embrace, sealing the memory in my mind, thankful we'd spoken earlier. "Be strong, Papa."

He kissed the top of my head. "Be happy, Daughter and remember God's promise, 'All things work together for good...'"

I gulped as he pushed away and nudged me into William's waiting arms, saying, "Somewhere I will see you again."

The fiddlers played softly as we swayed, unhurried, and I finished crying. His hand stroked my head. I breathed him in and melted into his arms. No longer needing Papa's comfort.

"Thank you," I whispered. "I'm all right now. Just that little girl letting go."

He twirled me once, then offered his elbow. I smiled and clasped his forearm. Ignoring the slow waltz, I led him in a skip toward our home. As we neared, he scooped me up and carried me into the pine-scented cabin, lit by the midafternoon haze and a flickering candle. After closing the door with his foot, he lowered me to stand on the floor, out of breath.

I scanned our one-room home. In the center of our table sat a vase of red, blue, and yellow wildflowers surrounded by snacks of bread, cheese, apples, and pears. The gifts lined the wall near the hearth, and in the center of the long wall stood a beautiful bed with polished headboard and footboard with a brightly colored patchwork quilt and fluffy pillows.

The fiddlers serenaded us a moment more, but I imagined the rattle of turtle shakers on my ankles as I stomped toward him in the Shawnee courtship dance. The candle flame flickered in his widening eyes. He wrapped me in his arms, swaying to the music until it ended.

No matter what trials lurk in our future, this "happy ever after" moment would stay locked in my heart forever.

I no longer shied away from the sensations his body caused. I caressed his back, then peered into his eyes. My heart pounded as heat swept across my cheeks.

I smiled and whispered, "Shall I tell you what I learned about lovemaking from the Shawnee women?"

His eyes widened with his grin. He blew out the candle, then kissed my neck while his wispy breaths tickled my ear. "Show me."

Acknowledgments

It took a village to write and complete this fourth book in the *Dangerous Loyalties Series*!

I'm thankful for everyone who gave encouragement, critiques, beta reads, and edits. Double blessings on the fan who prodded: "When will you finish? I'm ready for a good book to read."

I'm especially grateful for my family's love and support throughout my writing journey.

I acknowledge Certified Genealogist Patrick G. Meguire for his research. Thank you for corresponding with me through the years and for confirming the sibling connection between William and Christina.

If I could, I'd give a big hug to West Virginia historian Fred Ziegler and his wife Barbara. They met me at Cooks Old Mill on a freezing day in January so I could see the Shirley land and the location of Cooks Fort. His book,

The Settlement of the Greater Greenbrier Valley, West Virginia, is an excellent resource for those researching ancestors from western Virginia.

What Happens Next

I wrote the *Dangerous Loyalties Series* to highlight the historical events happening during Mary's early teen years. Although Mary and her family did not make the trip to Kentucky until 1779 or 1780, I set up the turmoil occurring in the Western territories, which led to the tragic events to come in their lives.

Whatever happened in Mary's teen years, she became a tough and practical—minded frontier woman by the time she was eighteen with an eighteen-month-old son they named Michael but nicknamed Bennie.

On June 24, 1780, a cannon blast shook her heart and changed her life forever. The rest of the story deserves a nonfiction book pulling in research and eyewitness accounts. This will be my next labor of love.

About Author

 Phyllis A. Still is living her dream as an award-winning author in Texas. She is an eighth-generation descendant of DAR Patriot, Mary Shirley McGuire, the inspiration behind the *Dangerous Loyalties* series. Phyllis loves her family, pets, road trips, history, and playing games with her grandchildren. Her adventurous childhood through seven states created her vivid imagination and a love for stories about people who have overcome hardships. She loves hearing from readers. Please consider leaving a review on Amazon or Goodreads. Join her Dangerous Loyalties Facebook group. Learn more about Phyllis at phyllisastill.com

www.ingramcontent.com/pod-product-compliance
Lightning Source LLC
Chambersburg PA
CBHW060852210726
48293CB00006B/1770